9109 LP

HIRED GUNS

**Center Point
Large Print**

**This Large Print Book carries the
Seal of Approval of N.A.V.H.**

HIRED GUNS

Max Brand®

CENTER POINT PUBLISHING
THORNDIKE, MAINE

This Center Point Large Print edition
is published in the year 2009 by arrangement with
Golden West Literary Agency.

The text of this Large Print edition is unabridged.
In other aspects, this book may vary
from the original edition.
Printed in the United States of America.
Set in 16-point Times New Roman type.

ISBN: 978-1-60285-527-4

Library of Congress Cataloging-in-Publication Data

Brand, Max, 1892-1944.
  Hired guns / Max Brand.
    p. cm.
  ISBN 978-1-60285-527-4 (library binding : alk. paper)
  1. Large type books. I. Title.

PS3511.A87H57 2009
813'.52--dc22

2009012646

CONTENTS

▪ I ▪
WHO CAN RIDE AND SHOOT?

Sitting the saddle, he looked a tall man, deep-chested and wide of shoulder, so that one could see why he had chosen a good weight-carrying cow pony. A burden bearer was needed to sustain that weight. When he dismounted, however, the loiterers on the hotel veranda at Peterville were surprised to see that he stood not more than an inch or two above the average height. His legs were very short; his inches lay chiefly above the waist.

Yet there was that about him which, after a second or two, made him seem a more dominant figure than ever. Between that width of shoulders was a nobly proportioned head and a broad, brown face seamed with the scars of experience. A sad face when he was looking down, one might say; but when he glanced up there was such brightness in the eyes, such infinite resource of invention, such ability to look into the brains and hearts of other men, that he immediately grew larger, so to speak, in the estimation of the onlookers. To sum up, there could be no doubt about the wisdom of that man, but whether he were good or bad was entirely another matter. One could make a thousand surmises about him and feel that all might be right.

His age might be between forty and forty-five, years which sat lightly on his labor-hardened body. He was a strong man, beyond doubt; and beyond doubt he was also an active man.

They had a chance to compare notes on him at once, for, having waved cheerfully at them, he at once took his pony and the sleepy, ranging gelding he was leading, and led them around the corner of the hotel to find the stable. Yet while he was gone they did not talk in more than a guarded whisper, and at the first sound of his returning footsteps they were still and looked guiltily one at another.

He came back whistling softly and fanning the alkali dust out of his trousers with the resounding strokes of his quirt. Climbing the steps, he selected a chair in the corner where the wind blew most steadily, loosened the bandanna around his throat, and produced a short, black pipe which he filled and lighted. During all this time he had not spoken a word. Not that there was anything either hostile or sullen in his silence—indeed, on the contrary, he seemed cheerfully aware of everyone about him. He ran his glances over their faces—a single glance at each one through the clouds of pipe smoke—and, having completed his survey, he turned his attention to the village itself and then over the sun-glistening roofs to the bare mountains beyond, pushed back behind a mist of heat.

For it was a very hot day. Passing from the veranda, no one sooner left the shadow than the sunrays beat through the clothes and seared the skin, and violent perspiration broke out under the hatband. Nothing dared remain quiet in that white burst of light. The very mongrel dog which had curled up in the dust for a sun bath quickly rose and skulked back into the shadow, where he lay down again with lolling tongue and heaving sides. The cow-punchers on the veranda kept turning and twisting from time to time, putting their hats on and taking them off and ever and again cursing softly. Sometimes, they rolled cigarettes. Sometimes, they tossed them away half burned. Sometimes, they drew out their guns and went over the action with frowning intentness. Sometimes, their voices rang loud and harsh as one took up a chance word from another. Sometimes, one would rise and venture to the edge of the shadow, saying: "This is a devil of a country!" But he never went out into the sunshine, and in his heart he knew that he lied. They loved even that white blaze of heat, these men, that dry heat of the mountain-desert which does not put one to sleep in the middle of the day but frays the nerves till they are ragged and wears out the mind and the body at once with constant irritation.

But presently, the talking, the attempted jests, the attempted tale-telling fell away. The wide-shouldered stranger had not yet spoken. Neither was he twisting and turning in his chair. But he smoked steadily and gazed out over the glimmering roofs of the village, though a child could have told that he was only seeing his own thoughts and never the mountains beyond. But the rest felt the power of that silence, and more and more keenly they began to wish that he would speak. His seamed face suggested that he could talk familiarly of every hell on earth. His twinkling eyes announced that he was familiar enough with every pleasure, also. Here, then, was a treasure for their ennui. When would he begin to talk?

At length, Perkins, the eldest of the men present, hitched his chair closer.

"Most like you come down from Brennan Springs over the range?" he suggested and waited without confidence, for it did not seem that so simple an invitation would invite a man this formidable to speak.

As a matter of fact, he returned at once, in an amazingly gentle bass voice—the sort of voice children and horses most love: "Yep, I come down from Brennan Springs."

But he did not continue to explain the goal of his journey or what his business might be; he did not break into anecdote; he did not speak of men and women and events. Having made his rejoinder, he fell into his former silence, saving that this time his glance did not turn to the mountains. It continued to dwell just above the head of Perkins while he calmly and steadily began again to look into his own thoughts.

Beneath that calm disregard—an actually polite disregard, if one might call it that—Perkins sweated and twisted.

"I used to know a tolerable pile of folks up to Brennan," he suggested again. "You been there long?"

"Nope, not long."

"But you sure must have seen old Withero. That's him that always sits alongside of the blacksmith shop. He was sitting there twenty years ago, I figure, and he'll be sitting there twenty years from now and never look no mite older. You remember him?"

"Can't say I do," answered the other, withdrawing himself from his meditations with the greatest kindness to respond to this chatter. "Only remember one man in Brennan—that is, only remember one tolerable well."

"And who was he?"

There was a general turning of heads. One might have thought that it was a great point of achievement to come to live in the memory of this wise head.

"A big young gent. Name was—lemme see—name was Kelly."

"Not Jack Kelly?" asked a dozen voices, everyone anxious to show his intimacy with the celebrity. And then they all turned and smiled on one another like pleased children.

"His name was Jack Kelly," answered the

stranger, quietly. Already, he was beginning to lose interest and slowly withdrew into his haze of thought; but, when they spoke to him, always his eyes flashed out through the mist, incredibly alive and alert.

"How was old Jack coming along?" asked a younger member of the group. "How was Jack doing when you seen him last? Fighting or making love or gone off to break in an outlaw hoss?"

"Didn't see him doing much along any of them lines," answered the mild voice. "Not when I last seen him."

"What was he doing?"

"He was trying to sleep."

There was a burst of laughter as though this were an excellent jest, and, indeed when the thermometer has mounted above one hundred burning degrees Fahrenheit, it takes a little thing to rouse mirth just as it takes a little thing to rouse anger.

"Jack was in bed, eh?"

"Yep, he was in bed."

"Well, that's plumb queer. Most generally, Jack is the last one to hit the hay and the first up."

"He's sort of changed," said the stranger. "Spends his time in bed now."

"The devil you say! Maybe he's been hurt?"

"Sort of smashed up," answered the other, with unbroken calm. "But the doc says he'll pull through—maybe with a couple of weak places where bones were broke bad."

There was a pause, then a chorus: "Who done it?"

"My hoss," said he of the bright eyes. "The old brown hoss I was leading."

There was a gasp and a side flash of eyes as though they were seeing again the old, long, brown horse disappearing around the corner of the building, but with what new connotations!

"Maybe he slipped up behind him and got kicked?" suggested Perkins.

"No. He was riding him," said the stranger.

It brought another silence.

"Then Jack Kelly's been throwed at last! I suppose the darned fool wouldn't pull leather—not him!"

"Wouldn't pull leather? You're plumb wrong, stranger. Maybe you and me don't know the same gent. The Jack Kelly I seen try to ride 'Brownie' sure pulled leather and pulled as hard as ever I seen a man do. But he was bumped off the saddle before he was through."

"Drunk, maybe?" gasped Perkins.

"Bone dry, partner. Bone dry and fighting hard, but jest not quite a good enough rider to back old Brownie. But it was a pretty bit of riding while it lasted."

"How come he to try riding your hoss?" asked Perkins.

"Well," said the stranger, "that's a tolerable long story."

There was an approving growl from the men, a satisfied growl. A story was exactly what they wanted. But they had to wait for it until the man of the wide shoulders had refilled and lighted his pipe, and then he spoke quite slowly, marking the important periods with long, white puffs drifting from his mouth.

"I got a partner," he said, "that's always arguing. Most terrible outtalkingest gent you ever seen when it come to hold up his end of an argument. Didn't make no difference what was right to him. Just let another gent get up and say a thing, and my partner hung his head and bit his lip till he got hold of a good way to disagree. Then he turned loose, and he talked so quick and easy that he sunk a shaft and lined it up so plumb smooth you couldn't tell where it was timbered. Well, that's his way. And him and me being old bunkies, it sort of riled me to have him go on that way all the time. Pretty soon he done most of the talking, and I done most of the listening."

"You got a kind of a patient look," remarked Perkins, chuckling, "like a gent that married a woman with a pile of jaw power."

"I got a patient look, and I'm a patient man," said he of the wide shoulders, looking down to the floor, "but after a while—after a good many years—I got kind of mad. Pretty soon I says to myself: 'The next time he starts arguing, I'm going to lead him around and trap him, and I'm going to trap him so plumb bad that he'll never forget about it. I'll make him bet, and I'll make him lose the bet.'"

There was a general leaning forward as the story approached this climax of interest.

"Come along a couple of days," went on the stranger, "and I got him talking about guns and hosses. 'Tell you what,' says I to my partner, 'it's darned queer how bad most gents is with a gun, when all they got to do is to line up the sights and the target and pull a little trigger—and there you are.'

"'Queer?' says he, quick as a flash. 'Not so queer. But, anyway, take any target you want, and you'll find a gent somewheres that'll hit the mark, long as it's inside of good range.'

"'I don't believe it,' says I.

"'You're the champeen doubter,' says he, 'and I never said you wasn't. Give you a chance to see the black side of a thing, and you sure always do.'"

"He must know you tolerable well for you to let him talk to you like that," suggested a voice.

"Him?" said the stranger. "Oh, him and me are like brothers. Besides, I ain't no fighting man. I don't believe in starting a gun play because a gent says some cross words to me. That ain't my style. I like living too darned much."

He said this with such perfect simplicity that for a moment the rest gaped and stared at him as though he were a monstrosity come strangely into a strange world. Then there was the beginning of the sneer with which hardy men look at a coward, but last of all came a peculiar look of doubt. No matter what he might say about himself, this fellow had the look of a fearless man.

"Anyway," went on the newcomer in Peterville, "my partner got riled a pile more when I said I figured they was hosses that no man could ride—real educated buckers. He sure hit the top of the roof when I said that. "'Find a hoss that I can't ride myself,' says he. 'Then you can start talking. But, any way you figure, you take your hoss and stop along at every town you come to, and you'll sure get your target hit and your hoss rode some place.'

"'Both in one town?' says I, leading him on.

"'Sure,' says he.

"I had him trapped. 'I bet you a thousand on it—that I don't find a gent to hit my target and ride my hoss inside of a month, me traveling steady.'

"Well, they wasn't hardly any way he could back out of it then, him being tolerably proud. So he picks me up, and I start. First I get the hoss, a real mean one, you see? And I teach him all the tricks of the trade till I wouldn't get on his back myself for ten thousand dollars. He's sure an educated bucker. He'd had a couple of years of experience before I got hold of him, and after what I taught him about hating men he sure is a man-killer now!

"Then I got a target. Easy one to think of. I just got a board. Stand off thirty paces and put six forty-fives side by side in it, and that board'll be cut plumb in two. But them bullets have to be side by side, or there'll be enough wood left to hold up the top half. You see?"

There was a gasp from his listeners. Obviously, the thing was impossible of accomplishment. Thirty paces was a long-enough shot for a revolver to hit a small target, but to keep six bullets perfectly in line and to make each hole overlap on the other—that would be indeed miraculous shooting.

"And you never got a gent to cut that board in two, I guess?"

"Never," said the stranger. "One gent took an hour for his shooting. He was a steady hand, and he done so well that the board began to sag after the sixth shot. Finally it broke of its own weight. But that wasn't really cutting it in two. Howsomever, I called it cutting the board in two to please him. That was Sandy Lawson in Crow's Nest that done that fine shooting."

"I've heard of him," said Perkins. "Smart hand with a gun, Sandy is. None better, I've heard tell. But more for target work than fighting, I reckon."

"If you'd seen the time it took him to get off his shots," said the stranger with the faintest suggestion of a sneer, "you'd of thought so. Take your real gun fighter, and he shoots quick. He can't help it. Every target is a man to him, and he shoots quick—to kill. That's the sort of gun work I like to see!"

His teeth clicked at the end of the sentence, and his eyes blazed. For a moment they were seeing the true man under the gentle exterior, and what they saw made the others wince and glance hastily one to the other. A moment later he was smiling again.

"But Crow's Nest didn't have no man that could ride Brownie. So they ain't much danger of me losing the bet. And they's only one week left in my month, unless Peterville can turn out a man, or two men, that can turn the trick."

A silence followed this incipient challenge.

"What does the gent get that cuts the board or rides the horse?" asked one of the younger men cautiously.

"Nothing," replied the stranger. "Not a thing. Don't need to offer no prize. But the town that turns out two men like that will be famous, and every town knows it. So they all sent out their best men to try. Crow's Nest has got the lead right now. But maybe Peterville'll do as well. Who knows? You boys are an upstanding crowd. Maybe one of you'll feel like making the try. I'm going to be around these parts till tomorrow morning. You talk it over and make up your minds. And if you want to practice on the target, you can sure do it. That piece of board in the top rail of that fence is the same size as mine. You cut off the same pieces of it and practice as much as you want. When you think you can turn the trick, just send for me, and I'll come out and watch. You don't get no reward but a pile of glory—but it don't cost nothing but the price of bullets to try. S'long. I'm going inside and get a bite to eat."

· II ·
PETERVILLE CALLS ITS BEST

They followed him across the veranda with their glances. Their heads remained turned toward the door after he had disappeared through it. Then:

"There's a cool devil for you," breathed Perkins.

He had voiced the sentiments of the rest so exactly that there was no comment.

"And him saying he wasn't no fighting man!" continued Perkins. "You hear him talk about gun play and the right way of a fighting gent? Well, I watched him tolerable close, and I seen that hungry look come up in his face—same sort of look that I used to see many a time in the days when they had a pile of hard ones around these parts. Them days fights blazed up in the saloons about as frequent as matches are lighted now. Just a word, and smash, bang—there you were with a man squirming on the floor and somebody backing toward the door and telling the rest not to foller less'n they wanted to get salted away with lead. Well, boys, they was the same sort of look, just for a minute, in the face of this gent that's just left us."

"He's no good, maybe?" asked one of the others.

"I dunno," said Perkins. "All I figure is that he ain't no common sort of gent. I guess he wouldn't hunt for no sort of trouble, but if trouble come his direction maybe he'd have ways of meeting it. A tolerable pile of ways, at that. But who's going to try to ride the hoss and shoot the board in two for Peterville?"

"If Jack Kelly couldn't do it," said one, "I'm free to speak out—which Jack's always been a better hand than me, and I don't take it to shame not to try what he couldn't do."

"I ain't meaning you," said old Perkins hastily. "I don't mean nobody here. All I say is that Peterville has got to turn out a couple of gents that can make a good try. Otherwise, we'll be laughed at by the other towns around these parts. And it don't take much laughing to make a gent hang his head or fight. And we got to hang around and find the best men we got."

"And have one of 'em get busted up by that devil of a hoss?" growled one of the men. "I say something had ought to be done about this gent that comes along and tries to get the necks of good men broke!"

Perkins raised his hand and shook a lessoning forefinger at the speaker.

"Listen to me, son," he said soberly, "when you talk like that you better talk soft. Don't let him hear. Maybe this stranger ain't out and out bad, but he sure ain't out and out good. And the gent that crosses him is going to have a handful of work all laid out for him before long. No, boys, the only way is to put our heads together and find the best man we have that'll take the chance and make the best of it. Who we got?"

"Young Price is a clean shooter," said one.

"But he's too young. Ain't got no steady hand. Still, maybe he's worth trying out."

"And Ewing has got a Mexican on his place that's a tolerable hand with a gat."

"He'll do for a try. But what about the hoss?"

"There's Anderson of the Creek."

"He never was one-two-three with Jack Kelly, though. I seen 'em ride against one another last fall, and Kelly won hands down."

"That'll make him all the keener to ride a hoss this time that Kelly couldn't ride. Then there's Josh Clark."

"Poor Josh! He's busted up bad already! Nobody better'n that to offer?"

"Wait a minute!"

Old Perkins bit his knuckles.

"What's the name of the young gent that went to work for Seymour last week?"

"The one that throwed the steer?"

"That's him."

"Buel, I think, Billy Buel."

"That's it. Billy Buel. Boys, he's the man for us! Billy Buel? Sure; it all comes back to me in floods. He's the gent that—why, he ain't much more'n a kid, and now he's got a name for himself already—a hard-riding, straight-shooting devil of a youngster, that kid is. We'll send for Billy Buel. And don't you make no doubt he'll come!"

"He ain't rightly part of us here in the town."

"What difference does that make? If he's willing to stand up for Peterville, is Peterville going to turn him down? But it's a long ride to Seymour's. Can we send a gent out there and get Buel back in the morning before this stranger leaves?"

"I'll go," said one. "The old roan'll get me out there quick enough. Besides, I've seen this gent Buel work, and I guess I can figure how to make him want to come."

"Then grab your hoss," said Perkins eagerly. "If Buel comes, they ain't a chance that he'll do both things, but maybe he'll do well enough to put Peterville as high as any other town in the mountains. Work your hossflesh, Slim!"

Slim replied with a wave of the hand and darted down the veranda steps. A moment later, the flying hoofs of his cow pony were beating up sharp spurts of dust as he fled down the street bearing the messenger.

The dust-muffled sound of those hoofbeats came clearly to the stranger as he sat over his ham and eggs. He continued to eat, but a faint smile grew up about his eyes, a gleam of humor and a quiet content. Peterville, he knew, had sent for its best man or its best men, and in the morning the finest the town could find would stand up to meet the acid test. It seemed to please the stranger immensely, though why he should have been pleased when it was to his advantage not to have a single man attempt the test was, indeed, beyond reckoning.

Perhaps there was in him something of the sportsman, so that he did not desire to win that bet of $1,000 from his partner until the money had been fairly earned. Perhaps, too, he had sufficient iron in his nature to enjoy these fierce contests between his fighting horse and the fighting men who attempted to ride it. Or again, still, it may have been only the imp of the perverse in him which made him glad to see his own $1,000 imperiled.

Plainly, he was a man of many motives. And an analysis of his own nature would perhaps have been quite impossible for him to make. Such an impression, to be sure, he was far from making as he sat at the table drinking his coffee and following the designs of water stains and cracks on the opposite wall paper. He seemed at that time to be one who admitted no doubts into his conception of life and the purposes of life. But, stirring the sugar into his coffee with a strong and steady hand, he drank it boiling hot the moment no grains continued to appear under the contact of his spoon; and when it was finished he went to his room.

That he was intensely weary only appeared the moment he was alone in his room. Then, as the door closed behind him, his knees seemed to sag, his head bowed, and in his eyes came that dusty look of complete fag.

He literally staggered across the floor, and, sinking on the bed, he dragged off his boots and his trousers and his shirt. Still, before he could sleep, he locked the door and made sure of the strength of that lock. Then he went to the two windows and saw that the approach to each was up two smooth stories of outer boards, and it was not until he had made all of these observations that he came again to the bed, drew out a long .45 caliber Colt, and, having stowed the latter under his pillow, he literally fell with arms outstretched and face down upon the bed, like a man who had been shot.

In fact, there was a suggestion of death in the sudden repose of this strong and self-centered man. Only once he turned and raised his head in the depth of his extreme weariness. It was to listen to the sound of revolvers exploding not many hundred yards from the hotel at Peterville. And the stranger smiled at the knowledge that the best men of the town were already using the best of their skill to perform one part of his great test, the shooting at the board. What would follow on the morrow, remained for the morrow to reveal.

Then he fell asleep, though the afternoon was still young, and though most men would have said that it was in the highest degree unwise to attempt to slumber in the heat of this day. He fell asleep face down, with his arms outspread like a child who is foredone with hard play. But what could have been a more foolish simile to illustrate the mind of this hardened fellow?

In the meantime, the rest of Peterville was by no means considering such things as similes. The word had gone abroad and had been heard. Challenge a Frenchman as to his love of glory, challenge an Englishman as to his love of verse, challenge a German as to his love of music, or an Italian as to his love of color, but do not suggest to a true Westerner that he can't ride a horse or shoot a gun. The answer is generally violent, and the result of the answer is usually lasting.

So it was in Peterville. If there had been no explosion immediately following the remark with which the brown-faced stranger challenged the manhood of the town, there was all the more response after he had left the veranda. First of all, most naturally, the report spread in a long murmur from kitchen to kitchen and from front porch to front porch where the wives were peeling potatoes or chopping onions in preparation for the evening meal. But the afternoon dimmed, the sun sank, during the sleep of the wide-shouldered stranger; and when the light grew faint the men returned, and with their return there grew up sullen and deep-voiced murmurs through the houses of the village.

They were men among men, these citizens of Peterville, and it was hard indeed if they could not do as well as the men of other towns had done. Mingled with their resolution was a hardy resentment against the man who had dared venture into their midst and give them the test.

But there were other things in the air. The story the stranger had told circulated. But was it true? Was it not very strange indeed that a man should travel across the mountain-desert merely to tempt gun fighters and horse-breakers to action, merely so that he would win $1,000 and quiet a talkative partner? What, then, was the true goal of him who now lay face downward on his bed, sleeping the sleep of utter exhaustion?

The morning, perhaps, would show.

· III ·
THE DELICATE CONTESTANT

That morning did not bring the stranger out of his bed early, in spite of the fact that he had retired in the middle of the afternoon. It was, in fact, not until eight o'clock that he rose. He had then placed behind him sixteen hours of solid slumber, during which time he had moved neither hand nor foot, but had lain face downward through the heat of the later day and through the increasing coolness of the night.

When he wakened, he was as a man stunned; he set about giving himself a sponge bath as best he might. That completed, he dressed and descended, to the lower part of the hotel.

The other men of the town had long since been up. And the buzz of stern, deep voices met him from the veranda. He paused with his foot close to the dining-room door and listened to those voices. His rest had not lessened the depth to which the lines were engraved in his face. Neither had it lessened the shadows about his eyes, nor made his step quicker or lighter. He had slept long and hard, yet he was essentially the same man who had thrown himself face downward upon his bed the afternoon before.

It suggested a man who had labored beyond his strength for many and many a day, who had now taken the opportunity to rest beyond the ordinary, and who nevertheless had still a vast deal of relaxation to make up for. It suggested a mine of nervous energy piled up and ready to be spent as occasion demanded.

Now he ate a quick breakfast, standing, and always straining his ears intently toward the voices on the veranda of the hotel. He gathered his information by fits and starts. All he could discover was that a man was coming who would make at least a bold attempt to win the double test. Peterville, it seemed, could not find two or more worthy men to make a serious effort, and it had consigned its fate into the hands of one Billy Buel.

The wide-shouldered stranger raised his head and considered the name with a frown of thought. But apparently he could not recall or place the name, and he continued hastily to finish his coffee. It was not ended, however, when one of the voices on the veranda rose in irritation at some remark.

"You sure talk plumb foolish, son. Sure he's been throwed, and sure he's been licked. He's been shot up, and he's been thrashed with bare fists, and he's been throwed fifty times by hosses. But the great thing about Billy Buel is that he can learn. He's a pile of scars from his fights and his accidents, but they don't take nothing out of him. If he's ever been licked, he's never admitted it while the fight was going on. He's never crawled while he was taking punishment. But when it was over he started in to learn everything that the gent that beat him knowed. And he always learned a pile more. And that's how we got the Billy Buel of today!"

All of this seemed to be unspeakably pleasant to the ear of the stranger. For an instant his eyes flashed, and then a gradual smile—a fierce pleasure, if there is such a thing—came on his face.

"There they come. That's him on the bay!" came a shout from the veranda. "I can tell by the way he rides—sort of slanting. That's Billy Buel!"

The stranger started hastily toward the door, but a moment of thought made him pause. Going back to his breakfast, he sat down at the table and quietly poured himself another cup of coffee and made it rich with condensed milk. Let the hero come to find him—he would not go to find the hero. In the meantime, he prepared himself for the meeting.

Billy Buel was a rider of horses, a fighter with hands or guns or knives, it seemed. He had been beaten in the early part of his career, according to the talk on the veranda, but he had learned from every defeat; and now, seamed with scars, and crippled, no doubt, in every limb, the terrible veteran struck awe into the hearts of even the men of the mountain-desert.

There was a goodly proportion of whim in the makeup of the brown-faced stranger. And out of what he had heard and guessed he drew even the face of Billy Buel. A pair of long, wind-blown mustaches, beyond question. A misty, long-distance eye. An expression of calm with infinite fierceness ready at the slightest provocation. Such was Billy Buel, no doubt. The picture became so vivid to the stranger that he was prepared to listen for a heavier tread when the champion came up the steps of the veranda with the crowd.

There was no such great distinction, however. The men on the veranda set up a cheer for their newly arrived champion; there was a confused scurrying of feet, and then the crowd rolled into the hall of the hotel and through the door of the dining room. Perkins, having made the suggestion, was now the hero of the hour, or at least the light which shone before the hero. The old fellow was pale with excitement, and, striking an imposing attitude, he waved toward the doorway behind him.

At the gesture, the little crowd split away and revealed the champion to the stranger. But what a champion was this! This slender, handsome, gracefully careless youth—could he be indeed the Billy Buel of the many battles and the many scars?

Even the imperturbable calm of the stranger was for a moment shaken. He even glanced sharply at Perkins, suspecting that the whole affair might be a farce; but the excitement of the old man was too real to have sprung from a jest. And the stranger turned his glance upon the man who was being introduced to him as Billy Buel.

Certainly, there was nothing formidable about his inches or his weight; and if he had received many scars none was visible in his face or on the long, slender hands. He took off his hat and bowed in the doorway and then advanced to shake hands. If there was nothing fear-inspiring in that handsome head of dark hair, it seemed to the stranger that there were many potentialities suggested in the straight-looking, dark eyes; and, though the features were a little too regular and too finely molded to speak of strength of will, at least there was an impression of boundless energy. Some of that energy had taken gay expression in the clothes of the cow-puncher.

Indeed, it was the clothes which had at first given him the appearance of irresponsible boyishness. All the extravagance of the cow-puncher was expressed in his outfit. The cattleman dresses to extremities of his body and does not pay much attention to the rest. His shirt and trousers are of no account. Why waste money on fine materials which sweat and grime will ruin in a single day's riding? But all the rest was perfection.

The shop-made boots of Billy Buel must have cost fifty dollars. They were tailored to the extremist point of stirrup comfort, and the soft leather molded his foot. Golden spurs sprang from the heels—the wide-shouldered stranger started when he saw that they were gold indeed—and a heavy chasing of gold appeared again around the buckle of his sagging belt; there was a rich band of gold around his sombrero. His shirt was yellow silk, his bandanna was the deepest of blue—mid-ocean blue. His gloves had, like his boots, been made to order at his dictates. And those fastidious dictates had forced the glove maker to turn out a mere film of leather to cover the hands of Billy Buel, lest the suppleness of those fingers should be in the slightest respect hampered by stiff-folding leather. It meant, of course, that a pair of gloves would not wear two weeks. But it was apparent from the first glance that expense meant nothing to Billy Buel.

In the meantime, he had not stayed longer in the doorway than was necessary to locate the man he sought. And the stranger took note that when Billy stepped forward it was without the swagger of the conscious hero. He came straight, with a perfectly simple and sincere smile.

"And your name?" he asked.

"I'm William Camp," said the stranger, rising from his chair and noting that he was a good inch taller than Buel. "And I'm glad to meet Billy Buel."

"You see how it is," replied the other, and it was a voice of well-nigh feminine softness. "I don't particular hanker to make a fool of myself, but the boys plumb insist that I take a whirl at your target and your hoss. So if it's the same to you, I'll make the try."

In the meantime, his large and gentle eyes wandered slowly over the face of William Camp. The latter was a hard man, a very hard man indeed; but, at the gentleness of those eyes and the silken apologies hidden in that voice, the delicacy came out in him.

"Son," he said, "I'd sure be glad to have you take a whirl at the target. It's the only thing that's been touched yet by any that tried. But you'll find the hoss hard—cussed hard. Better think twice before you try the hoss."

There was no sneer on the face of Billy Buel. He nodded in grave understanding and in gratitude for the warning, but Camp, looking past the other, saw smiles appear on half a dozen of the faces of those who stood about. They seemed to feel that it was ridiculous to warn Billy Buel about a horse. Moreover, they were watching their hero with a peculiarly expectant awe that baffled Camp. He knew men, and he knew that the interior and the exterior are often very far from matching. But that this slender and graceful fellow could be really formidable to man and beast, was beyond comprehension. For instance, at that very moment Billy Buel had drawn off his gloves, tucked them under his arm, and was rolling a cigarette with fingers as slender as the fingers of a woman. Work, certainly, he had never done—at least not for any extended period. Everything in Camp made him wish to shake his head. And just then, in the act of lighting his cigarette, the eyes of Billy Buel were raised to his.

They had been soft, mild eyes before. Now, catching the doubt and the frown of Camp, all the softness was banished from them, and they became concentrated points of light that pierced into the mind of his interlocutor. William Camp thrilled to that glance. He understood fighting men. He knew instantly the expression of the man who feels that he has been doubted, and that the doubt is an insult.

"It's your turn to talk, Mr. Camp," said Billy Buel coldly. "Do you want me to make the try?"

"It's your own skin," said Camp, not yet entirely recovered from his reluctance. "If you want to risk it, go ahead. I'll set up the target, and I'll furnish the hoss—saddled, which is a shade more than the bargain."

· IV ·
BILLY SUSPECTS CAMP

So saying, he started for the door. At once, the bystanders were transformed into a noisy rout pouring before him and behind; but what Camp was chiefly aware of was the youth at his side, stepping with the grace and the silence of a panther. He watched from the corner of his eye, but even that side glance informed him that there were qualities of strength in Buel that had not showed at the first glance.

One would have thought that, doubting the final result in spite of all his precautions, William Camp, in the danger of losing his $1,000 bet, would have become gloomy. But perhaps he was too sure of success. At any rate, his eye actually brightened, and something akin to a smile gathered around his wise eyes as he took note of the youth beside him. Doubtless, it was his love of a cleanly fought sporting event.

They came out into the open.

"I suppose you want to do the shooting first?" Camp asked. "That'll keep your hand from getting shook up by the fight with the hoss."

"I'll shoot before or after," said Billy coldly.

And he measured Camp with his glance. It was a very solemn glance, an ugly glance. The shadow of a doubt which he had seen in the face of the other had had an acute reaction in him, beyond question. Plainly, it was not wise to let Buel see that he was being pitied. It would have irritated an ordinary man, but William Camp, as perhaps may have been guessed, was far from the ordinary man. He met the grim look of the youth with unshaken kindness.

"If I'm to choose," he said quietly, "we'll have the shooting first."

So saying, he took from a hip pocket a piece of thin board about six or seven inches in length, and, having asked for and obtained a hammer and nails from the proprietor of the hotel, he went to the nearest fence post and affixed the board to the top of it.

The crowd was not silent while this was being

done. They informed Billy Buel in ugly whispers of their suspicions.

"He's made the board thin, you see?" they suggested. "That's so's if you nearly cut the thing in two it won't have no weight above to break itself off and give you the credit. You got to cut away every shred of that board or you lose, Billy."

He received the warning with a grave nod. His real attention was concentrated on the revolver which had come from the holster into his hand. And the mechanism became a live thing under his active finger tips! Every bit of the action was swiftly and carefully gone over, the cartridges looked to, and then in his open palm he weighed the weapon for a moment with a thoughtful manner. Plainly, that gun and the man who held it were old and intimate friends, but before going into action he was reassuring himself that he might be most closely in touch with his ally. And presently the lithe fingers coiled around the butt, and the gun dropped to full arm's length.

He was satisfied. So much was certain. He was sure of the gun and of himself. The only doubt was that at his very best he might not possess sufficient wizardry to perform the feat.

In the meantime, the faces of the townsmen presented curious studies. They were like students in the bleachers before the football game. The athletes in the field may be calm enough, knowing that physical action will soon put an end to their suspense, but those who sit and wait are in a double agony. The men of Peterville stood about with drawn faces. They looked at the target. They saw William Camp pace off thirty ample steps— steps so ample, indeed, that they brought a dull growl from the spectators. Plainly, this stranger was wasting no chance he could seize in order to make the task as difficult for Billy as possible. But when they suggested that their champion complain, he shook his head and without a word stepped to the mark which Camp had drawn in the dust with his heel. He did not even place his own heels on the mark—though every inch of saved distance counted—but toed it and stood erect, eying that bit of board. How painfully distant it seemed to the spectators!

They murmured a variety of comments: "Do your best, old man; they ain't nobody around these parts can do better." Or: "If you don't do it, son, they ain't nobody'll remember it agin' you." Or: "If you win, Billy, you sure got a home with me!"

As for William Camp, he said not a word, but stood with his chin resting solidly on the knuckles of his big right fist, and his eyes never moved from the grave, handsome face of Buel.

The latter spoke without shifting his eyes from the piece of board.

"Are you set, Mr. Camp?"

"The board looks tolerable set," answered

Camp, smiling at the cold antagonism in the voice of the youth. "And I guess it's ready when you're ready, son."

He expected a careful and painful moment of taking aim, but instead, while he was still speaking, the body of the gun fighter inclined forward a little into a crouch, or semicrouch, his hand whipped up after the fashion of one making a snap shot, and the last of Camp's words was blown into nothingness by the explosion of the revolver.

A yell came from the crowd when it was seen that a spot of sunshine appeared in the geometrically exact center of the board.

But that was only the beginning. The five other shots would have to be exactly in line with the first, or the board would not be cut; and each must be as widely spaced as possible, still making the holes overlap.

"Take your time, Billy," they called.

Again the explosion of the gun drowned the last of the words; and this time the spot in the center of the board widened. Barely overlapping the first was the second hole, as they could see, and exactly in line with it. Here was shooting such as men might dream of seeing, but shooting such as no man there had ever witnessed. There were no longer any shouts. And indeed there was no time, for the gun was exploding rapidly in the hand of Billy Buel.

To right and left of the original puncture the line

of light widened. But William Camp was not looking at his target at all. Strange to say, he was concentrating his attention purely on the face of the sharpshooter. And what a face it was. The lips had curled to a sneer of resolute scorn, so to speak. The head was thrown a little back with the jaw thrust out. And the eyes blazed as though each bullet were being driven into the body of a mortal enemy.

Then the sixth shot roared from the weapon, and not until Camp saw the villagers leaping into the air and yelling with joy did he reluctantly withdraw his eyes from the face of Buel and look at the board.

It was cut evenly in two, just above the top of the fence post—cut in a ragged line which yet held straight from side to side. Every bullet had done its measured work in exactly the correct proportion. The impossible had become the possible in the instant.

When he turned again, it was to see Buel calmly slipping a fresh round of bullets into his gun. And for some reason this seemed to please Camp more than the skill of the marksman.

"Looks to me," he said, and it was all he spoke in congratulation, "that you never take no chances, son."

Buel slipped the weapon back into his holster before he turned on Camp and answered grimly: "All depends where I am, Mr. Camp."

Plainly, he wanted to give offense. But Camp nodded and said no more. A sparkle of almost boyish glee was in his eyes.

"And now the hoss. I guess he's saddled? I guess old Brownie's all ready for you, Buel?"

"He's over yonder," said Buel in answer.

And he pointed to where the stable boy had led forth the formidable mustang.

Brownie the terrible, the man-killer, was as gentle as the proverbial lamb until someone actually swung into the saddle. Now he stood with sleepy downward head, his long ears wobbling alternately one back and one forward, as though he were enjoying to the uttermost this bath in the warmth of the early morning sun.

"Yep," answered Camp cheerily, "there he is— and good luck to you, Buel. Brownie looks quiet enough this morning."

But Billy Buel was tightening his belt as he answered with great gravity: "He looks tolerable bad to me, that hoss. Tolerable sight worse'n the worst hoss I ever rode."

His solemnity cut short the exuberance of the crowd. They drifted slowly toward the mustang, and Billy Buel followed them without haste. Never once did his eyes leave this new goal, any more than they had left the board the moment it was nailed on the post. But on his way he stopped near the hitching rack in front of the hotel and dropped his hand over the neck of the bay which stood there.

She was a lovely creature. She was not more than fifteen three at the most, but she was made with the care of a sculptor—with the care which the jeweler showers on the making of a fine watch, it would be more accurate to say. She had that length in the forehand which promises a bridle-wise horse answering to every pulse of the guiding wrist. Her sloping shoulders, her amply muscled quarters, her body girth at the cinches, told of the power to stand up under weight and work, and the heart and wind to endure. And her legs, black a little distance below knees and hocks, were fine as hammered iron—and like hammered iron in the strength of which they spoke.

Camp took in her points with one expert sweep of the eyes. Then he fell to watching the man and the horse together. They were friends indeed. Scarcely had she felt the hand fall on her neck when the bay turned her head and dropped a velvet muzzle against the chest of her companion. His other hand came up to pat it, and as though wondering why he did not swing into the saddle at once she lifted her head and whinnied softly, and even stamped lightly with a forefoot.

Billy Buel spoke gently to her, with a smile, but still his eyes did not leave the formidable and bony frame of Brownie, standing so placid in the sunshine. It was as if he were saying a farewell to the mare and acquainting himself for the last time with all of her faith and gentleness and bigness of heart before he went out to risk his life in the attempted conquest of a brute of her own species. And William Camp, watching, bit his lip with a singular anxiety.

There was a final pat for the delicate muzzle of the mare, there was a final passing of the hand along her arched, silken neck, and then Buel stepped out toward the sullen mustang.

He was stopped at once by wellwishers of the town.

"Give yourself a chance, son," said old Perkins, first to reach him. "They ain't no rush about this. Wait till long about the middle of the day when the sun comes up strong. Sure takes the deviltry out of a bad hoss, this sun we have around these parts. Lead 'em out in the morning, and pretty near any old hoss in the corral might give you a lively five minutes. But along about noon they ain't feeling so frisk by a pile. Take your time, Billy, and give yourself a chance. And don't you forget it—that's the hoss that throwed Kelly. He may look sleepy, but them sleepy-looking hosses are like mules. They think. And a thinkin' hoss is sure the devil."

There were other voices clamoring advice, but Billy smiled them away with a peculiar sadness.

"Gents," he said, "it ain't that I step around asking for trouble. Nope, I sure like to take things the surest way, but that old brown hoss ain't going to be changed by noon. There's fire in them sleepy eyes of his. He ain't been rode. He ain't going to be rode. He'll fight till his heart busts. And—"

He paused a moment. His solemn eyes swung above the crowd and rested bitterly on William Camp.

"It ain't a question of breaking Brownie," he said to the crowd, but plainly he was really addressing Camp, "because he can't be broke. It's only the question of can I bust his heart or is he going to bust mine? It ain't a hoss-breaking contest—it's murder, one way or the other. And I say—damn them that starts arguments like this one!"

• V •
THE BATTLE

His teeth clicked over the last words, and a devil came in his eyes and flared out toward Camp. It was a challenge so pronounced that the crowd winced back and left an alley between the two— an alley down which men or bullets might freely pass!

But William Camp had apparently no thought of taking offense. He eyed the youth with the most unbroken gravity, his head bowed, his big knuckles still supporting his chin. One might have said, had the surroundings been different, that he was a judge sitting on the bench and ready to pronounce sentence. There was neither joy nor anger nor anticipation in those wide eyes, old beyond expression. Rather, he seemed engaged in the dubious task of plumbing the very soul of the young fellow before him.

Billy Buel maintained his hostile survey for a long moment, and, seeing that there was no rejoinder, he stepped, with his teeth clenched, toward Brownie. The crowd fell back before him; he was not a pace away from the mustang when the voice of Camp sounded.

"Just wait a minute, son," spoke that smooth and large-compassed bass.

And Camp approached rapidly.

"I got this to say," he went on as Billy turned. "You've done plenty enough for any one man. In one day, any-ways. I say that I'm plumb satisfied. I ain't so poor that I got to count the dollars one by one. Let the hoss go. I'll pay my partner them one thousand dollars and say no more about it. But it rides agin' the grain for me to let you tackle Brownie.

"Listen to me, son. You sure said a lot when you said he wouldn't go down till his heart is busted. And I'll tell you some more. The man don't walk that can bust that heart of his. Because why? Because he's plumb loaded with meanness. I've known that hoss for always, pretty near. No good for work, because there was never a man good enough to back him. Quick-thinking, and always thinking nothing but deviltry—that's Brownie.

"Maybe you've knowed men that didn't have no wish in life except to raise hell with other men. That's Brownie. He lives for the sake of fighting. Turn him loose in the corral with other hosses, and he fights to kill 'em. He won't even let a mare alone. He gets her by the throat. He won't even let a colt alone—being about as bad as a mule when it comes to that. That's the kind of a devil he is. No good on earth, but sure trained to raise ructions with any gent that climbs into the saddle on him. It ain't just being throwed, but the minute he throws his rider he turns around and plants all four feet on him. That's Brownie. And I tell you what, Buel, you're too good a man to be wasted by hoss-flesh. Take my word for it. Forget about Brownie. Figure that you've rode him and let it go. I'll pay the money to my partner, and you can have all the glory you plumb want—but I don't want to see no massacre!"

There was a murmur of surprise and wonder at this generous speech—from all except Billy Buel. His expression had gradually changed, while the wide-shouldered stranger was speaking, from anger, to wonder, and finally to a deeply settled suspicion. And his answer was instant and decisive.

"Mr. Camp," he said, "I heard all you got to say, and if you had a hundred times more to say it wouldn't budge me none. I think I've got you figured, sir, and everything I figured is bad for you—mighty bad."

There had, apparently, been a cold rage gathering in Billy Buel ever since he met Camp, and now his face grew unutterably evil with anger as he talked. If ever the desire to kill looked out of the eyes of a man, it looked out of the eyes of Buel as he faced the stranger.

"The way I figure you," he said, "is this: You make a bet, or maybe you don't make a bet. Speaking personal, I figure there ain't no bet at all. You just happen to have enough money so's you don't care what you do with your time. All you want is to have the most fun. And the most fun in your eyes is seeing somebody else take chances and get beat. So you go around here picking up gents to shoot at your target, figuring that when they fail you'll have a little grin to yourself.

"And even if they win, they've still got your devil of a hoss to face. And he is a devil. I can see that by the ugly head of him. The only point is that I ain't cut out so's I can hate a hoss. I confine my hating to men. And I'm a powerful strong hater when I get started, pardner! But I'm going to ride this hoss.

"I know what's in your head. You seen pretty pronto that I didn't like you, Camp, and I'm here to state loud and plenty that I don't. And when I was lucky enough to cut that board in two you figured that maybe I'd be a bad one to have for an enemy, in case I lived through the hoss riding. So here you come at the last minute and act generous. You figure I'll think you're a pretty good gent, after all. But I ain't that simple, pardner. Not by a long ways. I know you, and I know you're no good.

"You've got Jack Kelly all busted up. And Jack is a straight gent from the word go—kind of hard, but honest and meaning no harm. And I misdoubt you've been going all through the mountains getting the best men killed or pretty near killed with your hoss. But I'm going to try my luck and do my best. And if I live through it I tell you, man to man, Camp, with all these here gents looking on and hearing, I ain't going to leave your trail till I've hunted you down and talked to you—with a gun. I guess that's final. Now get out of the way. I'm going to ride the hoss!"

There were in these words a spirit of denunciation so terrible, a spirit so far in excess of the actual words themselves, a spirit which spoke from the flaming eyes and the tense lips of handsome Billy Buel, that the crowd shuddered and shrank back still farther, ready to dive for shelter when the inevitable gun play would follow.

But there was no gun play. Buel stood tremblingly alert and ready to whip out his revolver, but Camp made no move toward his gun. He did not even seem to hear the words of the younger man, but only vaguely gathered their content while, with chin lowered on his chest, he studied

Billy's face from beneath gathered eyebrows.

It would have seemed in every man except one in a thousand a cowardly acceptance of the most bitter insults. But there was something about Camp which forbade the remotest suspicion of such a thing as a craven spirit. The utter calmness with which he eyed Billy Buel spoke volumes in itself. He seemed more than ever a man who knew much—too much, it might also be said—and who was ever thinking more of the causes than of the effects of action.

Had Billy Buel been himself a thinking man, he would have known that his accusations of cowardice were absurd; but Billy was distinctly not a thinking man. That smooth brow of his was eloquent. There were no wrinkles in it. He would be middle-aged before time began to be written into his face. He led a butterfly existence, looking never more than a day ahead, draining from each hour all the happiness and the excitement he could extract from it.

Such was Billy Buel. And this quality, which perhaps made him so terrible in action because imagination never made him dread the consequences beforehand, made it impossible for him to look behind the sober quiet of the older man and see the real force and courage of the other.

Had he known it, it required bravery of the most superlative nature for a man to hear such a taunt and endure it without a retort. But to

William Camp this was nothing—less than nothing.

He stepped back silently from between Billy Buel and Brownie, and with a half mocking, half regretful gesture he invited the youth to go out and do his best with an unsurmountable obstacle. Even then it was not too late for Billy to recede. Had he been a diplomat, he would have done so, for as he peered at the lined, grave face of the elder man he felt a glimmering understanding of the other. Indeed, he would gladly have opened a new parley at that moment, but a fierce pride prevented him. Perhaps he was damning himself to an early death with that pride, but, nevertheless, he could not break free from it. He bowed with gloomy profundity to Camp, and the next moment his left hand was gathering the reins over the withers of Brownie.

The die was cast, and the battle was about to commence.

But not until the foot of the daring rider had touched the stirrup—not until the weight of his body began to pull the saddle to one side—did Brownie awake from his pleasant dream of sunshiny pastures where men were not. And even when he awakened, it was only to put his ears cheerily forward. That was when the full burden of Billy Buel descended into the saddle and the knees of the young rider gripped the sides of the mustang.

At this he twitched his head about, and still with his long ears pricked forward he gravely and almost humorously examined the man who was seated in the saddle. It would have brought a laugh from the bystanders had they not seen that with all his might Buel was trying to keep that head from turning. Out of those slender shoulders, out of that set of slim fingers and femininely round, small wrists, he was producing an incredible power on the reins and on the bit, but in spite of the pull the head of Brownie twitched easily around. To be sure, the strain on the bit wrenched his mouth apart.

That made his pricking ears the more grotesque. He seemed to be laughing silently—the horrible human laughter in a brute beast—at the man in the saddle.

After that, he swung his head about and quietly surveyed the little crowd which stood around him. And beyond them he next looked over the field and the fences.

"They ain't going to be no buckin'," cried old Perkins joyously. "You sure talked when you said that hoss was wise, Camp. He's so wise that he knows he'd just waste time trying to get Billy out'n the saddle."

His voice was joined by a great clamoring. Brownie had begun to walk slowly ahead without sign of a hostile demonstration. Only William Camp failed to share in the general rejoicings. He remained watching, very thoughtful, almost removed from the scene by the severity of his contemplations.

The clamoring of the spectators stopped as abruptly as though a blanket had been thrown over their heads. Brownie, walking gently along, had flung himself sidewise without warning, a lurch so violent that Billy Buel swayed perilously far in the opposite direction.

Before he could regain his balance, the mustang, still with pricking ears, leaped high in the air and came down stiff-legged, his back arched so that Billy, sat, as it were, at the apex of a triangle. The triangle dissolved into a mad tangle when the mustang found that he had not really shaken the man on his back. It would require bucking of a supernatural virtue to unseat him.

Straightway, Brownie delved into the shadowy depths of his nature and began to pull out his tricks one by one. They were inexhaustible, it seemed. From sunfishing to straight, up-and-down, stiff-legged bucking there was nothing that Brownie did not know, and neither did he forget to season his antics now and again by flinging himself on the ground and striving to pin the rider under his rolling weight.

And still, every time the man slipped from the saddle, and every time as the horse rose, Billy Buel was clinging to him. But he was no longer the gay, the careless, the smiling Billy. The constant succession of shocks had numbed his mind and made his face a mask; covered with dust and seen dimly and uncertainly through that dust cloud which Brownie had knocked up. And in his eyes there seemed to the spectators to be a lurking horror.

Indeed, there was something truly horrible about the fighting of big Brownie. Most horses buck as though they were frightened more than angered. But Brownie fought as a savage man would fight against submitting to the rule of another.

His rage became a divine thing to watch, after a time, as he passed into a frenzy. He literally was living in the air, tying himself into strange knots and dropping to earth with a jar like a dead weight falling. Then up again and leaping from side to side, always with his head stretched out, and low, as a wise bucking horse will do. And though with all his might Billy Buel strove to pull that head in and up, he was utterly powerless to budge it.

Brownie had gone mad with a cunning insanity. He had become a super-horse. The shocks of his bucking were to Billy Buel like blows delivered with a club against the base of his brain. And the results were disastrous.

There is nothing so joyous to a man of the mountain-desert as a clean-cut fight between a bucking horse and a rider. At first, the men of Peterville stood about shouting and laughing and swinging their hats, but after a time they drew back and became silent.

Through the dust-mist they had seen the face of Billy Buel, and blood was trickling from nose and mouth after the violence of that relentless pitching. Yet, by some wizardry of horsemanship, he clung in the saddle when his brain must have been long since numbed. A splendid, subconscious courage, if it might be called that, sustained him. The balance which he had learned to maintain in a hundred battles with horses now stood him well.

Suddenly, old Perkins whipped out his gun.

"Boys," he said, "that hoss will kill Billy inside another five minutes. Before it happens, I'm going to shoot him through the head!"

"You're right!" they answered, and Perkins raised his weapon.

But William Camp appeared suddenly beside him and dragged down his arm.

"Let the hoss alone," he commanded, his face savage and stern. "I warned Buel. He took the chance. Now let him fight it out. The gent that shoots my hoss will answer for it to me, and he'll answer pronto!"

If there had been the slightest doubt before about the qualities of the stranger as a fighting man, they were removed in that instant. He swept the crowd with the eye of a lion and challenged them one by one, and one by one they frowned and looked away. Perkins slipped his revolver back into the holster.

"You're right," he said, admitting his weakness. "Besides, Buel has you lined up for his special meat. And I ain't going to interfere. But it's murder, Camp, and you'll answer for it if Billy comes out wrong!"

Then came a ringing shout from the others: "He's busted! He's done!"

William Camp turned to see Brownie standing motionless in the haze of dust which his own fury had thrown up. He was beaten and badly beaten; there could be no doubt of that. His head hung, his four legs were braced to sustain his weight, his body was racked with a heavy panting, and from his body the sweat dripped steadily to the dirt below.

It had been a terrible battle, and Brownie was far spent indeed. Through his rangy, ugly body a heavy tremor was passing, and his eyes rolled in the completeness of his exhaustion. As for the rider, he was a shapeless heap in the saddle. There was no responsive call to the bystanders when they cheered him. There was no waving of the hat. He sat bunched and helpless in the saddle, with his head bent forward on his chest, and his whole shirt was crimson stained from the fierceness of the battle. If Brownie were on the point of collapsing from exhaustion, certainly his rider was in no better shape.

"He's won!" shouted Perkins.

"He's won!" echoed William Camp, his eyes wide with astonishment.

And as they spoke Brownie showed that even his master had underrated his powers of vicious endurance. He started suddenly from his standing position, raced fifty yards at full speed, and, flinging himself in the air, came down stiff-legged.

At least, he attempted to come down stiff-legged. He was so far successful that the unexpected shock hurled the dazed Billy Buel from the saddle like an arrow from a bow. There he lay sprawling on his side in the thick of the dirt. But as for Brownie, his staunch limbs collapsed at the same moment. He had no time to rejoice in his triumph, but every muscle in his body relaxed, and he dropped heavily into the dirt and lay unmoving.

There was a rush for the fallen body of the rider, who had not stirred. William Camp was first beside him, and presently he raised his head and called to the crowd: "He's alive—knocked out, plumb alive!"

He did not heed the answering growl: "And lucky for you!" for another voice was calling from the body of Brownie: "The hoss busted himself plumb in two with that last try. He sure busted his heart fighting!"

"But who wins?" asked Perkins curiously of Camp. "Who wins? The man or the hoss—Buel or

Brownie? He sure rode that hoss till the hoss was all in, but the hoss throwed him before he died. Who won?"

"The question answers itself," said William Camp. "The horse is dead, and the man is alive. Billy Buel wins. Who knows what he might have done if Brownie had got up off the earth after his fall?"

· VI ·
HE WHO KNOWS MEN

Beyond doubt this was a display of good sporting blood. According to his own statement, William Camp stood to lose $1,000 to his partner, whoever that might be; and beyond question Peterville stood to win undying glory as the result of the double triumph. Not a man there but had seen many an outlaw horse do his worst, but no one had dreamed of such an exhibition of pure deviltry as Brownie had put up that day. Horses had been known to kill riders; they had not been known to kill themselves. But there lay the gaunt, lifeless body of the mustang. And there lay the limp body of Billy Buel, not far from death, it seemed.

They raised him with a reverent gentleness. Blood and dust and sweat stained his clothes; his body was like a rag for looseness of muscles. And so they bore him to the hotel and put him on a bed and called the doctor; and they stayed, a close-grouped, whispering crowd, until the doctor came out from the room to assure them that Billy Buel, in the morning, would be as good a man as ever he had been. It was a temporary exhaustion, he said, and it would pass quickly. He was like a prize fighter. He had been terribly stunned, but he would awaken.

With that assurance the crowd broke up and left Billy Buel to make his own way back to complete possession of his senses. That was a matter of some moments still. And when he awakened, it was only to ask: "Brownie? What happened to him?"

"Dead," they told him swiftly. "You beat him, Billy."

At that a smile of angelic peace came on the lips of the cow-puncher, and a moment later he had fallen into a renewed slumber. A real slumber it was this time, from which he did not waken until the gray of the next morning.

But when his eyes opened for the second time he sprang out of the bed fully alive and fully alert.

He had no sooner dressed than he cast open his door, and his call brought the proprietor himself. The conversation between them was swift and to the point.

"I've been plumb fagged," said Billy, "and I'm sort of hazy on yesterday. What happened when I rode Brownie?"

"You beat him fair and square. We all seen him

go down. He dropped the same time you did, but he didn't get up."

"He's done, then?"

"He sure is."

"Then get hold of Camp for me. I want to talk to him a pile."

But the other shrugged his shoulders.

"Camp's gone. He left last night."

Billy Buel started.

"When he left, did he leave any message for me? About where I could find him?"

The other smiled, reading the hungry face of Buel.

"He didn't leave no message, and he didn't want to leave none," he suggested. He added kindly: "And if I was you, Billy, I'd sure keep off the trail of that gent. He ain't an easy one to handle. I'd rather keep to bucking horses, a pile. Leave him be and let him foller his own road alone."

But Billy Buel was gritting his teeth.

"Which way did he take?" he asked sharply.

"The west trail," answered the proprietor. "But if I was you, Billy—"

"Hang all that," answered Billy Buel. "The west trail, did you say?"

The proprietor nodded and hurried downstairs.

"Buel has started on Camp's trail," he whispered to his wife; "and before the day's over they'll be a killing in these here mountains such as we ain't had in many a month. There he goes now," he added a little later. And they listened as the drum of the horse's hoofs began near by and died out far away. "That's Billy Buel starting!"

It was Billy Buel indeed, and riding as he had never ridden before. If the stranger had fled from him, it might be a long, an almost impossible, trail. But, if he had simply jogged leisurely out of Peterville with a light conscience, it might be easy indeed to overtake him.

So he plied Lou, the bay mare, with steady coaxing, and he was answered with all the speed and spirit that lay in the magnificent body of the mare. They dipped into Cumberland Valley before the sun was well up. They climbed the heights beyond and cut onto the main road.

It was very much like a stage entrance. He had scarcely put Lou to the level going again when a horseman turned an elbow of the mountain to the left, and William Camp rode slowly into view. Billy, watching closely, could have sworn that he was seen almost as soon as he saw the other, but William Camp came slowly and straight upon his way, neither retarding the pace of his horse nor increasing it. Twice Billy Buel reached for his revolver, and twice his hand came away. Then he placed Lou across the road and waited; a moment later Camp had halted his own mount before the obstacle.

He seemed a huge man sitting his saddle, though one with a careful eye might have noted that his legs were astonishingly short in the stirrups, considering the bulk of the body above. But Billy Buel had no attention to spare for such things as that. His observation centered only in the face of the man—the wise, sunburned face of William Camp, and the thoughtful eyes. Surely, this was not one to be accused of cowardly trickery. But Billy Buel, remembering what had passed between them, gritted his teeth.

For a moment they sat their horses staring at each other.

It was Camp who spoke first, saying: "Looks to me, partner, that you been riding kind of hard. Glad to see you, Buel, and to make out that you ain't been hurt bad by the riding."

"Yep, I been riding hard," assented Billy sternly, "but I'd ride a pile harder, friend, to meet you again. Camp, I been working Lou, here, pretty steady, and it's all been to meet up with you again."

William Camp smiled and nodded.

"That's sure a compliment," he said. "And what's in your mind, Billy?"

The lip of the latter curled.

"I reckon you know," he muttered. "I reckon you know why I've kept so close on your trail, eh? Didn't I talk out tolerable, loud and clear the other day in Peterville? Well, I hate changing my mind till I got a good reason for it! Camp, I'm here to fight!"

He leaned forward in the saddle as he spoke, a figure brilliant and savage at once. The least hair's breadth in the rise of Camp's brows would have meant the outwhip of a gun and a death or two deaths in the high road. Perhaps Camp knew this as well as if the mind of Buel were exposed before him in black and white printing. But, at any rate, no glimmering of fear showed in his eyes, nor of anger, either.

"I'm a tolerable patient man," he declared with his usual softness. "And I'm a pile interested in finding out what goes on inside of your head, Buel. Suppose you talk out good and loud and clear, and let me listen. I'll try to understand. Which sometimes I can do tolerable clear. What you got agin' me? Here you are with red blood in your eye. Why?"

The veriest coward in the mountain-desert might have shrunk from a speech as conciliatory as this in the face of Billy Buel's outright challenge, but Camp did not shrink. His eye retained its bright cunning, and not once did it desist from the careful scanning of the face of the younger man.

"What have I got against you?" echoed Billy, his voice hard, a flush of hot anger mounting to his forehead. "I'll tell you what, though it's something you know already. You take a murder hoss around through the mountains. You lead the gents on with a cock-and-bull yarn about you and a bet you've made, and then you get them to take a chance. You smash every good bone in the body of a gent like Kelly. You raise the devil liberal everywhere you go, and finally you pick on Peterville.

"It ain't that I grudge the fight, and it ain't by a long pile that I think I'm too good to take my chances with any hoss that ever walked. But I don't like the way you work, pardner. It don't look good to me by a lot. I say that hoss was a murder hoss, and I mean just that. It wasn't a question of breaking him; it was just a question of keeping from being killed by him. Is that plain? And if it is, I say I've come here to have a reckoning with you, Camp. And the way I make up my reckoning is that one of us is going to leave this place with two hosses, and leave fast!"

All the flame of his anger was in his face as he spoke, and trembling like the quiver of flame was in his voice. And still the marvelous calm of the other was not broken.

"You want me to fight with you, Billy?"

William Camp paused.

"Billy," he said at length, "ten years ago, if you'd said half of what you've said today they'd be a gun play."

"And suppose you pretend that this is ten years ago?" asked Billy through his teeth.

"Because it ain't. Not by exactly ten years, and during that time I been getting older and a pile wiser. That's why they'll be no gun play. It ain't that I'm afraid of you, Buel. Speaking personal, you're about the best hand with a gun that I've ever seen, but it ain't fear. As you know."

And Billy Buel, looking squarely into the eyes of the other, admitted in his honest heart that he saw no fear in William Camp. The man was as firm as a rock, and as steady in his glance.

"One reason I ain't mad," said Camp as though the silence of his interlocutor was an admission that he was understood, "is because you're right!"

The confession was so simply stated that Billy Buel started.

"You're right," said Camp. "I've been going through the mountains with a murder hoss. And the reason I did it was because I wanted to find a man that didn't have no fear in him. I had to have an acid test. Same as you got to have for gold. You might waste a year getting out yaller stuff and find at the end that it's all fool's gold. Same way with a man. I had to have a man; and I had to have an acid test for him. I have to have a man, and you're the man I want. But I had to try you out first."

"You had to have a man?" gasped out Buel. "You mean you got a use for me, Camp, and you took this way of getting me, or somebody like me?"

"That's it."

"Well, I'll be damned," growled Billy.

And his handsome face flushed again, in doubt as to whether or not he should accept the statements of the other at face value.

"Maybe you will be damned before you're done with me," said the astonishing William Camp.

"What blows up the things you've said," remarked Billy, though with less heat and more curiosity, "is that the minute the game's over you leave town. If you wanted me for something, why did you do that?"

"Because," said Camp, "I was quite sure that the moment you got on your feet you'd be after me as fast as your hoss could gallop."

"How would I know which way you'd gone?"

"I don't want a man who couldn't do a piece of trailing like that. No, I guessed that you'd come after me. And if you hadn't come, I'd have forgotten you. I knew you hated me. And a good hater is the sort of gent I want. Understand?"

"I don't understand," admitted Billy, with less and less anger as he began to see that he was face to face with a truly unique character. "But I'll hear you talk."

"Before you pull your gun?" Camp smiled, and he went on before Billy could answer: "I have to have a real man, a fighting man, the best the mountains can turn out. That's why I fished. And I've been lucky enough to get what I wanted—and you're he, Buel! The steadiest hand, the fastest eye, the quickest nerve for gun play, the best hand with a hoss. That's you, and they's not a man in the mountains that can stand up to you, all odds being equal."

Billy Buel flushed. Yet it was not mere wordy praise which he was receiving. The other spoke calmly, more like a judge than a witness. He was stating facts, not handing out mere empty compliments.

"Leave all that ride," said Billy, uneasy under the praise. "Just tell me what you got on hand that you need me to do and how you're so confident that I'll come along and work for you—me or the man you started out to find in the mountains?"

"I'll tell you why," answered Camp. "The man I want is the sort of man who'd leave a million-dollar job to tackle the work I got on hand."

"Why?"

"Because every day of the work I got to offer him is liable to cost him his life."

Billy Buel broke into uncertain laughter.

"Maybe that's a joke?" he said.

"Do I look like I'm joking?"

"Maybe not, I dunno. You're a queer sort, pardner. I suppose you offer big pay in this job you got on hand?"

"Pay?" said the other as though this practical thought had not yet occurred to him. "Why, yes, I suppose we offer high pay. Matter of fact, we'll pay anything you want us to pay. What would interest you, Buel?"

"For the kind of work that you got on hand," said Billy coldly, "I'd only ask five hundred dollars a week."

"Take you," said William Camp instantly. "Take you quick on that. five hundred dollars a week, Buel, and board and keep. And a hoss to ride, as good as you want."

Billy Buel blinked, thought of the salary he was receiving at that time, and blinked again. But it was impossible to doubt the sincerity with which the offer was made.

"I'm to go with you," he said, attempting to laugh but failing miserably in the attempt, "and take a chance of getting my head blown off every day, and get five hundred dollars a week and found for it. Is that the bargain you want?"

"That's just it," said Camp calmly.

"Then," broke out Billy Buel, "I say you're worse than I dreamed you were at first sight. More murder in your head, eh?"

"You'll take the job," was the reply of the astonishing Camp.

"I will, will I?"

"Sure you will. That's your weakness, Billy Buel. You can't keep away from the things that look dangerous. That's why I know you'll come along. You ain't even going to turn back and say good-by. You'll come along the way you are and write back to 'em to say that you've gone."

Billy Buel sighed.

"I come out here to pick a fight with you, Camp, and here you are offering me a job—"

"Which you'll take. Shake on it, Billy."

"Camp, I don't know you, and I don't know the work."

"It'll take a little time for you to know me. It won't take you long to know the work—maybe half an hour. What d'you say, Billy? Do we shake?"

Billy Buel strove to laugh the idea away—he could not; he strove to sneer the idea away—he could not; he strove to scowl the idea away—but in the end his hand went slowly out.

"I dunno how it is," he admitted, "but I guess I'll do what you say!"

· VII ·
BILLY IS PUZZLED

Yet the explanation for which Billy Buel was all ears was not forthcoming. Of a thousand other things the wide-shouldered Camp was ready and willing to talk, but when Billy pressed toward the all-important subject Camp avoided with easy and frictionless shifts that swung the conversation onto other topics before Billy was well aware of what had happened.

"Camp," Billy said as they jogged along the next day, "I misdoubt that maybe you've got a lot of wrong notions about me. I'll just start out and put you right. Is there any sort of hard work tied up with this job of yours?"

"Work?" said Camp. "That all depends. What sort of work d'you mean?"

"The kind that puts wrinkles between your eyes and an ache between your shoulders," said Billy instantly. "Is it that kind of work, Camp?"

"Not a bit. They ain't any lifting of weights, Billy." Buel sighed with relief.

"I'm sure glad of that," and he nodded, "because, between you and me, Camp, I sure hate work. I'm ashamed of it, right enough, and I don't brag none of being lazy. But just the same I sure hate callouses and sore muscles and all that. I'm tolerable glad your job ain't the kind that makes 'em."

And he smiled with winning frankness at the older man, while William Camp laughed aloud. He himself was one who must have labored many a day, to judge by the callouses on his hard hands, and by the vertical wrinkle of pain between his eyes. Yet he seemed to take no offense at Billy's confession of indolence.

"How do you make your living if you don't work?" he asked.

"I dunno. I just sort of pick along. Sometimes I got money, and sometimes I ain't. Used to be I had plenty and nothing to worry about."

"Inherited a pretty fat estate, eh?" asked Camp with quiet curiosity, and all the while his eyes searched and researched the face of Buel.

"Inherited nothing! I got nothing but good wishes handed down to me, pardner. Which they didn't put no heavy accent even on the good wishes."

"But where did you pick up the easy money?"

"Cards," said Billy Buel, "or dice, or anything else in the line of a game that a gent wanted to lay his money on."

His eyes glistened as he spoke.

"You struck bad luck and quit—like a wise gent," suggested Camp.

"I struck a girl," said Billy joylessly. "Account of her I quit."

"Ah," said Camp without enthusiasm. "A love affair, eh? Well, love has made tolerable big fools out of better men than you or me, Billy."

"It wasn't love," puzzled Billy. "Which I don't know just what you'd call it. I sort of wanted to please her, and she seemed to sort of want to please me. It sure rode her hard for me to gamble, so I just nacherally gave it up when she asked me to. And there you are!"

Camp considered this for a moment very thoughtfully.

"And where's the girl now?" he asked at length.

"South," said Billy Buel, more joyless than ever. "Away down South is where she is."

"Then you'll be bound that way one of these days."

"I dunno," and Billy sighed. "Being married ain't my idea of a good time. You got to settle down, Camp, and that means you got to stay in one place and work. And I ain't the working kind. I'm sure ashamed of it. But that ain't the main point. She's a pile too good for me. I don't figure to hang around and waste her time when she'd ought to be talking to gents a pile better'n I ever dreamed of being."

"Which means that she's pretty fond of you just the way you are," suggested Camp not unkindly.

"Her? You see," explained Billy, "I had the chance, and I done her a couple of pretty good turns. The result was that she took 'em to heart a good deal. That seems to be the way with a girl. You treat 'em the way you'd treat a man—just plain clean and decent, and act like they was a pal of yours—and the only way they find to pay you back is to dig down in their hearts and give you gold for silver—gold for lead. No, sir, a good woman is too good for the best gent that ever stepped—which I ain't one of 'em."

Full of his thought, he shook his handsome head and did not see that Camp turned on him a faint and quizzical smile as though there were many things he could have said on the subject had he cared to. But he left them unsaid, and Billy, clearing his mind with a heavy sigh, went on to the next subject in his brain.

"Another thing, Camp," he said. "Comes to me that maybe this work of yours ain't altogether on the level."

He paused, full of unspoken apologies.

"The reason I say it," he said, "is that the things that mostly pay the best are things that lie outside the law, far as I can see. Yep, they sure lie away outside the law. Now, I ain't hinting at nothing, but me and the law has always been tolerable friendly, and I mostly aim to keep on the same terms with it. So, if your job ain't in that line, maybe I'd better know right off the bat, pardner."

The direct answer of Camp was delayed for a moment.

"How come you're so fond of the law?" he said at length. "Here you are a gent that's handy with your gun, able to ride anything that walks on four feet, and knowing your country. How come you're so fond of the law?"

"And how come you to ask?"

"Because," said Camp, "them that like the law most is generally them that's got a lot to be watched by the law. Some old gent with money in the bank, or some old rancher that's made his stake—them are the kind that does most of the worrying about the law. Which I don't gather that you worry much about your ranch or your bank account."

Billy Buel chuckled.

"I sure don't," he admitted. "But I'll tell you how it is. They's only one thing you can be sure of. That's the law. Treat a gent pretty well, and you never know. Time may come when he'll turn you down cold and knife you when your back is turned, if he figures that he might make anything out of it. But the law's different. Treat it square, and it treats you square. Give it a fighting chance, and it sure always gives you the same chance. Besides, it sort of means this old United States, to me. And me not having any family, and no kid brothers or sisters to look down to and no father or mother to look up to—well, I just nacherally stick up America in the place of 'em and waste a pile of time thanking the Lord that I was born what I am with a country like this to call my own."

He uttered the latter part of this speech humbly, almost apologetically, as though he knew that it was not ordinary for such a man as he to say such things, and as though he instantly disclaimed any desire to preach. But William Camp had turned to him that fine, attentive head and listened gravely until the last syllable was spoken. Then he stretched out his hand and covered the fingers of Billy Buel with a grip that threatened to break the bones.

"You and me figure about the same way, son," he said, "except that when a gent gets along in years, the way I'm doing, he ain't quite so quick to take up ideas like the ones you just been talking about. This law you're so fond of sure acts like a blind man now and then, and steps on toes that it ought to let alone. But, take it all in all, it makes less mistakes than any one man would make. Nope, you don't have to worry about breaking the law if you work for us."

While he spoke, Billy eyed him with no little anxiety. Ever since his first meeting with the man of the wide shoulders, he had been a trifle over-awed, and no little ashamed of that very awe which he felt. He had finally taken the road to meet Camp and fight him to the finish when they encountered. And inside a few minutes he had found himself so completely persuaded that he was on the trail in the interests of a man who, before, he had considered unworthy to live. Not that he did not revolt against his own weakness of spirit and mind, as he was tempted to call it; but, no matter how often each day he forced himself to step away from Camp, mentally, and view him in cold perspective, in the end he was always won back.

It was the lure of the unknown that called him on. The nature of the business that Camp was leading him toward he could not guess, save to imagine shrewdly that it must have something to do with qualities embracing both gun play and horsemanship. And the great question kept him steadily on the trail.

They were climbing a long grade while the last conversation went on between them, and they continued on the upslant for an hour or more longer, until at last they broke onto level going which invited their horses to a gallop. Accordingly, they loped steadily for half a mile, and swinging around the shoulder of the loftiest mountain in sight so far as Billy could tell, they came suddenly on the view of a wide valley.

William Camp at once drew rein, and Billy followed his example. Spread beneath them was a broad tableland rather than a valley. Its greatest length lay east and west, and on all four sides the rectangle, sweeping over many a mile of rolling, heavily forested land, was roughly fenced by four ranges of mountains, the whole dominated by a great peak to the north. How many miles it was from mountain to mountain, Billy could not guess, but, with distance, the ranges were brown in the highlights and purple-blue in the shadows.

He turned to Camp and found his guide's face both stern and lighted.

"I reckon," said Billy Buel quietly, "that we've hit your country at last."

"I reckon," replied William Camp with equal gravity, "that you're right. There's your battlefield, son! All the way inside of them mountains. Look it over. You'll come to know it better later on!"

· VIII ·
THE CAMP HATE

It was a voice at once solemn and prophetic, and Billy Buel obeyed.

The whole of that broad region looked to Billy more like a piece of gigantic landscape gardening than like a battlefield in the wilderness. He smiled as he looked down on that scene of beauty, but the smile faded from his lips when he turned and saw the darkened, grave face of William Camp.

"You can get the landmarks in your eye now as well as any time," the older man was saying. "North, yonder, is Gloster Peak, and that's the Gloster Range walking away on each side of the big fellow. There's the Soutar Mountains in the west, and east are the Three Brothers—that's them three big ones side by side, but we call the whole range after 'em. This here peak we're on we call Lucky Mountain. I dunno why, except that the first gents that climbed it come in sight of the valley, yonder, and liked it tolerable well.

"There's your map, Billy. Print it pretty clear in your head, because you're going to need to know it a good many times before you get through with Gloster Valley—if you ever get through alive!"

This blunt frankness was not at all in keeping with the usual careful courtesy of William Camp, and Billy glanced at him in surprise and curiosity. Curiosity, because he was beginning to think that Camp never did anything carelessly; there was forethought directing him always.

"Why d'you say that?"

"Because," said Camp, "the minute you ride down off this mountain with me and into Gloster Valley, you take your life in your hands, son, and you'll keep on risking it till you leave the place. And because it ain't too late to turn back now.

Make up your mind quick. Do you ride on, or do you turn back?"

Billy removed his sombrero and smoothed his hair back.

"I got one tolerable bad fault," he admitted, "and that's curiosity. I guess you couldn't of said anything more to make me want to go on down into the valley."

"I sort of knew that," and Camp nodded, "but wasn't simply tempting you on, Billy. Fact is, I'm sort of sorry to see you take the big chance. I've rode all through the mountains trying to find a man like you, but, having found you, I begin to feel like a murderer. That ain't my ordinary way of talking, Billy. I don't throw away most things after I've found them. But, to tell you the truth, son, I like your style. And I'm telling you the straight of it. If you ride down in there, you got just about one chance in ten of living a year through!"

But Billy Buel smiled.

"I sure thank you for warning me," he said, "but I wasn't never cut out to live a quiet life. And before I die I want the fun of things. I'd rather get plugged young than live to be eighty and see nothing and do nothing. So blaze away, Camp, and tell me what's in the valley."

William Camp considered the thought for a moment and then nodded.

"Of course that's the way you'd talk. It's your

style," he said. "Well, I'll spill the whole thing to you, son. They's two parties down in that valley. Look there to the west, to the Soutar Mountains. That's where the Benchleys and their crowd live. All around through them valleys, they got a dozen houses where them and their friends live. They farm a little and they trap a little and they hunt a little, and altogether they make a pretty good living. Which old Jacob Benchley is a pretty tolerable rich man. And every one of 'em, from Jake down, I hate 'em all and all that belongs to 'em."

He said it with a snarling voice, his hatred overflowing to such an extent that for a moment it seemed that Billy himself was embraced in it.

"And over there to the east," went on Camp, his voice softening at once, his eyes filling with light, "there's where the Camps hang out. That's my tribe. The Camps and the Martins and the Walkers and the rest; they're my folk, Lord bless 'em. All clean men, Billy—the sort of men you'll cotton to quick. They mean what they say, and they say what they mean. All hard men, son, that'd rather fight than eat and rather eat than sleep. If they shake hands with you once, they never forget it. And if you ever cross 'em, they never forget it. They can learn to love you like a brother, and then everything they got from their money to their lives is yours. And they can learn to hate you like a snake, and then they's nothing that they won't do to make away with you. That's the Camps. Camp blood is like iron—it holds men together! And those are the gents you're going to fight for! Those are my people, and they're going to be your people, Billy Buel, if you ride down yonder with me!"

"They sound tolerable good to me," said Billy solemnly. "I guess we'll get on pretty well together."

"And yonder in the west under the Soutar Mountains," continued Camp, his voice hardening strangely again, "are those Benchleys. Well, son, they's one thing above all the rest that makes a Camp great, and that's when he's met a Benchley and left him dead! And they's one thing that makes the Benchleys take off their hats to another one of their clan, and that's when he's met a Camp and left him for dead! And in between all of Gloster Valley is their battlefield. But I'll tell you how come we hate each other. It's a kind of a long story. Want to get off your hoss and sit down?"

"That kind of story," said Billy thoughtfully, "I'd rather hear while I'm in the saddle. Kind of fits better with being on a hoss where you can see things."

Camp smiled grimly.

"All right," he said. "It started a long while back. We lived pretty close, the Camps and the Benchleys. Between us we opened up this part of the country, you might say. If the Benchleys had a hard winter, we helped 'em out; and if we run short of seed when it come to plowing time, the Benchleys would open up their granaries and give us all the seed we needed for planting. And nobody kept any close score about which had done the most favors and which side had something owing. It was all done liberal and free. Which Westerners had ought to live that way, as you'll agree."

"I sure do," said Billy with all due solemnity.

"Well," went on Camp, "it happened that Joe Benchley and Lew Camp was pretty thick friends. They hunted together. They rode together. They went to dances together. And, pretty soon, darned if they didn't fall in love with the same girl. Her name was Margery Moore, and she was sure pretty. They talk about her still as the prettiest girl but one that ever walked in Gloster Valley. Well, them being in love with the same girl, you'd of thought that they'd of fallen out. But them blue eyes of Margery Moore weren't enough to spoil the friendship of Joe Benchley and Lew Camp.

"Pretty soon she ups and makes her choice, and her choice was for Lew. Even then Joe didn't bat an eye. He just took his medicine, it looked like, and stopped calling on Margery on Saturday nights and Sundays and left the field plumb open to Lew. Pretty soon Lew and Margery agreed on a day, and it wasn't long after that Joe Benchley goes off and takes a trip and comes back with the word that he was going to get married himself. Which darned if he and Lew Camp don't get married on the same day, in the same church, by the same preacher. Joe's girl wasn't near the fine looker that Margery Moore was—which she wasn't no slouch, at that. Same dark kind of hair and eyes and clear-looking skin. It was easy to see that Joe had found the nearest thing to Margery that come his way. The name of his girl was Alice Clode, and that day he and Lew had a wedding dinner all together.

"They started out together. What did they do but go up in the hills, them two couples and clear some patches of land side by side and build their cabins, helping each other, and settled down like one big family. It was a kind of a fine thing to see, and many a time I've rode up there and seen them all four sitting out under the tree together and having no end of a party. Which Alice and Margery got to be pretty thick friends, though Margery was a pile the thicker of the two. Because it wasn't hard to see that Alice guessed that she was the second choice and that she'd been picked because she was kind of like Margery, with the same blue-black hair and the same black eyebrows and the same deep blue eyes. But that was only nacheral, her holding a little spite about it. Nobody could call that up against her.

"Well, things went along pretty well like that.

And pretty soon, in the middle of winter, we got the big news and the bad news.

"Both of them girls became ill. Joe and Lew matched to see who would go for help; and it was made up that Joe Benchley should stay there and help as best he could if the time came, while Lew Camp rode as fast as hossflesh would take him and tried to get a doctor.

"So off goes Lew, just about killing his hoss, and leaves Joe behind him.

"When Lew comes back, it was too late. Margery's baby had died. Alice Benchley had a little daughter in her arms.

"Well, Margery and Lew was near crazy with grieving, and Joe and Alice sure gave 'em a pile of sympathy. And after that for a couple of years they kept on living side by side. But when little Nell Benchley began to get big enough to walk, the loveliest thing your eyes ever got hold of, it was too much for poor Margery and Lew. They couldn't stand the ache of seeing little Nell Benchley playing around every day. So she and Lew moved off and made another clearing on the far side of Gloster Valley."

Camp paused, and it seemed to Billy Buel that some deep-seated emotion constricted his throat, shutting off his very breath. From his experience with men of the mountain-desert, men of simple honor, men stout of heart, Billy knew that what Camp was about to relate, had had a far-reaching influence on his life. Presently the inner tumult smoldered, died, and Camp continued in his outwardly calm way:

"Well, things drifted along for pretty near ten years. And all the time Joe and Lew kept pretty thick, though the two womenfolk had come to have mighty little to do with each other.

"Happened one day that Joe Benchley had come over to see Lew, them being pals. Lew was out cutting trees and getting ready to clear some more ground. So Joe gets him an ax and goes out to help. Well, they worked away pretty contented for about half a day and went back and cooked themselves some lunch, Margie being away. Afternoon comes along, and they were cutting down a big un and had it about through, when the wind gives a quick puff out of the north, and down comes the tree, pretty unexpected, and smashed Joe Benchley under it.

"There he lies groaning and sure bad smashed up, and with Lew Camp working like fury to cut him clear of the weight of the branches. Pretty soon he gets him out and drags him clear of the branches, and there he sees that poor Joe Benchley is done for good, with his legs plumb busted and his chest all caved in.

"He starts in and tries to patch up Joe as best as he can, but pretty soon Joe gives him a sign and makes him bend over.

" 'Lew,' says Joe, 'I'm pretty far gone.'

" 'The devil you are,' says Lew. 'You ain't near touched yet.'

"But all the time he knew pretty well that Joe was a goner.

" 'I'm no better'n dead,' says Joe. 'But before I die got to do some talking. Lew,' he says, 'I sure done you dirt. You and me being pals like we been, I've sure done you dirt.'

"Lew thinks that Joe is talking kind of crazy, like gents will when they're pretty far gone, but Joe keeps right on talking, and pretty soon what he says makes Lew's eyes plumb pop.

" 'Lew,' says Joe Benchley, 'go back to the day that Nell was born.'

"Lew gives a kind of a groan.

" 'I've gone back into hell many a time,' he says. 'Don't ask me to go back now.'

" 'I know it's been hell,' says Joe Benchley, 'but you got to go back this once more, and this time it'll make you happy; but it'll make you hate me the rest of your days. Lew,' he said, 'how would you like to have little Nell for your girl?'

" 'How would I like to have heaven?' says Lew, his heart coming up in his throat, because along about these days Nell was eleven years old and the sweetest, prettiest, black-eyed darling that ever walked Gloster Valley. Never a grown man that looked on her but felt the insides of him ache for the want of one like her; never a boy that seen her but go dizzy with wishing that she could be his sweetheart.

" 'How would I like to have heaven?' says Lew Camp, thinking of the long evenings at home and his wife that could never no more have a baby since the first one.

"And then up speaks Joe in a dying voice and says: 'Lew, she belongs to you!'

"It was like the lightning to Lew. He starts back, and then drops on his knees again beside Joe.

" 'For Heaven's sake, Joe,' says he, 'talk slow and soft and give it to me easy. Are you ravin'?'

" 'I'm only praying for the courage to go through with what I've started,' says Joe Benchley. 'But I'm near gone, Lew, and I got to talk truth to save my soul from the fire.'

"Lew couldn't hardly breathe. He did nothing but stare at Joe.

" 'It's true,' says Joe. 'Man, were you blind that you could look at her all these years and not see your wife's eyes in her?'

" 'My wife's eyes are blue,' says Lew, gasping. 'Margie's eyes are blue, but so are your wife's eyes—so are Alice's.'

" 'Alice has blue eyes,' says Joe Benchley. 'What difference does that make? The sky is blue, and so is the sea; but whoever said they had the same sort of blue? No more is the blue of the eyes of Alice like the blue of the eyes of Margie! No more, Lew. Lord knows I've seen it a thousand times, partner, and Lord knows I've wondered that you didn't see it!'

" 'Joe,' says Lew, 'you're going plumb mad!'

" 'Listen,' says Joe Benchley. 'I'm about to die, Lew. I feel it coming on. They's a sort of night swimming across my eyes, and the trees, yonder, are waving to and fro like a wind was in 'em, which means I'm about gone, Lew. So buckle to what I got to say and take it for gospel true.

" 'That day when the babies were born—well, it was a terrible day, Lew. There was them two women in pain—my wife that I love—your wife that I loved a pile more, no harm to you. And both of 'em moaning and calling at once. And me not knowing what to do, except as they told me—and them plumb mad with agony. But I done what they told me, best I could, running back and forth. Seemed to me like they was both going to die. No man could of stood it long. I only wished both the babies was dead and the women spared, before the end.

" 'But finally it was over. There I seen Alice lying, and the baby girl beside her was dead— dead! No beat of heart, no breath of lungs. And there was your wife, Margie, with a living child beside her—and both of them women plumb help- less and unconscious as though they was asleep. What could I do, Lew? Pity me now the way I pitied you and Margie then. But Margie was always the woman I loved. D'you think I changed when I quit her and went off to find another girl? It wasn't because I loved another girl, but just to keep my heart from breaking. I talked to Alice and made her believe. A woman that's fond of a gent will sure always go nine-tenths of the way toward believing him. That was the way she done, and when I told her I needed her, she thought I was telling her that I loved her. So she married me. And there we were.

" 'But when I looked across that day, Lew, my heart was sure spinning around. Seemed to me like I was the father of Margie's little girl. I loved her so plumb much! If it had been a choice between Alice and Margie that day, I wouldn't of stopped long to think what to choose. I would of asked for your wife to live, Lew, and mine to die. But then I looked across, and I seen the child of Alice and me dead; and I looked across, and I seen the child of you and Margie living. I couldn't stand it. You had all the blessings, and I had none. And I swore to myself that I would love your little girl enough to make up to her for what she'd lost—her real mother and her real father. So I just took her and put her down by my wife, and I took our poor dead baby and put her down by Margie—pitying her and you all the time, but just hungering to have Margie's baby for mine.

" 'Lew, I ain't asking you to forgive me, but I just ask you to step inside of my skin, if you can, and see things for a single minute the way I saw them then!'

" 'I think I see,' says Lew Camp, feeling as if the heaven had opened over him and that he was rising into it. 'And I forgive you. Little Nell Benchley is my girl—Nell Camp!'

"And Joe Benchley makes a face and says: 'That's right, but the new name sure grates on me, the old one being so familiar. But tell her never to forget me, Lew. And for the Lord's sake tell Margie never to forget. Will you swear that?'

" 'I'll swear,' says Lew. 'And Heaven help you.'

" 'That's what Heaven does,' says Joe Benchley. 'Passes the time helping honest gents like you, Lew. But keep me green in the mind of Nell—the sweet thing!—and when you kiss Margie to-night, tell her that I died loving her. And say a word to Alice. Good-by, partner!'

"That was the way Joe Benchley died!"

· IX ·
WILLIAM CAMP'S HAND AND HEART

Billy Buel had sat his horse through the thrilling recital with chills coursing up and down his spinal column. And now he gasped out: "I dunno how it is, Camp, but my heart sure goes out to Joe Benchley."

"And ain't that where it should go?" asked William Camp. "Sure, in all that I got to say, I ain't got anything to say against that man's man. Didn't I know him? Didn't I mourn for his death like he had been my brother?"

"Is Lew Camp your brother?" asked Billy Buel sharply.

"He is," said William Camp.

"Go on," said Buel.

"Well, Buel, you see how it was. They was no real blame for Joe Benchley. He'd loved Margie Moore, and he couldn't help the temptation of making her baby his when the time come. I can understand. So can you when you see her. What with grief and the years, she's the wreck of the woman that once she was; but still she's beautiful, Billy, and you can figure how she might have drove a man wild twenty years ago. You'll know it all when you see her. No, sir, I'm Lew's brother, but if I'd been in Joe Benchley's place I sure might have done the same thing!"

He paused a moment, his head bowed.

"Knowing Margie the way she was in her girl days, I sure can understand. And she's still a woman that's good to look at. Never been but one like her in Gloster Valley!"

He paused again, his wise face lifted, and for once the cynicism passed from it, and his expression was at once both pure and grave. Billy Buel saw and wondered and decided more than ever that he had not the ability to pass judgment upon his companion.

"But leave Joe Benchley out of it," went on William Camp. "He died, and he washed his soul clean with confession before he died. The blame falls on them that lived after him!"

The old, cold ring of metal came in his voice as he spoke.

"Here's what happened: Lew Camp—my brother—washed Joe that day and dressed him in his own best clothes and laid him out straight and clean, and closed his eyes and wept for him like he'd been his brother. And when his wife came home that evening he up and told Margie all that he'd been told by Joe, and didn't leave nothing out. Well, poor Margie, that had given up all hope of having another baby, just up and wept for the joy of knowing that she had a child. And then when she got through she wept again to think of taking Alice's little girl away from her. And such a girl! I've talked a bit about her before now, but little you know what she was—and what she is! All that's lovely and lovable in girls was boiled down and made into one bit—and that's Nell!

"But they was an end to the weeping. Pretty soon they had to send for the Benchleys. Down they came on their hosses, big men and strong men all of 'em. And down come the Camps at the call. There was me and the rest of us, and there was our friends all come to help at the burying of Joe Benchley. A Benchley in them old days was pretty near like a Camp, and never a Benchley that was loved by us the way poor old Joe Benchley was loved.

"I say we was all there, we Camps having shorter to come. And well I remember how the Benchleys come in! They're men for men to look at, the Benchleys are, curse 'em! First come Ames Benchley, and first at all places he is now!

"If it come to fist or guns or hosses, they was never a man like Ames Benchley in these parts. He's big enough to fight the strongest; he's quick enough to fight the fastest. And whether he fights or talks, he's always a gentleman. I'd like to talk a pile more about him. Lord knows I got reason to hate him. He's killed blood of my blood and bone of my bone. I've had brothers die under the hand of Ames Benchley, but I couldn't never teach myself to hate him the way I should. Curse him! Except that I wish I could get him face to face and be killed trying to kill him! But there was Ames Benchley come with his long hair blowing and his sombrero in his hand, for he'd heard that it was sad news that brought him to the house of Lew Camp.

"And there come next the father of 'em all— there come next the wise old devil with his white beard whipping around his face and his big horse dripping wet with the sweat of the gallop—that was old Jacob Benchley. A big man, too, like all of his sons, but withered up with his age so that his bones stood out in his face and in his hands. That was old Jake Benchley as he come in.

"And there was young Henry Moore, near as big as Ames Benchley and near as fine to look at, and a hard man to face in a battle. And there was Oliver Lord, next to them two; fine, big men, all three; as fine fighting men as ever stepped. And after 'em came all the rest—all the clan of the Benchleys ready to bury their dead man.

"Well, sir, it sure give my heart a leap to watch 'em ride in. Right there I thanked Heaven pronto that we Camps had men like that for friends and not for enemies.

"Down they got one by one, and they come and looked at Joe Benchley with never a tear. As, they was men that day, the Benchleys and their crew! I remember old Jake bending over his son—and sure he loved Joe more'n he ever loved the rest, even Ames.

" 'This'll be hard news to tell Alice,' he says and steps on with never a word more.

"And along comes Ames, like a king; and like a king he is, Billy, as you'll know when you see him. And he bends over his brother.

" 'He died like a man,' says Ames, 'working to help a friend—and so Heaven rest him.' Ames steps on with a dry pair of eyes, and so do the rest of 'em one by one and say their say or else say nothing, and stand ranged about the room. And when they're all done, out steps my brother—out steps Lew Camp, and he says: 'Gents, I know how grieved you are today, and you know how hard grieved I am, because they was never a brother of Joe Benchley that loved him more than I've loved him—him and me always being pals. But I got to tell you the death words that he told me—'

"And so he starts out, and he tells them just how Joe Benchley died, same as I've told you; and he tells 'em all that Joe Benchley said as he lay dying, same as I've told you. He didn't tell it with no joy, because he knew that there was one jewel among the Benchleys, and that was the little girl— that was Nell. And when he got done he stepped back with his head dropped, sort of grieved and shamed of having to claim his flesh and blood for his own.

"I stood there expecting somebody to groan, and one or two did groan. But in a minute out steps old Jake Benchley, tall and thin and bony, the wreck of the huge man he'd once been.

" 'You claim my Nell?' he says.

" 'I claim the girl that used to be called your son's Nell,' says Lew. 'Not yours.'

" 'She's mine,' says Jake, stiff as a poker, and his voice big. 'She's mine. My boy's dead, but his flesh and blood don't lack a father so long as I'm alive. The rest of 'em may stand by like sticks and stones and say nothing, them that calls themselves my sons and brothers of Joe Benchley, but I ain't going to be still. I say Nell was Joe's girl, and when he died she was my girl!'

" 'But don't you see?' says Lew, not understanding. 'It's all a mistake. She was never Joe's girl. She's mine. She belongs to me and Margie, there!'

"At that Margie folds her hands and lets out a little moan that would have gone to your heart to hear it. 'My girl!' she says, and all at once the picture of beautiful little Nell jumps into the eyes of all of us and takes our breath.

" 'I'd tell that story to Alice!' says Jake Benchley.

"It gives me a blow from the other side, hearing that. I couldn't help thinking of poor Alice Benchley that had raised that girl as her own.

"And while we was all standing there still and sort of shocked to hear old Jake Benchley talk, still not dreaming what he meant, out steps Ames Benchley like a king—he was always like a king even when he was a kid.

" 'Dad,' he says, 'am I hearing you right?'

" 'And what do you hear?' says Jake Benchley, sort of respectful, even when he was talking to his own son, because Ames Benchley raised that much respect even in his own family.

" 'I hear you say,' says Ames, 'that what Lew says about Joe's dying talk ain't hardly to be believed. Is that so?'

" 'You hear me right, son.'

"And, while the cold thrill went through me, Ames lifts that lion head of his and looks around the circle at us, and his eye was always a hard eye to meet.

" 'Then,' he says, 'I'll be a dead man before Nell is took from us!'

"And that, Billy, was the beginning of the war!

"I couldn't hardly believe it, saying that, hearing Ames Benchley speak, I knew it had to be so. He meant to fight, and fighting Ames Benchley was hell itself!

"And Ames Benchley went on: 'Miriam was right, dad,' he said. 'We all think Miriam is sort of light in the head, but Miriam was right when she said that Nell would bring trouble to us as great as the prettiness of her face. I see she was right; but if you think, dad, that we got a fighting reason to keep Nell, we'll keep her. She's worth fighting for!'

"By that time we was beginning to come to life. At first of all my brother Lew jumps to the door of the house and calls: 'Gents, if it's got to be fighting, they's no better time than now!'

"And he puts his hand on his revolver!

"And it was then that I made my big mistake. I couldn't look into the future. All I seen was that the Benchleys, that had come to take a dead man and bury him, was about to be killed in the midst of us, because we could of done away with 'em. There was a lot of 'em—all fighting men—and chief there was Ames Benchley like a lion ready to kill five men before he dropped. But it wasn't the hardness of the fighting that held me back. It was the fear that all them strong men should go down against odds, we having the odds against 'em. So I jumped out with both my hands held up, and I begged 'em to think and wait. I told 'em that we didn't want Nell unless we had a good right to her, and that the law would say what our right was! That we was willing to wait until the law had talked, and we'd abide by what the law said."

Here William Camp paused and struck his fist against his forehead.

"And what happened?" asked Billy Buel, filled with awe.

"What happened? Oh, I was a fool! What if they'd died in that room, all of 'em, and enough of us to square the count? It would have been cheaper! A pile cheaper. But how could I tell? Like a fool, I forgot that the judge of that district was Jake Benchley himself. So the case come to a trial, and of course there was Lew to give the testimony of what Joe had said when he died, and there was Margie to weep and hold out her hands to Nell. And how beautiful Nell was that day!

"But what did she know, poor baby? All she knew was to hold close to Alice, that she thought was her mother, and there was Alice Benchley, sitting white as a ghost and stiff, and hugging Nell to her with a fear in her eyes that was a horrible thing to see.

"And there was old Jake Benchley on the bench telling the jury that only one man had heard the confession, and there was no signed confession to offer to the court, and him that had heard the dying confession had the most to gain by it because it meant gaining the girl—and he had only to point to beautiful little Nell to make all the jury feel how much she was worth having and worth lying for, all of 'em knowing that Margie and Lew had no babies.

"What was the end of it? Why the end was just that the jury took about a minute and a half, and then without leaving the box they said that Nell had ought to stay where she was with Alice Benchley—meaning that Lew had lied in all that he said. And no sooner had they spoke out than Nell throws her arms around the neck of Alice and bursts out crying with happiness, and Alice sits there straight and stiff and looks a million pounds of hate across the room to Margie, and Margie sits there with her head bowed like a weight was hanging from her forehead—like it sure was hanging from her heart!"

"And then?" asked Billy in a husky voice.

"And then it was war!" said William Camp gloomily. "Then the good days in Gloster Valley was done. Every man's hand was against the hand of every other man. We fought, and we fought to kill. They ain't many questions asked. We're the law all to ourselves away out here, and nobody comes in and asks to bring cases into court. We fight hard, and we fight like Indians to get scalps, you might say. But they ain't no end.

"My brother Arthur that has so much money, he comes up from Richmond and puts all he has into the fight. We kill off a pile of the Benchleys and a pile of old Jake's sons, but still they's Ames Benchley left. For everybody we kill, he comes back and drops one of us, pretty near. And he brings in his allies. It ain't hard for him to get allies, having a girl like Nell for bait.

"It's gone on for nigh nine years. Now she's twenty years old—old enough to marry. And she's growed up more than all she promised to be when she was a little girl. She's made out of night and fire and dew, that girl is. She's like a breath of wind coming through the pine trees, all pure and calm. She takes the hearts of men and brings 'em up in their throats, does Nell. Lord bless her, for all the harm she's done to me and to mine! They's nothing wrong with her—just the fate that makes her think Alice is her mother and Ames Benchley her uncle and Jake Benchley her grandfather. And here's poor Margie and Lew breaking their hearts for her!"

Camp paused again after his long speech and looked soberly down into the hilly woodland below them.

"And so it's been war?" said Billy Buel calmly, but all the while he was afire with excitement. He was seeing that the calm William Camp was not calm at all—simply the wise man whom long sorrow and worry had given an impervious mask.

"War?" echoed Camp. "For nine years, lad. How many good men are rotting under the trees down there, I won't try to say, but they's many a one—they's many a one, Billy Buel! Some we've killed, but more have been killed among us, because, for all we're fighting men and ready to meet any man that walks, we have no Ames Benchley among us. He's as sure as Heaven above him that he's right, and that Nell belongs to Alice and to his dead brother, so he fights as only Ames Benchley knows how to fight, and no man that ever walked Gloster Valley could stand up against him.

"And that's how I came by my thought, Billy Buel. No, there was no partner that I made a bet with, but I made a bet with myself that I'd go through the mountains and find a man who fought for the love of fighting and who was as good a shot and as cool a head as Ames Benchley himself. And I've found you—a kid like you!"

He shook his head, looking at Billy.

"I dunno how it is, Billy. Anybody else would say a kid like you didn't stand a chance. And maybe you don't. That's to be seen when you face Ames Benchley. In the meantime, I've got a hope that I've found the man who'll stop Ames

Benchley—and, if I have, sooner or later we'll get Nell! But the point is this—are you willing to take the chance against men like them I been talking about? Keep in your head that for nine years we been fighting, Billy, and for nine years we've been beat—then tell me yes or no. And if you want to turn back, they's no shame to you. I've told you the whole story."

Billy Buel sighed.

"I dunno," he said. "Maybe I'd ought to have enough proof to satisfy a court, but I ain't built that way. If the proof is good enough for you, it's good enough for me, Camp. Maybe I'll die down yonder in that valley, but I'll sure die hard. As for Ames Benchley, I'm tolerable ready to meet him, just out of plumb curiosity!"

"Good!" said William Camp. "Then give me your hand."

He took the hand of the youth, and, holding it in a long and fervent grip, he stared into the eyes of Billy Buel.

"Billy Buel," he said, "I've sure used you hard. I've fooled you and I've lied to you and I've treated you bad every way from the start, but, now that you've made our cause your cause, here's my hand and my heart with it. It may not mean much to you now, but it'll mean a lot to you before you're done with the Camps of Gloster Valley. If you're well, I'll ride and fight by you; if you're sick, I'll stay by you and tend you like my own flesh; if you're dying, I'll plumb pray for you; and if you're dead, I'll put the stone over your grave and put the writing on it that tells how you come to die for folks that wasn't your folks. Here's my hand, Billy Buel, and my blood with it!"

About his burly hand he felt the sudden coiling of lithe fingers which became iron-hard, iron-strong, and crushed his hand to the very bone. Into his eyes looked the eyes of Billy Buel, grown steel-bright.

"And I give you my word," said Billy, "that I believe the things you been telling me, and that I figure they're worth fighting for, and that before I'm done I'll bring Nell back to you or die trying for her."

· X ·
BILLY SAVES A LIFE

They swung down off the mountain and into the pleasant shadows of Gloster Valley. Valley it was not, but a gently rolling tableland, yet from the floor, looking up to the tall mountains on either hand, it seemed a valley indeed; and one half expected the slope at any moment to pitch down again to the bed of a water-course which must have formed the depression.

Through the mottling of sun and shadow, Billy Buel rode with a grave face. He had done things wild enough in his short life, and he had done them all carelessly, thoughtlessly, following the emotion of the minute. But what had he gained from life that was really worth prizing? The revolver at his hip, the gaudy clothes upon his back, and neat-footed Lou, the bay mare who danced beneath him.

He looked down fondly at her dainty head. She was a companionable horse. No matter how she hewed to the line of direction her master laid out for her, her head was continually swinging from side to side as she seemed to take note of and be tempted by each place of interest. And if her master changed his place in the saddle, or if he spoke, her short, nervous ears were instantly in quivering play, and her head went up on the alert. She was a watch-spring mechanism, was Lou. With one sharp command he could make her leap from a stand into a full gallop. With a pressure of his knees and the least swerve of his body, he could make her spring to right or left. There was no questioning in Lou. She obeyed him almost by instinct, as some highly sensitive dogs which actually received silent commands from a master through a glance, through an inclination of his head. And Billy loved her as only a brave man can love a brave horse.

He had Lou, and he had in the holster at his side a revolver which, he was convinced, was a little truer, a little easier to his grip, a shade more perfectly balanced, and a vital particle speedier in action, than any weapon on the whole range of the mountain-desert. He had a fine horse, he had a fine weapon; and there were the boots on his feet and the gold braid on his hat—but beyond?

He turned to William Camp. The latter had changed the moment he entered the shades of Gloster Valley. He rode alertly erect with his feet well braced and the stirrups thrust out from the side of his horse with a stiff leg, as a man rides who is on a horse that may spring in any direction without warning. Billy knew that attitude. More than this, the eyes of Camp were at ceaseless play among the tree trunks of the forest. Never once did his glance hold steadily down the road, as is the fashion with men who have ridden a great distance since sunrise. Instead, it flickered from side to side, and sometimes his head turned sharply at some small thing—as when the upper branches of a tree swayed by the wind and a shaft of sunlight was admitted suddenly to a new place.

Plainly, he feared attack even so soon after his entry into the valley. Surely, the Benchleys could not know the date of his return. But perhaps they were always abroad, always hunting. And this attitude of silent watchfulness on the part of his companion spoke to Billy more eloquently than words of the fear that was never absent from the trails through Gloster Valley.

"And how do you keep up this war, pardner?" Billy asked. "Benchleys killing Camps and

Camps killing Benchleys, without the law stepping in and hanging some of both sides."

"Didn't I tell you that before?" asked Camp, and after flashing one look at his companion his eyes resumed their task of probing the unseen distances of the woodland. "Well, it's this way," he went on. "The sheriff and the sheriff's deputies are always Camps or Benchleys. Sometimes, we elect him; sometimes, they got a few more votes. And they's an unwritten law that when Camps and Benchleys are killed by one another they ain't to be any calling in of the law. We fight it out by mutual agreement the way we been doing all these years. They's always a coroner's jury called, but that coroner's jury is always made up of just Benchleys and Camps, and they always bring in the same sort of a verdict—'killed by accident' or 'suicide' or 'death by causes unknown.'

"That's the way it's worked. And they ain't nobody allowed to come in here and settle down unless he's on one side or the other, and the minute he takes sides he's in the fight and follows the same ways that we got. There was Sam Wall come in with his boy and took sides with the Benchleys. Well, one day Hugh Camp meets up with Sam's son. Young Wall was a growed-up man and a hard one, too. And Hugh was just a kid—not more'n sixteen, I guess, then. But he was a cool head and an old hand, and he filled Wall full of lead.

"Well, old Sam was sure cut up about his son dying. And first he wants the whole gang of Benchleys to go on the warpath and burn us out. But fire ain't allowed in our little war. So Sam got plumb mad, and he rode over to Exeter to get the law on us. Well, when the Benchleys found out what he'd done they jumped on their hosses, a couple of 'em, and they follered Sam and caught up with him almost at Exeter. They tried to argue with him. He told them to go to the devil. He wanted a head for a head. They said they'd do their best to get even for the sake of his son, but they asked him to wait. Well, he wouldn't wait, and the short of it was that Sam Wall was left dead in the road, and the Benchleys rode back home." Billy Buel set his teeth, shivering. This killing in cold blood was almost too much for him. He could understand even the most terrible slaughter in the heat of battle, but for two men to shoot down one old man—

He turned gloomy eyes on Camp.

"Still," he said, "they's something good about that. The Benchleys wouldn't call in the law to help them. That's in their favor. They must be some good men among 'em!"

"Good men? Good gun food, son," growled Camp with that sudden and fierce widening of the nostrils and hardening of the eyes which Billy Buel had noticed more than once before when his friend was on this subject. "Don't you forget it.

They're good targets for your lead to be pumped at. They're good for nothing else. And when—"

For a moment he had grown so warm with talking that he lost his usual attentiveness in surveying the road, but Billy Buel had caught that uneasy habit; and now, in the heart of a stretch of bracken, something moved and winked. Sunlight will glint on glossy foliage. But there is no glimmer like the sudden and eyelike flash of the sun on the blue steel of a revolver barrel. And at that glint Billy lunged to the side.

One sharp call, one pressure of his knee, was sufficient to make Lou swerve like a pugilist dancing away from the blow of an antagonist. The quick motion carried the mare across the head of Camp's horse and diverted it, also, and not more than a fraction of a second too soon.

A gun barked from the bracken; a small, wicked, humming sound darted past the ear of Billy Buel, and before a second shot could be fired his own revolver had been whipped into his hand. He fired with that instinctive sense for direction which was his gift.

A yell and a curse from the growth of ferns told that his shot had taken effect. And Billy, filled with an honest frenzy of rage, drove Lou straight at the ferns.

"Come back!" shouted Camp. "Keep to the trees! Ride in a circle! You're throwing yourself away!"

He followed his own advice, but Billy Buel was

too furious for calm thinking. Straight through the bracken he dove, and on the far side he saw the enemy, a slender figure in the very act of swinging into the saddle. His right arm was held clumsily far to the side.

So much he saw; then the rush of Lou carried him past the other. Far to one side he leaned, gripping Lou with all his might, and shot his right arm, revolver and all, between the stranger and the horse. There was a violent wrench which almost tore Billy from his saddle—and then he was riding with his foeman crushed in his arm across the pommel of the saddle.

It was like carrying a wildcat. The slender body writhed and twisted like an oiled bundle of muscle in his grip. He caught for a knife with his left hand. The grip of Billy shifted to the wrist of that hand, and under that burning, twisting pressure the other groaned, and the knife fell from his nerveless fingers. Still he struggled and twitching himself about, struck Billy twice in the face with his crimson-stained hand.

That was the last. In a moment he had been turned face down and was paralyzed in the coiling grip of Billy's arms. Lou had come to a quivering halt, and Billy swung from the saddle and brought his captive to the ground.

All of this had taken only a few seconds; but it had sufficed to bring William Camp into view, galloping through the bracken. He was shouting and waving his arm with a peculiar, wild joy. But Billy Buel was staring gloomily at the helpless, trembling figure before him. The muscles were only half formed along the arms which he held with a crushing grip; the shoulders had not yet widened to the full strength of manhood; the neck was round and graceful as the neck of a woman. So far as Billy could make out, he was not more than a child of fifteen, grown almost to the inches of manhood, but a man in height only. Otherwise he was a child indeed.

And this was the danger that had threatened him from the bracken! And yet the shot, after all, had been a perilously good one. Only the instant leap of Lou, he knew, had saved him from receiving that bullet through his head!

He glanced up. Camp had arrived, drawn up his horse and was sitting the saddle in complete silence.

"He's drilled through the forearm," explained Billy Buel slowly. "Nothing serious. Didn't touch the bone—didn't tear no sinews. He'll be as sound as ever inside of three weeks."

Camp's face was working, but he said nothing.

"If you got any spare bits of cloth about you—" began Billy Buel again.

He was interrupted by the voice of the boy. Its quality was that uncertain and tremorous note which still has something of the shrillness of childhood, and which is also wavering toward the bass that will develop in another year or so.

"I won't run away. You can let me go. And I ain't got no gun left on me."

Billy ran his hands swiftly and expertly over the body of the youth and made sure that what he said was true. Then he released his arms, and the boy stepped away. He turned on them a handsome face, finely modeled, with a singular nobility in the brow, a singular sensitiveness about the mouth. He was pale with a mortal terror; but he was erect with a mortal pride. He looked straight at William Camp.

"You don't need to tie me," he said, "and they ain't no call to blindfold me. I'll take it standing, with my eyes open."

And Billy was astonished to see the boy come still more erect, clench his hands at his sides, and stare wide-eyed straight before him. Suddenly, he blanched and shrank a trifle, and Billy turned, bewildered, in the direction of the gaze.

There was William Camp, who all this time had not uttered a syllable, bringing down his revolver on the mark with a look of inexpressible and savage satisfaction. He was about to shoot down the victim.

For an instant Billy was frozen past speech, past movement, then he sprang before his captive with a hoarse cry.

"Don't shoot, Camp!" he called. "Lord man, you ain't in earnest?"

The face of Camp convulsed; the revolver did not waver from its aim; and for an instant Billy thought his own chest would receive the first bullet to clear him from the path of the second.

"Ain't I in earnest?" said William Camp. "Ain't I in earnest? Maybe the bullet that he sent at me and that you just saved me from by the wink of an eye wasn't in earnest. Stand aside, Buel. I'll show you if I'm in earnest!"

"Not in a thousand years!" said Billy with growing anger. "Camp, are you going to murder this kid? I don't believe it."

"Didn't his father, 'murder,' as you call it, young Hugh Camp, him that I told you about? Wasn't Hugh shot down—and didn't they pump a bullet into his head while he lay there helpless?"

A shrilling voice behind Billy answered: "And he's proud of it—and I'm proud of it. And Hugh ain't the last of you skunks my dad will kill. He'll get even for me. D'you think I'm afraid? Shoot, Bill Camp, and get it done with."

Billy turned on the youth with speechless amazement, and he found himself facing a savage. The first fear was gone from the youngster. He was quivering and flushed by a new ecstasy of courage and rage.

"Yep," said William Camp. "Look him over, Billy. That's Harry Runyon, and old Hank Runyon is his dad, Hank Runyon that finished Hugh. Curse him! This ain't a Benchley, but he's on the

Benchley side, and he's got the Benchley poison in him. See it boiling out at his eyes? See it writ all over him? That's the kind of snakes they turn out. You can crush him easy now. Turn him loose, and he'll be as hard as any of 'em in a couple of years. They grow up quick. Stand aside, Buel, and lemme finish!"

Billy Buel spoke without turning, snapping the words over his shoulder.

"Put up your gun, Camp. I've made up my mind. He's not going to die, not if I got to fight you for him. Put up your gun and help me tie up his arm."

"I'll see the buzzards get him first!"

"Then stay where you are. I'll do it alone!"

· XI ·
CAMP IS PLEASED

It was with the deftness of one to whom wounds of all descriptions were an old story that Billy Buel set to work, and yet he worked gently, also; and all the while the tirade of Camp was poured at him from behind.

"You're wrong, Billy. You're coming in here and trying to set up new ways, but they ain't no room for new ways here! No room at all! You show you got a chicken heart, and d'you think they'll give you any credit for it? They've seen that you're fast as a wink with a gun—and it was the prettiest gun play, bar none, that I ever seen—

you shooting at a flash in the ferns and landing him this way! That'll make 'em dead set to pot you, and pot you they sure will if you go around letting snakes live under your foot! I've known 'em a long time, and I've never yet seen a Benchley or one of the Benchley kind that was worth the skin of a dead dog!"

But Billy Buel paid little heed. He was too busy with his work. And finally he had completed the rough bandage. There had been a painful task of cleansing it as well as he could, but the boy had never winced, never murmured.

Billy stepped back and nodded.

"I guess that'll keep you till you get home, kid."

Young Harry Runyon was looking at him with eyes as large as saucers, incredulous eyes that surveyed him from head to foot as though he were viewing a new and monstrously strange specimen of humanity. A little more, and he would be agape.

"Get your hoss," said Billy, "and ride home."

The boy made a side step, halted suddenly as though in fear there were a jest, and then, keeping his face steadily toward William Camp, he backed toward the place where his horse was standing. Camp groaned with impotent rage.

"The day'll come when you'll curse yourself for this," he said to Billy through his teeth.

But Billy Buel paid no heed to him.

"Wait a minute," he called.

Harry Runyon stopped as though a bullet had overtaken him.

"Get your gun," said Billy Buel. "There it lies yonder, and there's your knife."

"Are you plumb crazy?" asked Camp. "Going to give him a chance to shoot you the minute he gets behind cover?"

Billy raised a silencing hand. He was more interested in the stupefied air of the boy as the latter went slowly, timidly, toward the gun and picked it up with a sudden gesture. With the weapon in his left hand, a glint of savage satisfaction came in his eyes again.

"Look at him!" snarled Camp. "He's ready to murder again!"

But Billy deliberately turned his back and swung into the saddle on Lou. As he turned the mare, Harry Runyon had followed the example. He sat in his own saddle, armed again, none the worse for his adventure, save for a wound which would heal in a few days. Billy rode straight to him and halted Lou by his side.

"Now hark to my talk, son," he said gravely. "Seems to me that lying behind a tree and waiting to get a shot at a gent ain't a man's way of fighting men. Out yonder in my country they hunt a skunk that does that and kill him like a dog. But down here in Gloster Valley they seem to have queer ways. I suppose you fight the way you been taught to fight. Is that so? I guess it is. But it ain't my way, and it'll never be my way. And murdering kids that ain't half growed up ain't my way.

"Go back and tell your dad that you're to go out no more gunning for scalps. Tell him another thing—that Billy Buel is in Gloster Valley, and he's lined up with the Camps, and that he's going to do what he can to bring Nell back to the folks she rightly belongs with. Understand?

"Tell him another thing—that I've heard how he killed young Hugh Camp, and that, because of that, when I meet up with him—which I'm going to try special to do—I'll drop him if I can.

"They's one thing else. I give you back your knife and your gun, because it's a hard thing for a kid to lose his first gat in his first fight. I'd have grieved considerable about a thing like that when I was your age. Use the gun well, son. Learn how to shoot. And don't shoot till you have to. When you have to, be sure that you kill. All I ask is that the next time you want to drop a gent, don't do it from cover, but step out and hail him and give him an even break on the draw. Will you do that?"

The wonder had been fading from the face of Harry Runyon; the light of understanding was dawning on him.

"I'll do that!" he said huskily. "And—I'm ashamed, Billy Buel!" He extended his hand. "I got no right to ask it, but will you shake hands, Buel?"

"I sure will, son!"

113

Their hands met, and that of Runyon clung to his for an instant while the youngster said: "You've showed me a new way of seeing things, including myself. I'll sure never forget. And—and I sure wish to Heaven that you was going to be on our side, Buel. That's all!" Twitching the head of his horse about, he rode rapidly away, as though in fear that he might show weak emotion before the eyes of another man.

As for Billy, he went gravely after William Camp toward the trail which they had just left. He found that the latter was waiting for him. All his excitement was gone. His usual wise alertness was the only expression in his face. But Billy called him back to the subject.

"And as long as I'm in Gloster Valley," he said firmly, "I'm going to see no murder done, and I'm going to do no murder. You can lay to that, Camp. I'll fight fair and square with any man that wants to meet me; but I'll do no more. Maybe that ain't enough. If it ain't, we'll call the bargain off."

William Camp shook his head. However enraged he might be over the escape of one of his enemies, he concealed it perfectly from Buel.

"You'll be worth the five hundred dollars," he said quietly, "no matter how you fight." He broke off with a faint chuckle that had not altogether a pleasant ring in it. "Know what I'm thinking about now?"

"What is it?"

"I'm thinking about how Ames Benchley will look when they tell him about you; how you got away from that first shot; how you fired at the flash of the gun and nailed your man; then how you was so sure that you'd hit him that you rushed the ferns with your hoss!"

"But I wasn't sure," said Billy Buel gravely. "I was just sort of out of my head, being so mad that they'd fired on me from cover like that. I was just plumb crazy, Camp, that was all!"

"They won't see it that way," said William Camp, "and you can lay to it that the kid won't tell it that way. He looked at you all the time like you was more of a devil than a man. Besides, it's been a long day since a Camp got a Benchley and wouldn't kill him, old or young! And they'll think that you despise ordinary gents and just wait for the big game!" He chuckled again and slapped his thigh. "That'll give Ames Benchley something to think about—him and his name for being the best fighter that ever stepped in Gloster Valley!"

"He has that name?" asked Billy Buel.

"As big a name as you could guess for him— that's how much they think of him!"

"And what do you think of him?" asked Billy.

"I think," said Camp slowly, but frankly, "that if I had a good chance to meet up with him, I just wouldn't take the chance. Not that I'd run with folks looking on, but it ain't for me to face Ames Benchley, nor any other like me. Not even 'Slow'

Joe Walker could face him—let alone me. Not even Buck Martin would have more than one chance in three against Ames Benchley. And you—I dunno, Billy. That's what my hope and prayer is—that you'll be able to give him a rub—but I dunno!"

As he spoke, they came out over a gentle spread of meadow land with a group of red cows grazing on the far side and other cattle, beyond, wandering among the scattered trees. Utter quiet and bright sunshine lay on the place, and the wind in the trees made a continual, soft rushing sound like running water not very far away. At this sight William Camp brought his horse to a slow walk and finally halted him.

"You're plumb in the open," said Billy anxiously, "and if any Benchleys heard that shooting and came in this direction—"

Camp did not seem to hear him.

"In the old peaceful days it was like this everywhere in Gloster Valley, but the old days ain't no more. There were the young folks marrying—Camps and Benchleys and Benchleys and Camps—and pushing out and setting up new homes. But they don't set up no new homes nowadays. They hold on to what they have and are glad if they can keep it. The old men have lost all interest except for hunting on the man trail, and the young gents have growed up to know nothing except fighting. They laugh at the idea of working. They lie about, gamble and drink moonshine that'd tear the heart out of a giant, and talk big about what they're going to do when they meet Ames Benchley. But here ten years back they was meadow after meadow like this in Gloster Valley."

He shook his head and sent his horse out at a sudden gallop, speaking no more, but Billy Buel felt that he had looked at a new man inside the William Camp he thought he had come to know. He had begun to feel that there was not a real touch of tenderness in the whole make-up of the man of the feud country. But now he guessed how shrewdly the bitter fighting of the past nine years had changed him. They were swinging along at a brisk gallop now, and presently they cantered into a broken country of thickets and groups of the huge spruce, among which they wound rapidly. Presently, the alert manner of William Camp, his uneasy erectness in the saddle, left him, and he adopted a quieter manner. In a moment a whistle shrilled above them, out of the central air; it seemed to Billy Buel, after his first experience in Gloster Valley, that every unknown sound was a danger signal. He shot Lou with one leap to the side of the clearing and drew his revolver, but he found that William Camp remained unconcerned well out to the center of the opening, with his head raised, searching the thickets of foliage above him.

He whistled in answer, and in return there was a slight commotion in the branches of a great spruce. After a moment Billy saw a figure swinging down with incredible agility, from branch to branch and bough to lower bough, until at last, clinging by bare toes and hands, the guard scampered down the trunk of the tree and stood before them—a boy even younger than Harry Runyon, clad in trousers which ended in a fringe of tatters just before the knee. His shirt had once, perhaps, been blue, but many washings by the rain and fadings by the sun had reduced it to a remarkably dirty drab. His face was brown as the face of a half-breed, and little black eyes glittering under an unshorn mop of black hair completed the impression of the savage. At his back was slung the most murderous of all short-range weapons—a double-barreled, sawed-off shotgun, each barrel capable of sending a spray of big slugs, and each slug ample to kill a man. This barefooted warrior and out-guard received them with twinkling eyes of attention and not a word of greeting until he had produced a slug of black tobacco from a hip pocket and worked off an ample chew which he stowed in one cheek.

Then: "Howdy, Bill."

"Howdy, Jeff," answered Camp. "This is Billy Buel, and here's Jeff Camp, Billy."

Billy stretched forth his hand, but Jeff approached very slowly, regarding the finery of the cow-puncher with a careful, bright-eyed gaze; finally, he accepted the hand with a brief, vigorous shake, then quickly stepped back after the manner of one who has been so long on guard against men that he treats even known friends with a deep degree of suspicion. Billy regarded the child with a mixture of respect and pity and amusement.

"What's up? " asked William Camp.

"Ain't nothing worth talking about," said little Jeff Camp. "Times is tolerable dull since you left."

"Where's the folks?"

The boy flashed a glance of uneasy suspicion at Billy Buel.

"Buel is all right," put in William Camp hastily. "He's one of us. You can talk right out."

The boy nodded, apparently only half convinced. Then he said: "Art has come back. He's over to his house, and most of the folks is around there with him."

"That's good. Are they planning anything?"

"Appears to me like they're waiting for you to come along, Bill."

"They won't wait long. S'long, Jeff. Come on, Billy."

Billy followed his leader at a gallop, and looking back he saw little Jeff in the act of climbing back toward his sentinel post in the trees. William Camp rode in silence for a time; but, when Billy drew up beside him on a well-

119

beaten road, Camp said: "And d'you wonder now that I hate the Benchleys, Billy? You see the boy back there? That's what fighting the Benchleys has made us—plumb animals, Billy!"

· XII ·
BILLY'S RECEPTION

That the Camps had been as bad for the Benchleys as the Benchleys had been for the Camps was an obvious comment which Billy Buel was too wise to make. He had begun to see that, no matter how wise and mature William Camp might be on other subjects, he was a child on the subject of the Camps, neither extending broad-mindedness for his part nor expecting broad-mindedness from others. It was, with him, a religious conviction that all Benchleys were evil.

Billy Buel took note and wisely said nothing. He took it as a singular privilege that, on his first venturing into the valley, he had seen two sides of a great question, namely, the young men of the Camps and the young men of the Benchleys, each exemplified by an adequate specimen. Whom he favored more, he could not say. Unquestionably, it seemed to him that young Runyon was a far higher specimen of manhood than Jeff Camp. But the Camp story as he had heard it from William seemed beyond doubt the only just side of the main argument.

He was wondering what the Benchley side of the same tale might be when William Camp raised his hand as a signal for halting. He obeyed and, looking ahead at the same time, through the mass of foliage directly before him, saw the outlines of a house. It was a large structure, sprawling shapelessly to the right and to the left.

"Here's Arthur Camp's house," remarked William. "And before we get there I might as well tell you that Art is kind of the chief man of the clan. Meaning by that, that Art's the king, and we're the workers. I dunno just how it come about, but Art ain't any more'n my brother—he ain't any more'n me. But somehow he seems to lead—partly because he's the rich man among us, I guess. But we all take off the hat to Art and ask him to lead the way." William paused, much embarrassed. "Now that you're working on our side—" he began.

"They ain't any apologies needed," remarked Billy with decision. "If Art Camp is to be my boss, enough said. I'm working for five hundred dollars a week and for Nell. That's about enough thinking for me. You pay me five hundred dollars every week and I work to get Nell back to the folks she belongs to. Outside of that, I don't think, Camp!"

The answer seemed to be highly satisfactory to William. He nodded to Billy.

"Starting out with that spirit," he said, "you'll go a long way, son. But here we are!"

He had led the way at a walk during the last part of this conversation, and now they were breaking through the last screen of foliage and came in full view of the house itself. What first struck Billy Buel was that, in spite of the fact that this family was occupied with a feud, the main dwelling, for such this appeared to be, was not at all planned for defense. It spread on either side of a quite old central building and had apparently been added to from time to time as the whim of the homemaker dictated rather than the caution of one who makes, at the same time, both house and fortress. Billy, observing, was so struck that he mentioned it to William Camp. He had the more reason since Camp had stopped as soon as they reached a clear view of the big building, very much as one who is proud of the place to which he brings a guest.

"Look here, Camp," said Billy, "it appears to me that you, or Art Camp, or whoever built this house, ain't been very careful to make it bullet proof and easy to hold. Look at that hill over yonder. Anybody could get up there and make life tolerable bad for the gents inside the house."

William Camp turned on him with a snort of mingled surprise and disgust.

"From that hill—" he said coldly. "Son, d'you think that the Benchleys ever will have the nerve to come that close to us? Not them! Not even with Ames Benchley to lead 'em! No, sir, they'll keep their distance while Buck Martin and Art and myself and Slow Joe Walker are stepping about! You lay to that! Billy, they ain't any fear of even Ames Benchley giving us a rush right here where we live!"

Billy Buel nodded slowly. He began to understand that, in spite of anything that might be said to him, the Camps were the aggressors. Their object was to bring back Nell; the object of the Benchleys was simply to keep her safe; and, no matter how justified the endeavor of the Camps might be, he could not help a thrill of sympathy for the Benchleys who, obviously not having the strength to attack their enemies in their homes, could only skirmish at a distance and struggle to preserve the girl.

And what was she, then, for whose preservation so many strong men were willing to bleed? What was her grace of mind? What was her physical beauty? He could only guess at it blindly. But, looking on the stern face of William Camp, he was sure that it must be a lovely creature indeed who could tempt him out to battle, he and all his clan.

In the meantime, William had ridden straight to the door of the house and beat upon it with his fist without dismounting. The door was opened immediately by a heavy-faced fellow whose scowl was immediately exchanged for a grin at the sight of the man who knocked.

"Take my hoss," said Camp, dismounting, "and take the hoss of our friend, Buel."

The dull eyes glinted with sudden pleasure at Billy Buel, and the servant stepped out and took the reins which Camp and Billy gave him, and passed around the corner of the house with the horses. In the meantime, the two had entered the house, and passing down the hall, they heard on the left the indescribable murmur which comes from a dining room where many hungry men are eating.

"This way," said William, and throwing open a door he led Billy into the presence of the Camp clan.

They were ranged about a long table, five men and four women—four fighting men and one old sage; one beautiful, dark-haired girl and three mature women. At the sight of William and the stranger, they started to their feet with a single exclamation. But their eyes were not for William. Every glance was turned burningly, hopefully, on Billy, and only gradually the hope grew dull and the foreheads began to frown. Plainly, they knew why William had left Gloster Valley, and, plainly, they were not pleased with the champion he had brought back.

Then there was a general settling back into chairs, save for one woman of kindly middle age, who came to William and kissed him. His arm was still around his wife while he presented his guest.

"Gents," he said, "I've got the man I started for.

This is him that shot the board in two with six clean shots—cut it clean as a whistle."

There was no exclamation of surprise, but a new focusing of sharp attention on Billy.

"And this is him that rode Brownie—to death!"

This time a hum of wonder passed around the board. The women were now staring wide-eyed; the men were more stoical.

"And this is him," said William Camp, "who's thrown in his luck on our side to stick with us till we've got back Nell to her real father and mother. This is Billy Buel."

He took Billy around the table, and one by one the men rose and took his hand in mighty grips. First was the white-haired, ancient man, bowed of shoulder, his face misted over with beard, and through the mist were two keen old eyes watching the face of Billy.

"It's a good day for us that brings you here, son," said the man, who was introduced as "Judge" Camp. "And a fine bit of work you've done, Willie, my lad."

And Billy saw that William actually smiled and flushed a little under the applause. Plainly, the opinion of the "judge" was considered its weight in gold among the Camps.

Next rose a man of very much the same build as that of William, and of the same general cast of feature, save that there was less keen wisdom in his face, and a cast of melancholy lay over him. It was Lew Camp, and Billy Buel thrilled as he shook hands with the true father of Nell. He understood the wild hope and the gloomy doubt which struggled together in the eyes of Lew. Was this young stranger to be the means of bringing Nell back to him? Was there force enough in him to accomplish what so many big and strong men had failed in attempting all these years? He was more doubtful than hopeful, yet he gave Billy a kind word as the latter passed by and met Margery Camp, the wife of Lew.

She, indeed, was no doubter. In her worn face, where the beauty of her youth was still traceable, there came a flare of color, and tears rushed into her eyes. With a sudden impulse she drew down the head of Billy and kissed him on the forehead.

"Heaven bless you, Billy Buel," she whispered, "for coming to help me. And I have a feeling—a strange, light feeling about my heart—that you will do it!"

He pressed her hand silently. The smallest man at the Camp table had arisen before him, and that smallest man was both taller and heavier-shouldered than Billy Buel. He was no heavy sluggard, however, but a flame of manhood. His arched chest spoke of his strength and endurance, his erect head told of his pride, and his fiery, pale-blue eye was the eye of a fighting man. His hair was a flare of red, a wild flare which no comb or brush could effectually smooth, so that he had the appearance of standing in a steady wind. To see him standing still was to know he would be fleet as a deer in running; to see him smile now, in taking the hand of Billy Buel, was to know that his wrath could be terrible and edged with danger.

It was Buck Martin. Billy wrote his face down in large characters to be remembered in time of need.

He passed Buck Martin and was face to face with that slender, dark-eyed girl he had noted in a first keen glance around the room. She was Sally Camp. It seemed to Billy that she greeted him with a curiously cold and impersonal manner, her head canted a little to one side, her smile rather judicial than friendly. It was as though she were making a close estimate of the qualities of this stranger and very much doubting his ability. For he had hardly passed her when her eyes sought Buck Martin, and then the big man on the far side of the table.

Her mother was far kinder. The big, queenly woman at her side, who was introduced as Mrs. Arthur Camp, received Billy with a strong hand-shake and said: "You're a youngster to be here in this business, Billy Buel. But I speak for all the rest when I say that I thank you for coming."

Billy smiled frankly back to her and shook hands with her husband just beyond.

He sat at the table, this Arthur Camp, as much of

a king among men as his wife was a queen among women. As he rose from his place at the head of the table, the fingers of his left hand were tangled in his short, thick brown beard, so that he was still estimating and judging Billy while he shook hands. His clothes were far better in quality and make than the clothes of the other men at the table, and his whole manner was that of a rich man, the head of a household sufficient unto himself. Withal, he was a big man, a manly man, with a rolling, bass voice. And in spite of his beard the facial resemblance of Lew and William was striking. Obviously, he was the third of the brothers.

"All I got to say, Buel," he remarked in greeting, "is that if you do as much for us as Will seems to think you can do, you'll never have reason to regret it—so long as my bank account holds out."

It was not altogether the sort of warmth which Billy had reason to hope for. He began to feel that he was only a hired man, and he regretted that contract which he had made for five hundred dollars a week. His gloom was intensified in a different manner when he met the last party at the table.

He was a huge fellow. Rising from his chair as Billy came toward him, the big man, it seemed to Billy, would never stop erecting himself toward the ceiling. Billy might have met bigger men, but none who showed such imposing size to strike the eye of the onlooker.

"Here's Slow Joe Walker—Billy Buel," said the introducing voice of William Camp. "Joe has done a pile for us, Billy. And I sure hope that you and him will be friends, because, with the two of you working together, it looks to me that there ain't very much that you can't do. Here's hoping!"

His conciliatory manner suggested that he was far from having the assurance of which he spoke. And the gloomy face of Slow Joe Walker, the shrug of his immense shoulders, intensified the impression. It was not hard for Billy to guess that the giant, before the coming of this new champion, had been the chief stay and upholder of the cause of the Camps against the Benchleys. His huge, deep-throated voice strengthened the same idea.

"I'm tolerable glad to meet you," said Slow Joe Walker. "Will, yonder, has always had the idea that what we needed is a gent that can meet Ames Benchley and get away with him. Here I've been for a long time ready and willing to meet Ames Benchley and try what he could do. But Ames ain't showed none too ready to meet me. Well, be that as it may, now you've come along, and he may be a pile more willing to meet you. I hope you have the luck."

So saying, his hand, his immense, thick-fingered

hand, closed over that of Billy Buel. The moment these fingers touched his, Billy guessed the purpose of the giant. He would crush the hand of the smaller man in his huge grip and then laugh in the face of the would-be conqueror of the formidable Benchley.

His impression proved to be the correct one. The grip increased, strengthened slowly. With all his might Billy Buel fought back and, maintaining his smile, put all his power into the grip of his own right hand. It was useless. He was attempting to outface a colossus. He felt the nerves along the back of his hand go numb. He felt muscles and bones begin to give.

With a sharp effort he wrenched his hand away. And there he stood, no longer the mild-eyed, gentle-faced youth who had entered the hall bashfully with William Camp, but a tiger-eyed fighter. He had wrenched himself back a full stride from the other in that struggle to get away. Now he stood swaying a little, risen to tiptoe, his jaw set, his fingers working, those long and nimble fingers which meant so much to any man with eyes to see them!

"I sort of understand the kind of luck you wish me, Walker," he answered slowly. "But in my part of the country a gent don't get along by good wishes. He gets along by being able to fight his own way. And the way he fights is to meet every gent that has any hard feeling against him. Day or night, morning or evening, he's ready to fight. Is that all clear?"

Vaguely, he sensed that the other people in the room had stiffened and grown tense as they caught the note of soft fury in his voice. And in the face of Slow Joe Walker he saw a vast surprise deepening. But before either of them could speak again William Camp pushed in between them and carried Billy Buel away.

"Here's our two places waiting. Come along, Billy. You've met everybody now, I guess."

And he whispered fiercely as they walked away: "Watch yourself, Buel. Don't pay no attention to Walker. He's too stupid to count, but he's a real man and a real fighter. Don't hold no malice, or everything is spoiled before it's fair started."

· XIII ·
THE ENEMY COMES

He raised his voice again, turning back a little: "You knew I'd come back with the man I started out to find, Art. You talked doubtful all the time, but down in your heart you knew, and so you've kept these two extra places set all the time waiting for me to show up. Is that right? Admit it, Art. Admit that you knew all the time I'd bring back the man I wanted!"

"I'll admit that I hoped you would, Will. But I knew you'd bring back someone, whether he was the man or not. So I had the two places ready."

There was a not altogether hidden imputation that Billy Buel would not be in fact all that William Camp had said he was. But before Billy could take offense, William was speaking again.

"You ain't the only one that was waiting for me to come back. The Benchleys was waiting, too!"

The announcement had on the company the effect of an explosion. There was a general stiffening in chairs. And Mrs. Lew Camp, shivering, cast a glance over her shoulder and toward the window as though she dreaded that the face of a Benchley might at any moment appear behind her with leveled gun ready to take life. It meant much to Billy Buel, that little side play.

"The Benchleys was waiting," said William Camp, apparently content to have won the thoughts of big Joe Walker away from his offended pride. "We come down the valley pretty careful, but nobody can be careful enough when there's foxes afield. I didn't see nothing. But Buel did. Caught a flash in the ferns ahead of us, swung his hoss and mine to the side, and got me away from a bullet that was sure meant for my head. It pretty near clipped my hair as it went by. Before I could get my gun out of the leather, Billy had fired—at the flash, mind you!—and, by the Lord, if he didn't hit his target! Because we heard a yell, and then, the first thing I knew, there was Billy charging straight at them ferns. How did he know that they wasn't a dozen Benchleys in that thicket instead of just one?"

He paused to let his story take effect. And every eye was fixed in terrified wonder on Billy Buel.

"There he went like a madman and busted through and caught Harry Runyon, with a bullet through his right arm, and caught the kid as he was about to climb into his saddle."

There was a deep, short cry from several of the men.

"Then," said Lew Camp, "they's one snake less in the world right this here minute? Son, I sure want to shake hands with you again!"

"Didn't kill him," added William. "He don't like that way of working, particular when the others are as young as Harry Runyon. So he just let Harry go and told him to take a message to Ames Benchley, that Billy Buel was come to Gloster Valley, and that he was all set to meet Ames Benchley first of all, or any other Benchley whenever they was willing. I tried to talk different and show him that a young snake was as bad as an old one, and that inside of a couple of years Harry Runyon would be as bad as any of the Benchley tribe that ever stepped. But give him time, gents, and he'll come around to our way of thinking. In the meantime, the important thing was he beat a Benchley and beat him bad, and then showed him that he scorned 'em! That'll hurt 'em worse than another death could do!"

Indeed, the narrative had brought a sharp chorus of exclamations from the people about the table. Embarrassment had kept Billy Buel from looking frankly about him. But he was aware that Sally Camp was flushing and smiling at him with pleasure, and that the men, one and all, were distinctly not pleased with his adventure of the day. Their opinion was unanimous, coming in ominous growls. Never had there been a Benchley who was worthy of the slightest mercy. And that young dog of a Runyon should certainly have been killed without mercy.

Billy wondered. All these were probably brave and generous men, yet they talked like common murderers. It could only be explained that the feud had lasted so many years that those who partook in it had been brutalized in that one respect at least. Even the women, aside from Sally Camp, showed no particular pleasure at the mercy with which he had treated young Harry Runyon.

There was only one common impression when the whole story was ended, however, and that was obviously the impression which William Camp had wished to create that here was a fighting gun-toter of the very first caliber; one who not only could ride and shoot at trick targets, but who also had the requisite nerve and the willingness to face the worst forms of danger. They had glanced at him at first with great suspicion—now, all in a moment, they accepted him as

William Camp wanted his protege to be accepted. Even Slow Joe Walker had raised his head with eyes that flashed admiration when he heard how Billy Buel had so rashly charged the covert from which the first shot had been fired. And since that time he sat dreamily, as before, his great, dull eyes conjuring up visions of other adventures where he could play a similarly brilliant and daring role.

In the meantime, a kindlier spirit had come over the conversation. Talk waxed freer and more gay. There were anecdotes now and again of a playful nature. And as the dinner progressed and the sun of the long summer evening began to lengthen toward the twilight, an actual touch of joviality appeared. And finally, speaking of the feud, Lew Camp ventured to suggest that the time had come when, with an ally like Billy Buel, they should gather all of their forces and try to settle the long war in one brilliant, headlong, terrible attack.

His speech was met with shouts from the men and bright eyes among the women. And then someone was beating with his knife loudly at the foot of the table. It was he of the long and snowy beard—Judge Camp; and the moment he was observed a respectful silence circled among the others, and all heads were turned gravely to await his opinion.

"You got reason for talking sort of foolish along them lines now and then, Lew," said the old man.

"You got reason so long as your Nell is up there calling another woman mother and grieving for a dead man that she thinks of as her father, and hating you because she thinks you and Margie want to steal her away. So you sure got reason to talk foolish and want to get the fighting ended quick."

He paused. He had placed the case against the Benchleys indirectly in the bitterest possible light, and there was a growling of rage among the men at the table. Even Billy felt a fierce desire to stand up and instantly start against the Benchley strong-holds.

"But this ain't a thing that's going to be finished by brute force," said the seer. "So long as Ames Benchley is up yonder, you'll never take their houses by force. We're stronger than them in the open. But when it comes to just sitting back and waiting for trouble, one gent that waits is about as good as two men making the attack. And that's why they're so strong when we start hunting 'em. Besides, they got Ames Benchley, and he is as good a man in a fight as ever stepped, and as wise a man when it comes to figuring things out, and as just a man when it comes to talking straight man-talk. So as long as he's up there, it ain't any use attacking 'em!"

"Seems to me," muttered Slow Joe Walker, "that you folks down here think a whole pile about Ames Benchley. I dunno why. He's sure killed enough of you—and the best of you, it appears to me!"

The brutality of the giant was like a blow with a club. An angry silence spread around the table, but no glances were exchanged. Not one there but had lost brother or father or son in this cruel war that had no ending. The heavy silence was again relieved by the subtle William Camp.

"We think a lot of him," said William, "but it ain't because we don't hate him. But we just admit that he's a powerful bad man to face. He's about as great a fighter as I've ever heard of. Not that I say he's quite as good as you, Joe. You're stronger, that's sure; and if you ain't quite as quick, maybe—why, still, you're a pile surer; about as sure a shot as I ever seen, you are, Joe. But, besides being a fighter, Ames Benchley is a lot of other things. He's clever, and he's a fox when it comes to seeing through the plans we make."

"I dunno," said the pacified giant, who had drunk in the praise with eyes that half closed in the intenseness of his delight. "I sure got my doubts about a man being quite so brave as they say, when he just sits around and waits for us to do all the forcing. But maybe you and the old judge are right."

"Thanks," said Judge Camp with just a twinkle of mirth in his wise old eyes. "Me being so far along in years, Joe, I begin to figure that maybe

I'm plumb out of touch with things, and it sure means a lot when a bright young gent like you ups and tells me that I'm right. But I say it again. We'll never be able to rush the Benchleys till we've killed Ames Benchley! And there, maybe, is the gent that will do it for us!"

And he turned, as he spoke, and pointed straight at Billy Buel.

There was a little dramatic pause at this place, and, before the silence ended, a door opened, crashed to, and a man burst into the room, running headlong. He flung himself at Art Camp, gasped for breath.

"Ames Benchley!" he breathed. "He's coming. Ames Benchley is coming here pronto—right now!"

· XIV ·
"WHAT FAITH HAVE THEY KEPT?"

Utter consternation swept through the room. Partly, no doubt, it was because of the awe which the name of the great enemy inspired in the Camps. And now, to intensify the fear which he ordinarily struck in them, his entrance had been prepared for by the conversation which had just been turning around his formidable name.

If anything were needed to give added point, it was the figure of the poor wretch who now cowered at the side of Art Camp, quaking in every limb, his face heated from the running which had exhausted him, but nevertheless strangely pale with terror.

In that crisis, as the women drew into a huddling group and the men started up, with guns coming into their hands, it was plain that one man was the acknowledged leader, for all eyes turned instinctively upon Art Camp.

He had risen more slowly than the rest, and now he towered above the ragged messenger.

"You seen him coming," he said, "and he's still on the way? Maybe your gun clogged, or something? You couldn't shoot?"

The latter wiped his forehead with a trembling hand. That hand alone was ample explanation of why he did not shoot.

"He was riding straight down the middle of the road, and far as I could see they wasn't anybody with him."

"Idiot!" snarled Art Camp. "The rest of his men is hiding in the trees and coming along under cover. That's why you didn't see 'em! I'm cursed with having fools to foller me!"

"Be-besides," stammered the frightened messenger, "he was carrying a handkerchief on the end of a little branch above his head and waving it while he rode."

"A white flag!" exclaimed Art Camp. "He's coming under a sort of a flag of truce, maybe?"

"Flag of truce—hell!" said William. "Send a

forty-five-caliber slug into Ames Benchley and look for his flag of truce afterward—that's what I say!"

"And me—and me!"

Every voice echoed that sentiment, until old Judge Camp spoke: "Boys," he said, and Billy saw that even this antiquated fellow carried weapons and was ready to use them, for he was looking at the condition of a short-barreled rifle which he had taken from the rack against the far wall, "you're plumb wrong. I know what you think about the Benchleys, and mostly you're right. They're snakes. But Ames Benchley is different. He fights square, he talks square, he acts square. I say, if he's come here with a flag of truce, the best thing we can do is to let him come and let him talk."

"I'll go out and meet him," said Slow Joe Walker, his eyes burning as the thought came to him. "I'll go out, and when I'm through talking to him maybe he won't have so much to say to the rest of you. Maybe he won't never have nothing to say to anybody when I get through with him!"

He started for the door with a vast stride as he spoke, a true giant among men, and doubtless a giant in courage, also. But little, withered Judge Camp barred the way with lifted hand, and his small, shaken voice was even more imposing, in its way, than all the unsurveyed bulk of Joe Walker.

"You stay inside, Joe. You stay here, less'n you want to make us all out fools and cowards. Ames Benchley comes along with a flag of truce. Are all the Camps going to jump up and grab guns the minute they hear he's coming? No, sir. I say let your men keep a sharp lookout, Art. But the rest of us, here, will go right back to that table and sit down and put our guns away and start eating and talking like nothing had happened. And we'll not let Ames Benchley come in and find us all standing around with guns in our hands and ready to fight a shadow. Not six men afraid of one man, I hope— when the six are the Camps! Go back, Joe. And the rest of you go back. We'll have our outlook kept. We'll see there ain't no chance to rush the house. But don't let all of us be shamed by one man!"

His words were strangely persuasive. His actions were even more so. Putting the rifle back into the case, he went calmly to the table, resumed his chair, and nodded to pretty Sally Camp who stood with the rest of the women, uncertain, at the far side of the room.

"I'm kind of lonely over here, Sally, eating all alone," he said. "Ain't you coming back and join me?"

"I'm coming this minute," said the girl, flushing and smiling, and Billy Buel admired her with a silent pleasure. "And—and I'm sure glad that the Camps have you among 'em to keep our heads all level!"

And with that she came straight back to her place at the table.

The example was quickly followed. One by one the others returned, and there they sat, while Art Camp gave sharp and swift orders to his messenger that a close lookout be kept from every place of vantage around the house to make sure that Ames Benchley came in truth alone—but upon Ames Benchley no shot was to be fired. He was permitted to come freely straight into the dining room.

After that the dinner was resumed, or at least a pretense was made at resuming it. But only Judge Camp was truly at his ease, or seemed to be. He kept on talking gaily to Sally Camp, who was plainly a great favorite with him, and the others did what they could to imitate him. Ames Benchley must be received as though his visit were the most ordinary thing in the world.

Billy Buel looked from face to grim face, and then at the frightened, whispering women, and then at the illuminated face of Sally Camp. Her beauty was beginning to grow on him, and all her fresh courage. It was in her straight-looking eye, as steady as the eye of a man. It was in the steadiness of her hand, which raised the glass without a tremor. And she, seeing his admiration, smiled straight at him, as if to invite him into a sudden entente of which she and Judge Camp were the two other members. Billy smiled in return.

But he was far from being as calm as he pretended. Into that room, before many minutes, would step the man who, he felt, he must either kill or be killed by before his stay in Gloster Valley had ended. What would he be like? Similar to the Camps, perhaps? A great, huge-shouldered man like Joe Walker, it might be?

While his mind was still full of conjectures, voices sounded and footfalls passed down the hall beyond. There was a tightening of the facial muscles all around the table. Then the door opened, and in it stood that man!

At a single glance, Billy Buel recognized Ames Benchley. It must be he. On every line of his face, in every contour of his tall, strong body, was written the tale of the conqueror and the ruler. A handsome man, without weakness; a stern man, without cruelty; a just man, without coldness of heart—he seemed to Billy, in the first flare of approval, all that a human being should be. Not even in the faultless and ample proportions of his body could a single flaw be found. While he had not the immense size of Slow Joe Walker, yet he was a big man indeed, and who could tell what combined sheer muscular power and nervous energy would make of him in the crisis of action? Might there not be in him the same crushing strength as in Walker? Might he not also possess even the lightning speed of a Billy Buel or a Buck Martin?

Billy saw that Walker and Buck Martin were eyeing the stranger hungrily, but with awe. The same hunger and mingled awe were, he knew, shining from his own eyes. But the stranger was quite unmoved. Round that circle of eager and hostile faces his own glance went with an utter calm. In the excitement of the moment, indeed, he even smiled faintly, so that for an instant he lost the grave weight of his forty years and seemed more a youth. Only one man rose to greet him, and that was Art Camp.

Billy, with a beating heart, watched the two archenemies as they drew together, but, if he feared an explosion, little did he know the full strength of the laws of hospitality which ruled those households in Gloster Valley—and little did he know the true strength of Art Camp's character.

He did not, indeed, offer to shake the hand of the visitor, but he said very simply: "It's been quite a pile of days since I've seen you as close as this, Ames. Gimme your hat, and then go and sit down and rest yourself. They's a chair over by the judge."

"It's been nine years," said Ames Benchley. "Nine years since I've come under your roof, Art. And the longest nine years and the saddest nine years of my life. But—we'll talk a bit more about that later on."

He went over to the chair which had been pointed out to him. Standing by it, he surveyed those who sat about it and named them carefully, and kindly, one by one. In spite of consuming fear, hatred, curiosity and bitter anger, his courteous smile was unchanged. His voice was as smooth as the voice of William Camp himself as he uttered his greetings.

And Billy gave half of his attention to those at the table as they met the glance of the great enemy. Buck Martin was boldly erect, very pale, his eyes afire; Joe Walker sat with his head bowed, scowling up at Benchley as though his great body were as fearless as ever, but his spirit had been bowed before the calm pride of the latest comer. From the eyes of Lew Camp came a spark of utter hatred. From Margery's eyes came the coldness of utter fear. Mrs. Art Camp kept a patient sneer on her lips. And a thousand emotions were in the pretty face of Sally, as though against her will she were being forced to admire the big fellow who stood so straight and so quiet and so gentle in the house of his enemies. But in Billy himself there was a wild and a growing panic. There stood the man in whom he recognized his great antagonist. What might happen when they stood face to face?

For one instant his heart leaped in the joyous anticipation of the battle. The next moment he was conscious of the pallor of his face and the cold sweat which lined his forehead.

Last of all, his attention rested on the two who, next to the judge, he felt to be the most intelligent of the Camps—William and his wife, Ruth. The wife looked nowhere save at her husband, patiently, almost smiling. And William Camp was staring down at the table with a frown of the most complete concentration, as though he were bent on the solution of some grave and abstract problem, and as though the enemy of enemies were not in the room with him. For some reason it made Billy Buel respect the fox of a man more than he had ever respected him before.

"Have you had dinner?" asked Art Camp as Benchley sat down.

"I had dinner before I started," said Ames Benchley.

"But a cup of coffee, maybe?"

There was a pause. Straight across the table peered Benchley and into the eyes of his host.

"Don't mind if I do!" he said.

A hush passed softly around the table. It was plain that even to Ames Benchley this was a moving moment, and Billy could guess why. Under the house of the man whom he had most wronged, and who, no doubt, had most often wronged him, Benchley was about to partake of food, and by so doing he was to invest himself, while he was under the roof of the Camps, with all the sacred character of the invited guest.

The coffee was brought by an old Negro who came agape and with staring eyes, holding in both hands a cup that chattered on the saucer with the violence of the old fellow's trembling. Doubtless, that expression had been his many a time before, hearing the wild stories of the battles and the killings of the great Benchley. But even he was disarmed by the kindly smile with which Benchley received the cup.

Still the silence held. The stirring of a lump of sugar into the coffee was a grave part of the ceremony, for such it was rapidly becoming. All eyes followed it, glittering with excitement. And finally Benchley raised the cup and tasted the contents.

There was a little sigh of excitement among the rest of the people at the table. The thing had been done. Ames Benchley himself sat at that table and tasted the food of the Camps!

"Art," went on the visitor, addressing himself to the host on the far side of the table, "I guess I can say that none of us ever expected to see this time come. A Benchley sitting at a table with Camps all around him!"

"I guess we didn't," admitted Art Camp.

"And it ain't anything that I'm too glad to see!" burst out Lew Camp.

A sudden cloud passed across the brow of Benchley, and as he glared at Lew Camp it seemed to Billy Buel that the character of the fighting man was painted in bright colors and stood out from the rest of the nature of this many-sided hero.

"That's something you're ashamed for saying to a guest under my roof," said Art Camp sternly.

But Lew started to his feet, mad with rage and excitement.

"I say I see the gent that's keeping Nell. Without him the rest are nothing. And I see him here in our power! Are we going to let that chance go? Are we going to? You want us to keep faith with him? What faith have the Benchleys ever kept with us?"

And, in the deadly hush that followed, Billy Buel saw William Camp softly draw forth his revolver and hold it on his knee, ready for instant action, with the barrel trained upon the broad chest of the visitor.

▪ XV ▪
WISE TALK

It convinced Billy that a real climax had come. He had deemed it impossible that any courageous men could take such cowardly advantage of a guest who had, of free will, placed himself so entirely in their power. But, as he scanned the faces around the table, each one was set and stern. Even Art Camp, the host, wavered and did not speak again; and old Judge Camp settled back in his chair with a frown, rather as one who has seen many bitter things before and is ready to endure the sight of another, than as a man about to spring up and intervene with the full weight of his authority.

But if Billy Buel wanted a full confirmation of the crisis, he could find it in the face of Ames Benchley. The big man had not stirred in his chair, but his lionlike head had raised, and his tawny eyes moved steadily, fiercely, about the table from man to man. He was gathering his strength of mind and nerve to prepare himself for his death fight which plainly he felt to be not far away. A hopeless fight, to be sure, but here was one who would not give up even a hopeless battle. And Billy Buel's heart went out suddenly, after his own impulsive habit, to the cornered champion.

It was not until the full horror of that silence about the table and the shrinking of the women —and even they showed no pity!—had entered the comprehension of Billy Buel, that he leaned forward and suddenly swept every eye toward him and arrested all action for the moment. He did it very simply, for as he leaned a little forward he laughed, and the almost feminine lightness of that laughter shocked all attention toward him— as though, in a room of silent tragedy, the careless voice of a child playing outside the house should break through the windows and call those who were about to fight back to the daylight reality and true happiness of life.

And, indeed, there was something of the child in

the careless grace of Billy Buel as he faced Ames Benchley.

"Don't you see, pardner," he said gayly, "that it's all a joke—that that's why I'm laughing? It's all to try you out. They seen you fight before; they wanted to try out your nerve inside a house. You can lay that that's all they is in the air!"

"I hope you're right," said Ames Benchley gravely, but without cringing. "Art Camp, this is your house. Talk up and tell me what's what! I'm under your roof, and I'm eating your food. Does what Lew says go here?"

"He's under your roof, Art!" cried Margery Camp, springing to her feet, with her tired, sad face transformed to a fury. "But ain't there been times when Camps were under the roofs of the Benchleys? Wasn't they a time when my cousin—"

The deep, calm voice of Ames Benchley cut into her talk, wisely guessing that if she continued her narrative of outrages very long his death warrant would be signed. "You're right, Margery. They's been hard things done on both sides in this cursed war. But they's never been a man born that can say that Ames Benchley ever took an unfair advantage. That's why I risked myself here!"

The maddening, shrilling voice of the woman cut in on him again. And in spite of the horror of it, Billy Buel could not help sympathizing with her and pitying her; for was she not, after all, simply a mother making a desperate appeal for her daughter and the return of the chief obstacle which existed between them? But her voice was a thrilling call to war; she trembled with her eagerness!

"You never took advantage!" she cried. "No, Ames Benchley, because you was born and trained a man-killer! The best of our men meet you, but you know that you ain't got a thing to fear. You got a quicker hand, you got a steadier eye; and you know you ain't taking any chances. That's why you've played fair. But I ask you, Judge Camp"—and here she whirled on the patriarch at the far end of the table—"are you going to sit quietly by while the man that murdered your only son is—"

Billy Buel rose in turn. He could tell that the Camps were being rapidly driven to the point of frenzy by the tragic recollections which the woman was forcing on them. And truly, Ames Benchley must have done much indeed to be so feared and so hated. His calm, by contrast, made him appear greater. They were all big men, fighting men—but, looking about the room, it seemed to Billy that a lion was being badgered by wolves.

"Lady," said Billy Buel, "maybe you'll let me explain my little joke?"

She paused for a moment, rather exhausted by emotion than because Billy had asked for attention.

151

"You see why I know it's a joke, Benchley," said Billy Buel without lifting one silken syllable above a monotone. "The Camps come to me and asked me to come down here and help 'em. But they know that I come from parts where killings are terrible frequent, but where murder ain't done. And they know well that I won't sit down and see a helpless man butchered. That's why I say it's all a joke—just done to try you. Rest easy! Rest easy, Benchley. When you die, it'll be under the blue, open sky, fighting one man hand to hand, with everything fair!"

As he spoke, the fighting passion which was, unfortunately, the great controlling impulse in Buel's life, rose hotly to his throat and cast a red mist across his eyes and set him atremble with eagerness like a terrier on a leash—or, better still, like a panther mad with hunger and waiting for his spring and kill. Here was his man of men! Here was the one man he had ever seen capable of draining all of his powers as a fighter. It ceased to be a generous desire to help Benchley. It became rather a jealous urge to save this man for the great test, for, as his tawny eyes glimmered at him across the table, Billy Buel for the first time in his life knew fear. In those mighty shoulders he guessed the strength; in those finely molded, big hands he guessed the speed and gesture of striking; and in the eye he recognized the dauntless spirit and the iron nerve of the warrior. He fell in love with his own fear, so to speak. It dazzled him and taunted him. He played with it, as a man is tempted by a great height, or as a child is tempted toward the "haunted" house in the woods.

"Because they know," continued Billy Buel, "that if it come to a pinch, they'd be fighting not you alone, but me, too. That's why you're safe in this room, Benchley. You see other men in here—gents that've done a pile of fighting in their days—but I don't see enough all told to down the two of us."

And as he spoke, his wild black eyes, so different from the tawny, calm ones of Ames Benchley, flared from face to face with a question and a challenge—William and Arthur and Lew Camp, Buck Martin, and big Slow Joe Walker, who had not yet understood the meaning of Billy's words. Old Judge Camp, of course, hardly counted one way or the other. But, in that case of five men against two, not one of the five, with the exception of Slow Joe, had the slightest doubt that Billy Buel and Ames Benchley could actually conquer. About them both was the irresistible air of the champion who is quite used to conquest. Moreover, in the manner in which Billy was eying Benchley again, there was something curiously fascinating—curiously terrible.

Ames Benchley did not wait for the argument to start again. He rose.

"Buel," he said, "I'm sure thanking you. After

what you done for Harry Runyon, I was tolerable sure that this was the way you'd act in a pinch, but I'm sure glad to make sure."

"You've hired a man for the Benchleys, William," cried Margery bitterly, "not a man for us! He's saved Ames Benchley's life before he's been a day among us!"

"But he'll have a chance to take that same life again," said Benchley, "before this same day is clear ended. That's why I come here, ladies and gents. That's why I took my life in my hands to come here and make a fair and square proposition to you.

"Today, Harry Runyon came home with his arm tied up. He'd been clean drilled by a gent he said was the fastest and straightest shooter he ever seen or heard tell of. And the same gent that shot him tied up his wound and sent him home with a message for me.

"Well, gents, it sure made a big hit with me to hear about that kind of a man being in the valley. It didn't make so much of a hit with the others. They figured that it wasn't altogether on the books for you to send out of Gloster Valley and get gun fighters to clean up on us. But—"

"Wait a minute," broke in Art Camp. "What about Hal and Henry Moore, and what about Ollie Lord? Since when have they belonged to the Benchley's outfit? Since when have they had your blood in their veins?"

"They come for the love of Nell," said Ames Benchley angrily. "And never did they ever get a penny of money from us!"

"No!" cried Lew Camp. "You lure 'em with a girl that don't belong to you. Ain't that worse'n hiring men for money?"

The deep bass of Judge Camp cut in with: "Steady, lads. That's going back to the beginning of everything. No use arguing about things that words won't help."

"But I've come today," said Benchley, "to cut right down to the beginning. I want to go from the beginning to the end, and you gents and the Lord willing, I'll do it! Boys, they's an end to the fighting. Look how many years it's been going on already. Look how many years it's still apt to be going on. And what's been done but killing of men and breaking of the hearts of women? That's all. Well, Art Camp, I know you've a heart of oak, you and the rest of the true blood. And I know Martin and Walker there would fight to the last drop in their bodies. And I know why!"

"Why?" asked Buck Martin nervously.

"Not for the love of the Camps, Martin, but because, back at the fair three years ago, you seen Nell. She was only a slip of a girl then, but the promise was in her. You seen Nell, Buck; and so did Walker, and that's why you threw in with the Camps, hoping that if Nell was got by them they'd marry her to one of you out of gratitude. Am I right?"

"It's a lie!" cried Buck Martin.

There was such savagery in his tone that Billy Buel was startled. He had not dreamed that any man in Gloster Valley would dare rush against terrible Ames Benchley after this fashion. He was yet more amazed by the perfect equanimity with which Benchley received the insult.

"Better take the time and think that over, Buck," said Benchley quietly. "I ain't aiming to grab off a quarrel every time I got a chance!"

Buck Martin said no more, and his head lowered a little, as one who has ventured beyond his depth and received a reproof.

"To go back," went on Benchley in his much interrupted speech, "I say that the five or six of you would fight to the last, and then your women would take up the guns and keep on! But the men you got following you ain't the same. They're dead tired of this murdering and the fear that keeps walking up and down Gloster Valley and gives us all a chill in the middle of every night for the fear of what the next day'll bring out to light. Your men are plumb tired, Camp!"

"That'll be seen in the end," said Art Camp gravely. "I think my men will hold as long as I hold."

"They won't, Art," answered the other. "I know, because I know about the way our men feel. They're sick and tired, Art, which I don't mind telling you, because you know as well as I do that

156

they'll not give up Nell as long as she wants to stay with us. But they know that every year she spends with us costs a tax of lives. It turns me sick when I think of the price that's paid for that lovely, innocent girl with no harm in her. It's saddened her, as well as the rest of my men. How can it help? The boys that's her playmates—how can she tell when they'll die for her sake? The gents that come wooing her—how can she tell how long it'll be before they die fighting for her? And it's thinking about it that puts the fear in her face, and the sadness in her eyes. We have her, but we've lost her while we still have her. And I've made up my mind and persuaded 'em all—except her mother, poor woman—"

"Her mother stands here!" called out Margery Camp.

"No matter," said Benchley with a peculiar gesture of resignation. "The point is that I've persuaded my folks that we've got to make one final trial of it and risk the keeping or the losing of Nell for the sake of peace."

Breathless silence fell over the Camps as they listened.

"The idea come to me," went on the big man, "when Harry Runyon told me the story of the first generous fighting man that's stepped in Gloster Valley these ten years, pretty near, since we started cutting throats for the sake of sweet Nell and her pretty face. But I made up my mind that if you had a man like that among you, you had a man you'd put up. And I tell you this, gents: I'll meet that man alone this evening, any place you say. And no Camp will be near; and no Benchley will be near. And one of us will come back living; and one of us will lie there dead. And the dead man will be the loser, and the live man'll know that Nell belongs to his side forever, and no more fighting. Is that a square and fair end to the war?"

The men were struck dumb. Margery Camp, wringing her hands, moaned softly to herself. Here was a chance to have her child at last. But how terrible to risk the end of the long hopes on the chance of a gun fight!

"Speak up!" cried Benchley.

"Ames," said Art Camp gravely, "I got to ask a bit of advice from the wisest head in Gloster Valley. Judge, what shall we do? If one of us meets Ames Benchley and loses, we've not only lost a good man from among us, but Margery, yonder, will die of a broken heart. They ain't any doubt at all of that. And Lew will have no interest left in life. What'll we do, judge? We've been bleeding and suffering a pile these nine years. My own life's been a hell. My money that I had so much of is near all gone; I've seen my people, half of 'em, going about in rags. And I say, like Ames Benchley, that it's time to make an end!"

Judge Camp nodded, passing his lean, purple-veined fingers through his mist of beard.

"It's got to stop," he said. "But him that faces Ames Benchley is facing the best man in these parts. It's got to stop, if only we can get a fit man to face Ames Benchley. But where is he?"

He paused, and his eyes, wrinkled of lid but undimmed in intense brightness, passed about the room.

"Me!" cried the bull voice of huge Walker. "I'll meet him!"

"Just hold on a minute!" The slender, active-stepping form of Billy Buel flitted past the approaching giant. "This ain't a fight with hands or with clubs. Gents, I'm going to meet Ames Benchley, I'll tell you why. I've been seeing the place where my bullets would hit him!"

He turned on big Benchley with a working face, and at a glimpse of that terrible passion, that hungry eagerness of the fighter, the men in the room started and the women shrank.

"Choose me!" pleaded Billy, shaking like a man in fear. "I've been sitting there watching Benchley and killing him in my thoughts. Choose me—or else we'll fight for the place. Walker and me—Buck Martin and me—whoever wants, stand out and fight me for the sake of meeting Benchley!"

Walker undoubtedly would have responded, and Buck Martin, also, for very shame; but wise William Camp prevented.

"I brought him here for this purpose Art," he said. "Don't let Walker or Martin take the job.

159

Billy Buel's our man. Why, with him coming at this time, and all, there's a fate in it!"

"There is," said old Judge Camp with a sudden emotion. "With Billy Buel, by the chill in my blood, I feel we'll stand or fall. Buel, we put our cause in your hands!"

· XVI ·
THE BENCHLEY PATRIARCH

The coldness of eighty-five winters lay on the head of Jacob Benchley. Eighty-five winters advisedly, for it seemed that no summer had ever warmed his blood. He sat now wrapped to the waist in a heavy fur rug, unstirring in his big chair except to draw the upper edge of the rug a little higher from time to time. Yet the air in the long low room was warm enough. Another would have sat in shirt sleeves and been comfortable. But in Jacob Benchley the vital spark was flickering so dim and low that it must be cherished, it seemed, against every possible chill.

Eighty-five years, and what a history was wrapped in that length of time! Once—how far away!—he had been the dashing, handsome, the spendthrift trapper. Not until well nigh middle age had he learned the graver lessons of existence, and then he changed slowly and became as the world afterward knew him—crafty, patient, industrious, frugal, stern. He was well past forty-five when he married, but after the first child, Ames, there had been a long list of others. And as his family grew, his wealth had grown also until, out of nothing, he came to be a figure in Gloster Valley almost as impressive as William Camp, nine-tenths of whose wealth had been inherited. And to this day, perhaps, the one thing which could make the old fellow show life in the purple-stained, sluggish lids and bring the vital spark blazing and glowing in his eyes, was a question of trade; profit and loss were his twin gods. He had never been known to gamble since his marriage; business he found to be a new form of gambling, with the authority and sanction of the law behind it.

Watching his face—the sparse, stiff-standing brush of snowy hair, the sagging muscles, the depressed, lipless mouth, and the tide of beard that rolled down his chest—one could not easily have guessed whether that gathered frown meant that Jake Benchley was bending all his energies toward the maintenance of the life-spark within him, or whether he was meditating some deep plan. But there was about the old man an air of many potentialities, and so impressive did the still figure become after a few moments of observation that one would not have been surprised had the stiff and bloodless hands, which were folded in his lap, suddenly aroused to strong gestures and actual feats of muscular power. Indeed, the body of Jake Benchley was fast crumbling to the grave, but the dynamic will still lived in the wrecked frame of the man.

He sat, as has been said, in a long, low room. It had originally been the main frame of the first cabin he built in Gloster Valley. Since then the partitions had been knocked out and the walls torn down, and the hall now extended over a far greater area than the whole first cabin had covered. And from either end of the hall the house of Jacob Benchley stumbled up and down over uneven ground, a step up or down from room to room— and the whole made a big rambling structure which had come, in process of time, to wander in a great circle, embracing barns and corrals and mighty storerooms and huge granaries and dairy sheds—a little city in itself rather than the house of one man.

As for this main hall of the house, one could see at least three periods and kinds of architecture, from the sagging rafters of the central section to the well-paneled ceiling at either end. And there was evidence of the strong planning and dominating influence of Ames Benchley in the finely arched doorway which opened into the hall at the center. And Ames Benchley, too, had ranged the prizes of the hunt, head after head, along the walls. And Ames Benchley had caused the brown and grizzled bear skins to be made into the rugs which were flung here and there upon the worn floor. And Ames Benchley had caused the cavernous fireplace to be built at the southeast corner of the big room. But, nevertheless, it remained distinctly Jacob's hall; and, though it was Ames who built the fireplace it was Jacob who insisted that the fire never be allowed to die in it.

It was a freak of the old man's fancy, one of those few symptoms which told of the disintegration of mental as well as muscular powers under the weight of years; but whether it were in the humid, warm days of spring or in the full mid-blaze of summer mountain heat, that fire must always flicker on the hearth. And when the old man entered the room or was wheeled into it in his chair, if his nostrils did not at once catch the sweet and penetrating fragrance of woodsmoke, he became suddenly, foolishly alarmed. His head rose, his hands froze on the arms of his chair, and a look of unspeakable terror came into his eyes.

Always, he had found that his first alarm was groundless and that the fire still burned on the hearth, with however meager a flame; and so it always had burned. And so, too, the Benchleys had come one and all to believe that the fire on the broad hearth would continue to burn unflaggingly until the instant of Jacob Benchley's death—and then miraculously it would go out.

Close to the hearth was the big easy-chair of the patriarch. His eyes seemed closed, but now and again the lids flickered up enough to make sure of the friendly blaze upon the stones. Or, again, his glance wandered little by little and step by step down the big hall and enjoyed the unpouring of the yellow sun just before sunset.

Sometimes, he turned a little. Looking eastward and down through the windows, the whole slope and sweep of the length of Gloster Valley swept away before his vision, a glorious flood of silver water and green trees. That had been his dream—to march his fences rank by rank down Gloster Valley until the whole was his. And how close he had been coming to it, how close, how close, when the cursed war burst forth!

He turned his head sharply away at the thought and glanced through the western windows of the hall into the great patio, if it might be so called, around which the buildings of the estate were grouped. For though the Camps, through the strength of greater numbers, dared to spread here and there through the valley as they pleased— only keeping well to the eastern end of it—the Benchleys, few in number, had gathered closer and closer around the main bulwark of the family fortunes. They left the cabins where they were apt to be surprised and cut off by the terrible Camps in the middle of any night; they left those cabins, and coming back to Jacob Benchley, they added their own section onto the main house, helped in raising another groups of sheds, another bay to the immense barns, another stack in the center of the corral. And so the little city had grown in a nucleus.

Here, at the end of the day, old Jake Benchley listened to the confused sounds—someone with stentorian lungs cursing a refractory mule—the lowing of the dairy cows and the rattle of the three-gallon tin pails as they were carried out to the milking—and the singing of some sweet-voiced child going up among and above all else like a light. All of this Jake Benchley heard, and saw the barns with their old sides bulging out from the bulk of good hay within, and saw the glimmer of the sun on the strawstacks like heaps of tarnishing gold, and saw a group of wild-riders streak across the corral in the midst of some dangerous frolic, and saw in another corner men busy throwing out sacks of feed from the door of the granary—aye, his eye even penetrated into the heart of the granary itself and made out the multitudinous rows on rows, heaps on heaps, of sacks. For he had held back the sale of that year's crop of grain. Those of his people who needed money, he himself would supply. And when the winter was at its height—that was the time he felt confident the price would rise—their profits would be doubled.

And it was sweet, infinitely sweet, to the old man to see these sights and hear these sounds, for, though all had a share in the properties, he was the overlord. When he bade hold, the crops were held; when he bade sell, the crops were sold; if there were bargaining, his dictates were the price of buying and selling; not a seed was planted before the oracle had spoken; not a blade was cut before he gave the word. And his bloodless hands still held the reins of government more tightly than ever before—more tightly because what he decreed, the terrible right hand of Ames Benchley was ever present to execute, and because, moreover, everyone felt that any year might bring the death of the tyrant, and then it would be well indeed to stand high in his favor. Old Jake knew it well, and he played upon the emotion; but always it made him smile within. Little did they know him! What, die at eighty-five? Nonsense!

There were too many things to be done. His life had barely commenced. Here were the Camps to brush out of the way, curse them; and there was Gloster Valley to gain and hold, and the trees to clear, until the plows of Jacob Benchley ran over that whole sweep of mellow ground long enriched past reckoning by the mold of the forest! And die before this was done? Little did they know him! Had not men lived to ninety and a hundred? And were there not records of those who had lived to the tremendous total of one hundred and twenty years in the full possession of their faculties? What if the body withered and decayed? The brain was the seat of life, the only life that mattered and could be projected into the future!

Somewhat in this manner the old man's thoughts

were running as he sat with gathered brow and stone-cold face in the corner shadow of the room. And only now and again one hand drew the fur rug higher about his waist, and the other hand wandered out feebly toward the yellow glimmer of the firelight.

But presently his head rose, and a smile, or a faint suggestion of a smile, appeared on his lips for he knew the steps that were sounding heavily on the floor of the hall before he glanced at the man who approached. There was only one with a stride so masterful, so long and strong.

And that was the prince of Gloster Valley, his eldest son, Ames Benchley. But when the head of the old man was turned to the newcomer there was no vestige of a smile of welcome on his lips. It was as though he feared that the expression of any great emotion would sap that inner vitality which he was hoarding, hoarding for the great work and the long work which lay ahead.

"Father," said Ames Benchley, "they've accepted. They've put up their man against me! And the war ends, one way or the other!"

· XVII ·
AN OLD MAN'S WILL

Now, indeed, the smile broke on the face of the ancient father of the Benchleys.

"The fools!" he cried softly. "The fools! But the war ain't going to end, son. It'll go on, except that it won't be brute force against force. That's the way they've held me off—numbers and money, son. But when they's a time of peace—then I'll show you real war; I'll show you how I'm going to push my fences down Gloster Valley until the last of the Camps mortgages his hut over his head and rents his land from me!"

He rubbed warmth into his bony hands and then beamed on Ames Benchley.

"But how'd they come to be such fools? Are they gone blind and forgetting everything all at once? Have they forgot how many of their men you've met already, and how many men you've killed? Or is it that thick-witted fool, Slow Joe, that's took up the challenge and got the Camps to back him?"

Ames Benchley looked down to his big hands sadly, and shaking his head answered: "I've done my share of the killing, father. And they's time when I gloried in it. But I figure my time is come!"

That glance of wild alarm which had been noted

in the face of Jacob more than once when he dreaded that the fire might have gone out, appeared there again, and the age-slackened lips parted in horror.

Ames Benchley went to his father and placed his hand kindly on the bony shoulder.

"I ain't aiming to get you scared for nothing," he said gently, "but you and the rest have always been figuring that nothing in the line of a fighting man could ever kill me. And maybe I've been thinking the same thing for myself. But now I've seen a gent that can give me a hard rub. It ain't Buck Martin or Slow Joe Walker, though they're terrible men, both of 'em. It's the new man—the man they went out and hired. It's Billy Buel."

"That wild spark that shot young Runyon," and Jacob Benchley nodded slowly. "But, Lord in heaven, son, what manner of man is he to make you afeard of him?"

"Afraid? I ain't afraid," said the champion of the Benchleys, "but I figure that I've met my match. Figure a wildcat turned into a man if you want to know what sort he is. He stands on his toes; he sits on the edge of a chair; he's got a voice that purrs and bubbles at you, and eyes like the eyes of a girl pretty near, with fire waiting behind 'em. That's the sort of man he is, father. I'm fast for a man, with a gun. But where's the man that's as fast as a cat? And, besides, he's filled up and overflowing with hunger for a fight, like a wild beast that's hungry for meat!"

He shuddered at the thought, and then, controlling himself, he went on: "Have the bell rung. I'll go out and talk to 'em."

"Wait," said old Jacob slowly. "Son, if you've lost your nerve—"

"I ain't lost it," insisted the big man. "I'll fight as well as I ever fought, but I just got my doubts, and I want to tell you to break the shock. Now get the bell rung."

It was the bell which only Jacob himself could order rung, or, after his death, his eldest surviving son. So much the Benchley clan had agreed to. And when that mighty old church bell sent its peal over the gorges and the valleys and up to the crowning hilltops, there in the domain of the Benchleys, each grown man, and each boy old enough to bear arms, seized his weapons and rushed with all the speed of his horse to the gathering place; for the ringing of the bell meant that an event of the greatest communal importance was about to take place.

But still Jacob Benchley shook his head.

"If it means that," he said, "you ain't going to fight."

"Not going to fight?" breathed Ames Benchley. "After I've give my word and defied 'em all, and near got killed for trusting 'em, if it hadn't been for this same Billy Buel? But what a man of fire and powder, ready to blow up any minute—because I give you my word that if they'd raised a hand agin' me he'd of been at my back fightin' 'em, with two guns smokin' in his hands. He's that kind!"

"Then get him for us—get him for our side, Ames; and with him and you together we'll drown the Camps in their own blood!"

"You couldn't hire him," said Ames Benchley gloomily, "because the reason he wanted to save me from the mob, chiefly, is because he wanted to fight me man to man by himself."

He sighed and shuddered at the memory. And it was strange to see him. The man had so often, so many, many times, proved his indubitable heroism that now he was not afraid to exhibit horror and fear as he felt them, certain that when the need came he would not fail.

"There'll be another side to it now," said old Jacob after he had carefully considered his son. "Maybe there'll be another side to it, and I'll not give my consent. They'll be no shooting match, son."

But Ames Benchley smiled.

"I ain't a child, father," he said quietly. "I've given my word, and with or without your consent the fight comes off."

"Fight whom you want to fight," said the old man, apparently losing all interest, "but you ain't going to fight for Nell. No matter how the fight comes out, she stays where she belongs—with her mother and me!"

There was a moment of pause. Beyond a doubt the old man could refuse to sanction the removal of Nell, no matter how the fight came out; and in that case the whole point of the battle was lost. Ames Benchley, his rage growing, ground his teeth.

"Listen to me," he said fiercely, shaking his leonine head as though to get rid of his own passion. "Do you know what you'll be if I leave you? Nothing but a rotten stick with nothing to support it. The minute I say the word, two men out of every three around you'll follow me and leave Gloster Valley. And that's what I'll do unless you have the bell rung and let me go out and tell every man of 'em the arrangement that I've made to end this feud."

His father peered at him from under the shaggy, lowered brows. His own vast age and experience made all other men, particularly his children, seem like infants before him. And now and again, with a shock, it was borne in upon him that Ames Benchley at least was a man among men. This was one of the times. And indeed, for the first time old Jacob had come to realize that Ames had something which he himself had never had—the magnetic power which makes others follow a leader, not for the sake of reward or for a cause, but for the sake of the man himself. He,

Jacob Benchley, had bought or traded for everything he possessed in the world; his son, it seemed, had gained as much through pure affection of his fellow men as the father had by labor and cash. But Jacob brushed aside such ponderous and uncomfortable thoughts. It was not his habit to waste time on speculation, particularly painful speculation. It was sufficient for him to realize that what Ames said was true—one word from the son could strip the father of followers.

"D'you want to know why that fight ain't going to take place?" he said.

"They's no reason that can stop it," said Ames.

He took the knob-headed cane of rough wood which leaned against his chair, and beat the floor with it. The stroke seemed to take all of his strength, and after the effort the cane remained unraised, but dragged the skinny old arm and skinny old hand down to full length and hung suspended as though about to fall.

Ames Benchley started forward to take the cane from the feeble fingers, but he checked himself. He knew that the wise old seer was striving to work upon his sympathies through his physical weakness contrasted with his son's physical strength. A servant appeared, grinning and nodding and scared, as most men in Gloster Valley were scared when they came into the presence of Jake Benchley.

"Get Nell," was the order, and the house servant disappeared.

"You're going to tell Nell," said Ames bitterly. "You're going to get her to plead against her being risked on the result of my fight? You're going to get her to beg to stay here with her mother?"

"Give my solemn word of honor," answered the ancient, "that I'm not going to do a single one of those things. I won't have her say a word to you. But where is she?"

The wait had been only a minute or so since the servant disappeared, but the irritability of Jacob was immense—on a few points.

"A lot she thinks of me—a lot she thinks of her granddaddy!" he was growling before the girl could possibly have had time to appear. "Where is she gadding about? Never near me no more. Never wastes no more time on me, Ames!"

The big fellow smiled.

"Wasn't she with you all morning?"

"All morning? Only a minute. Confound it, those young rapscallions—the Lord boy and Hal Moore and Henry—they take up every hour of her time."

"Lord knows, sir," said Ames Benchley, "that they've come to fight on our side out of love of her. Why shouldn't they try to see her?"

"And d'you think that she cares for one of 'em?" asked the old man, his voice quaking a little.

Ames Benchley covered a smile.

"Hal Moore has always been pretty thick with Nell since she growed up."

"Bah!" growled old Jacob, jerking up the head of his cane and chewing the knob with his toothless gums. "She don't give a snap of her fingers for Hal Moore. He's too common for her, a big sight too common for her. I'd rather see her dead than have her marry him."

"I think you'd a pile rather see any gent dead than have Nell marry him, eh? You'd rather have her stay with us here at home, eh, father?"

"Why not?" was the surly answer. "Why not, I ask you? Ain't she got a pretty good home here? Ain't we kind to her? Is they anything she asks for that she don't get? Besides, she ain't made for hard work and labor, and such-like things, lad. She's made to be looked at, that's all. Hush, hush! She's coming, Lord bless us!"

And he leaned forward in his chair until the fur rug slipped half away from his legs and remained there disregarded, while with a smile of utter pleasure, the octogenarian fixed his glance on the farther extremity of the hall.

· XVIII ·
STRENGTH AND CUNNING

The door at that end had been tossed open, and now a girl ran down the length of the hall toward them. As has been said, the hall was darkening toward the evening, but the very last gold rays of the sun, before it set, streamed through the western windows and made regular splotches on the opposite wall. Through these alternate streaks of shadow and golden light the girl ran, her yellow dress turned by that rare illumination and by the wind of her running into a garment of delicately tinted flame; and each time she struck the light her smile and the beauty of her face flashed out at them; and each time she entered the shadow all this was dimmed.

But in a moment she was before them, laughing and happy, and even as she paused she seemed about to break into a light-footed dance.

"You sent for me," she said to old Jacob.

"But Ames is the one that wants to see you," said the wily old ancient.

She turned to the bewildered Ames with a laugh.

"The very first time since I was as little as that, that you've ever wanted to see me, Uncle Ames, and the very first time—oh, the very first of all— that I've ever made you smile."

And she caught those large hands which every Camp knew, which all of Gloster Valley dreaded

176

so, as though, having chanced to win his favor with a glance, she was going to try to hold it with the strength of her grip. And the big man, smiling down to her with all the innate kindliness of his nature, suddenly freed his hands and took her face between them.

"And to think, Nell," he said, "that I've got here between my hands the whole cause of the trouble—the whole cause why growed-up men have been doing murder these nine years back!"

It was a brutal thing to say. His big, kind heart jumped with remorse the moment he had spoken, and the girl winced back from him.

As for old Jacob, he was speechless with rage.

Then: "Come to me, lass," he said. "Come to me, dear. And of all the—Ames, are you a son of mine? Do you have no gentle blood in you? Come to me, Nell! Ah, girl!"

"It—it just came out all of a sudden," said Ames Benchley miserably. "I'm a thousand times sorry, Nell!"

He admired her more in this minute, he thought, than he had ever admired her before, for she did not turn from him and hide her face in the arms of her grandfather, as any other girl of nineteen might have done. Instead, she merely backed away, always facing him; and, though she dropped her hand into the icy fingers of Jacob Benchley, she kept her eyes for the eldest son.

"I know you've never loved me, Ames," she

said steadily. "But I've never blamed you. Even with your brother's blood in me, Uncle Ames, I don't expect you to care much about me, because I'm bringing such danger on all the Benchleys— oh, such danger! And now that you have a wife and a baby boy—ah, I don't blame you a bit! But what can I do? I'd be quick—a thousand times eager to do it. But can I leave? Those wise, crafty Camps—ah, how I hate them, how I hate them!— they'd follow me and take me and make me go to live with—with a strange woman—and make me call her mother; and—they'd make me marry that huge Joe Walker, or that terrible Buck Martin with all his swearing; and—and I can't go, Uncle Ames! I can't give up granddaddy here and—my mother, Uncle Ames! Please!"

Ames Benchley wiped the sweat from his forehead, for he was suffering torments.

"Leave us? Lord in heaven!" cried Jacob Benchley. "Is the man mad to be asking it of you? And would I let you go? I—I'd see every Benchley under the ground first. Hush, lass. Hush, Nell. I'm sick for the thinking of it. Ames, are you a son of mine, I ask you? Have you a man's heart and a man's blood in you and—"

Over those old lips, stammering with their anger, the white hand of Nell was laid, and the old man did not remove it, but looked up to the girl-face above him with one flash of worship that told a thousand tales.

"Nell," said Ames Benchley, "you'd better be trotting along now. And trust in me that I ain't thinking but how to do best by you and all of us."

She nodded obediently.

"And they's no hard feelings between us, Nell?"

"Never in the wide world, Uncle Ames. But sometimes, you see, you're so grave and so just and so wise that—that you frighten me just a wee bit, you know."

"And you're never a bit afraid of my father?" asked Benchley.

"Granddaddy Jake is a darling," declared the girl, slipping her arm about that formidable and skull-like head of age. "And if the rest knew him as I know him, they'd all love him too much to be afraid."

And so, somewhere between defiance and appeal, she went out of the room as swiftly as she had come, and paused against the opposite wall to wave back to them, like a yellow flower under a shadow. Then she was gone.

"They was never no heart in you, Ames," said the old hypocrite. "If you'd been born with a heart in you, you'd of been a pretty near perfect man, lad!"

His much-enduring son smiled and said nothing. As a matter of fact he loved, in his strange father, the one golden vein of love and generous pity which Jake Benchley poured forth for the sake of Nell.

"They was never no heart in you," repeated the ancient. "There she comes like a flower of flowers—like a white rose with a hulling of yaller petals on the outside, wouldn't you say, Ames?"

"Ay, more'n that. She's the loveliest that ever walked, father."

"Tut, tut. You admit all that, and then you talk about me risking the loss of her by a fight?"

"You were free enough about letting me fight before."

"That was before I knew they was a man like this new devil—this Billy Buel, d'you call him—and be damned to the black heart of the dog!"

He laughed feebly: "Risk her? Am I mad? Ain't she mine? Ain't she my son's girl? Ain't my son dead? Don't that make her mine? And in all my life-work ain't she the jewel? And every minute ain't the Camps eating their hearts out with hate because I've got her? What? Risk the loss of her? Never in a million years, lad! Ain't she the jewel I've saved out of a life of work? I'd let you fight any of the rest and know you'd win, and Heaven knows I want peace—and Nell. But not peace without the girl! Never, Ames."

"And yet," said the son sternly, "I tell you're going to give orders for the bell to be rung."

"Not I, Ames. Never!"

"Listen!" said the big man, and striding close to his father, he lowered his lips until they were an inch from the ear of Jacob Benchley.

"They was a night about fifteen years ago when poor old Joe come home from his woodcutting tolerable sick. You remember? And he hadn't gone home to his wife—he'd come home to us right here. Maybe you've forgotten?"

"I dunno," said Jacob, his long fingers freezing tighter and tighter around the knob of his cane.

"But you'll remember what Joe said, I reckon. Because I was lying close to the wall in the next room with a crack between, and every word come plumb clear to me. He said he was feeling tolerable bad with the world, that he wanted to make a clean breast of a rotten thing he'd done, and then he told you the same story that he afterward told to Lew Camp. Father, I heard every word!"

He straightened and stepped back.

"That being the case," said the old man, blinking very rapidly, "how come you've kept so quiet about what you know all these years?"

"Partly," said Ames Benchley, "because I knowed that it would kill Alice to lose her; and so, in spite of the fact that the Camps ought to have had their girl, I kept putting it off and putting it off till finally Joe died. And then I was plumb sure it would kill Alice.

"Besides, the Camps was now coming to fight for the girl, and it sure goes agin' me to give up anything when somebody comes around asking for a fight instead of plumb justice. And, besides, Nell had growed into a flower of a girl by that time. At ten years old she was sure a sweet thing, father. And it went agin' me to think of giving her up. And so, somehow, all these years I've let it drift along and seen all the men in Gloster Valley turned into brutes and never said a word until this new gent, this Billy Buel, comes galloping in and does the first bit of man's work in nine years, the first plumb clean and decent and gentlemanly bit of fighting that we've seen since we started cutting throats over Nell. And I made up my mind that to have no girl was worth turning so many growed up men and women into slaves and brutes. Which is what the feud's making us."

He paused, and his face grew sterner than ever, looking down into the icy, defiant eyes of the old patriarch.

"But it's more than I could bear, all this talk of yours about Nell being your blood. By the gods, sir, that ain't a clean way to talk to the poor girl, lying about her own parents. Some day I'd tell her the truth myself. But will you tell me one true thing?"

"I'll try, son."

The softness of the crafty old fox, Ames Benchley knew, was to ease the force of the blows which were coming.

"Tell me straight, father. Have you been keeping Nell because you loved her, or just because you hated the Camps?"

"Which do you think?" asked the old man.

"I don't know," said the son with a touch of sadness. "I've tried all my life to find just one thing you'd be clean and honest and worked up about, and now I'm about ready to give up. But maybe it's a touch of both reasons, eh?"

"Maybe it is," admitted Jacob Benchley with frankness astonishing for him. "I dunno, Ames; maybe I love Nell a pile mostly because every minute I keep her I'm sticking a thorn in their sides, curse 'em! But what are you going to do about it all, Ames? What are you going to do? You see I'm helpless. Besides, I'm an old man and a tired man, Ames. I ain't got quite the strength to argue up to a big young man like you, and a smart young man like you, too, Ames. So you tell me what's to be done, and I suppose I've got to do it."

The son eyed him gloomily. He knew perfectly well that the assumption of humility was a snare and a delusion, and that all the time his father was craftily seeking for some way out of the matter.

"There's only one thing for me to do," said Ames at length. "It's what I should have done long before, Lord knows; and something I'll be damned for not having done. Well, I'll do it now. I'll go to Nell and tell her the truth—who her real parents are!"

"Would you do that?" gasped Jake Benchley.

"It's got to be done."

There seemed to be a sort of distant admiration in the eyes of the patriarch.

"I sure admire you for that, Ames," he said. "I sure admire you a pile for that!"

"Why?" asked Ames Benchley.

"Why? You know why. You're a brave and a noble boy, son. Hang what the others may think!"

"What the others may think?"

"Aye, you know, what they'll have inside their heads—that you was afraid to meet Billy Buel, this new man-killer, and so you patched things up and gave Nell back to the Camps so's you wouldn't have to stand before Buel's guns!"

"Lord!" breathed Ames Benchley, and his great hand went back in the agony of the thought.

"But hang what the others may say!" craftily exclaimed old Jake Benchley. "You and me, lad, we'll know the truth, no matter how the others may smile behind their hands and sneer when you pass—all them that've secretly hated you all these years and envied you for your name of the bravest man and the best fighter in Gloster Valley. I can hear 'em talk—but never mind that. You and me, lad, we'll know the truth and shake off what we may hear!"

"Do you think it would be that way?" asked the big man huskily.

"Do I think? I know, lad. I right well know! And inside of six months every little sixteen-year-old lad that's been looking up to you like a kind of dog for these nine years will be putting out his chest and talking big to you. I'd rather be in my grave before I see that day come to Ames Benchley, but let it come! Maybe the truth is best; maybe it would be best, after all, for Nell to go to the Camps, which she hates them like snakes. And maybe it would be better for her to go to Lew Camp and learn to call him father and to Margie and call her mother, while poor Alice withers and dies in the midst of us, Ames. Only one thing—after you've sent Nell away, keep clear of Alice, because she'll look such things at you, lad, that she'll send a poison to your heart!"

He said it all in a tone of kindly sympathy, of gentle and friendly advice, keeping his old voice smooth, and a faint smile upon his lips.

But Ames Benchley knew his father too well. He neither saw the face nor paid heed to the oily voice; but every word was barbed and burned in his flesh. It was much to him, much indeed to give up his place of first man in Gloster Valley, and now he knew perfectly well that his cunning father was right. They would interpret the surrender of Nell in that fashion, and nothing he could do would make up for the lost ground. He had been all his life the man without a flaw, of stainless integrity, of bright courage. He had seen the faces of young boys brighten, and he had seen them stand straighter when he passed. And it had been sweet to him to have the leadership of all the stern, fighting men of the Benchleys freely rendered into his hands. But if he gave up Nell, that leadership would pass away. How could they follow one who was even remotely suspected of having been cowardly for even the least part of an instant?

And when he lowered his head it was to say sadly: "You win, father. You most generally do. Which I ain't got the craft to stand up against you. But give the word—let 'em start the bell ringing.

"Aye, now I've seen all sides of the thing, I guess you're right."

Ames sank into a chair. The cane of his father struck the floor, and the house servant came hastily and softly again and stood bobbing and grinning in the background.

"The bell," and Jake Benchley sighed. "Have the bell rung, and have it rung loud and long."

From the shadows of the corner the servant gasped, then fled. And still the father and the son sat in silence until at length the deep-throated voice of the bell began to peal.

Far away the sound passed, trembling and ringing.

It came to a woodchopper on a distant hillside. He dropped his ax, seized the rifle which stood by him during all of that exposed and dangerous work, and drawing up his belt a notch he started toward the Benchley house with a long and free-swinging stride.

It came to a teamster on a valley road. He listened with awe-struck face raised as though the voice of a ghost were fleeing above him. Then, as understanding came, he sprang up on his seat, whirled his whip high, and sent the team forward at a gallop.

It came to a woman sitting at the dark doorway of a distant cabin, and at the sound she lowered her head to her arms and wept.

· XIX ·
THE TEMPTRESS

The clamor of the bell had long since ended, though still it seemed that a tremulous memory of the sound brooded over the hills. Now Jacob Benchley sat alone in the hall once more. He had heard the voice of Ames in the big corral telling the assembled clansmen that the war was at length to end—that he was to go forth and meet a new champion of the Camps and decide in one battle what had remained unhinged for nine long years, and he had ordered the clan, each man and all, to stay at home and not dare to follow him when he set forth, not dare to attempt to aid him, just as, he knew, the leaders of the Camps would forbid their men to go out to help Buel.

And when that speech ended it was met with a mingled cheer and groan—and at the end the long, wild wailing of a woman. That would be Alice, the old man decided calmly, weeping for thought of the loss of the girl she considered her daughter. He nodded and grinned to himself; truly, his heart was a cold stone!

After that the corral was filled with a subdued muttering of voices, and he was still left alone until a door opened and into the hall came Ames Benchley and his wife, Martha, a tall woman and nobly made, a fit mate for the chief man of Gloster Valley. Jacob sighed, not from pity, though he saw the infant son in the arms of Martha, but from weariness. Here would be another scene of sad farewell, and to old Jacob tears were disgusting and hard on the nerves.

He was agreeably surprised. There was iron, indeed, in this tall, bright-haired girl. He saw her give the child into the hands of Ames, saw Ames lift the baby into the air above his head and laugh at its struggles, saw the wife cling for one instant to her husband, and then take the infant and leave the room without a word.

The nostrils of the old man curled with pride. Here, indeed, was something which appealed to the Spartan heart of him. And then Ames was kneeling before him—an old custom in that household when the men went out to know battle. He laid both withered hands on the thick curls of the head before him and murmured the blessing; and then Ames Benchley was gone with that long, heavy stride of his.

But still, in the full, steady light of the early evening, Jacob seemed to wait, and his quick eyes oved ceaselessly from one end of the room to the other. When at length a door opened again and a woman entered, he sank back in the chair and closed his eyes as though exhausted, but a secret smile had come for an instant on his lips and then vanished. This was what he was waiting for—Alice, the widow of Joe Benchley, kneeling beside him, weeping, begging for help, for comfort, for assurance that Ames would not fail, and that even if he failed Nell would not be taken from her.

And finally he leaned above her, and with one of his cold hands he raised her face, tear-stained, tremulous of lip, wild of eye. In her girlhood she had been pretty, but plain indeed compared with Margery, the wife of Lew Camp. But the long years of happiness for her, and of grief for Margery, told their tale. She had reached a noble middle age, and, though her hair was silver, it flowed pleasantly above a smooth brow. And there was in her face the pride of maternity that one would expect to find in the reputed mother of Nell.

"But what can I do, Alice?" he asked her gently. "Ain't it clear that I don't want to see Nell risked—no more'n I want to see Ames risked? But what can I do? Can I go behind my boy's back?"

"But if you did—then you know some way?" pleaded Alice Benchley.

"Ah, they's a way, right enough," said the old man, "but one I can't tell you, my girl."

"What way, for Heaven's sake?" she breathed "Oh, I know that Ames is strong and brave and a terrible fighter. But there are so many chances Who can tell if his gun may hang in the holster, or if it may fail to go off when he pulls the trigger? And this new man—they say he is a tiger. I heard young Harry Runyon talk about him He's a tiger of a man, Grandfather Jake. And for Heaven's sake find some way!"

"They's only one, lass, and that ain't honorable—and we got to fight honorable!"

"Any way's honorable that saves Nell for me—for us."

He shook his head.

"It wouldn't be right, girl," he said. "It wouldn't be right, you see, for you to go to one of the boys that loves Nell—to Oliver Lord; no, not to him, because Oliver wouldn't stir a step in such a thing—but it wouldn't be right, say, for you to go to one of the Moore boys and give 'em a whisper in the ear—and tell 'em it means making sure of Nell—and tell 'em that they might sneak down the valley after Ames, you see? One of 'em! And when Ames meets this Billy Buel, what would keep the gent in hiding behind from lifting his rifle and drilling Buel through the head before ever a shot was fired? And what would keep us, then, from claiming that Ames done the shooting? And then Nell would be ours for good, eh? And Ames wouldn't dare admit that he didn't do that killing of Buel, so—but you see, Alice, them are things that I couldn't do myself, me being the chief of the Benchleys. And that's a thing that you couldn't do, Alice, because it ain't honorable."

She had risen to her feet, her face hard, her breath coming quickly.

"It ain't honorable, no," she muttered, and all the while her eyes held on the far wall of the big room.

"So you wouldn't do no such thing as that, my girl."

"Me? Of course not—of course not! But I've got to go now and sit by myself and think!"

"Go along—and pray for Ames' luck, Alice!"

She nodded and hurried from the hall, and the old man settled back in his chair again, this time smiling openly and rubbing his hands together. Had he not achieved a double victory of incalculable value? Would he not, by this stroke, save the life of his son, the champion of the Benchleys, from danger, and at the same time insure the undisputed possession of Nell to the Benchley family? And, after all, was not Nell really the brightest jewel in his crown?

He dismissed these thoughts to pass to others of a far greater importance—the march of the fences down the valley and the steady increase of his farms at the expense of the Camps.

In the meantime, Alice had passed out into that central enclosure around which the buildings of

191

the farm ran, and where the clansmen and the adherents of the Benchley faction were still gathered in clusters discussing the great event and wondering that a man had been found whom the Camps were willing to risk as their champion against Ames Benchley himself.

She found the men she wanted standing close together, young, tall, straight—swarthy as Italians and with eyes of Italian darkness—handsome as two young gods. They were the Moore brothers, Hal and Henry. They had come into the world at one birth, and since that time they had been inseparable, so that, naturally enough, but by a sad irony, they fell in love, finally, with the same girl—Nell Benchley. For that matter, half of Gloster Valley was in love with her, but the rank and the file shrank away from advancing any pretensions.

Yet the Moore boys had reason to hope. Their farms beyond the mountains were wide and rich in cattle pastures and in plowed grounds; they could ride with any horseman in the mountains; their hands were as sure on a gun as the hands of any man. So they had come together, leaving the farm to be cared for by a manager, and they had devoted their lives to the battle for Nell. If there were envy between them—if from time to time one felt that the other were gaining an advantage in the attention of Nell—none of the envy and none of the anger was ever shown.

And so they stood now, a little apart from the other groups, rather looking on than taking an active part in the discussion. And Alice noted that their faces were stern and anxious. She studied those faces carefully as she approached. They were much alike, save that the frame of Hal was more heavy in the bone, and his face was broader, stronger about the jaw, and a little smaller of eye. Instantly, she made up her mind—Hal was the man for her temptation.

She did not come too close; there must be more secrecy in this than in anything she had ever attempted in her life. From a little distance she nodded and signaled to Hal, who was facing her more directly than his brother Henry; then she turned her back abruptly and hurried back into the house.

She had hardly closed the door behind her when it was opened again by Hal Moore, and she signaled him to follow into her room.

It was a pleasant place, rich with color that bloomed softly, now, in the light of the early evening; and in the window, it seemed, a fragrance of lavender was blowing—a strange place and a strange setting for what she had to say. In the midst of all her anxiety, she could give a thought to this. And then she turned on Hal and took both his hands.

"Hal," she whispered, "you know what's going to happen tonight?"

"I know. Ames is going to drop that fellow from the Camps the way he's dropped others before him."

"But suppose Ames misses?"

The young fellow winced.

"I know. I been thinking the same thing over and over agin', trying to get a chance out of my head, but somehow it won't stay out, you see?"

"And if Ames fails, Hal?"

Hal Moore gritted his teeth.

"Then Nell goes to the Camps?"

"And that will break her heart!"

"No matter how the fight turns out and who drops," he said fiercely, "we won't let Nell go! We won't!"

"You can't help it. Jake Benchley has made up his mind."

The face of Hal Moore grew gloomy. He knew what the making up of that mind meant to the whole of Gloster Valley.

"No matter. Ames can't lose."

"But Ames himself ain't sure, Hal. And did you ever know a time before when Ames wasn't dead sure of himself when it came to a fight?"

"I watched while he was talking to us all," and young Moore groaned. "And he didn't seem none too cheerful. And this new gent, this Billy Buel, they say he's fast as a whiplash when it comes to getting his gun out, and straight as a whipstock when it comes to shooting."

"He is. He must be. And—Hal, we must not lose Nell!"

"What's to help, if Ames has no luck?"

The woman paused, and though there is little conscience in womankind when they speak for the welfare and happiness of those they love, yet now she hesitated before she played the role of the temptress. And she looked into the clear eyes of young Moore and thought of the untarnished reputation which he had brought into Gloster Valley and kept there, untainted, through all the battles which he had fought for the sake of Nell and in the interest of all the Benchleys. But the pause was only momentary.

"If I tell you how you can help, Hal Moore," she said gravely, "will you keep the secret of it forever?"

"So help me," he declared eagerly.

"It'll mean more'n just keeping Nell. It'll mean that if she's kept for us I'll find ways of rewarding you, my boy, by keeping you in Nell's mind. I'll find ways for you to see her often. I'll keep talking you to her and—"

"If you do that!" breathed the boy.

"But raise your right hand, Hal, and repeat after me!"

And he raised his hand as the woman began to speak.

· XX ·
AT THE APPOINTED PLACE

That ringing of the bell had been heard by the other scouts of the Camps sent to listen for the sound, for it was known that not until the bell had been rung could the Benchleys possibly keep the word of Ames to remove all their watchers from the valley so that the two men might wander out and meet, in solitude, at the appointed spot.

So, when the horseman dashed out of the shadows of the trees and halted at Arthur Camp's house with word that the bell was ringing, there was a distinct sensation in the house, and chiefly in that little group of the main warriors, the main councilors of the clan, Martin, Walker, Arthur, William, Lew, and Judge Camp.

And to Billy Buel all eyes were turned.

"They's only one question," said William after the first solemn moment of silence. "Does that bell mean that Ames is keeping his word, or does it mean a trick?"

"No trick with Ames Benchley in it," declared Billy Buel.

"I'd trust nothing that comes out of a Benchley," said the cynical William, "and if I have my way we'll send a couple of good men along to keep watch that the fight is square."

"Well," said Billy hotly, "if you do that I won't

take a step to the fight! I go alone or not at all. That's what I bargained for with Ames Benchley."

"He's right," said Arthur Camp. After all, his voice was the decisive one in all argument, and the cunning of William and the wisdom of the judge were nothing when Arthur spoke as the head of the family and of the clan. "He's right. That's the bargain. And if the Benchleys don't play square and fair, then we know that we got to deal with snakes and mad dogs, not men; and we'll burn 'em out of Gloster Valley instead of fighting them out. Let Buel go alone, and good luck is all we'll send with him!"

They came to him one by one, those big, quiet men, and wrung his hand. Only Slow Joe Walker had a bitter word.

"If I'd had a little luck," he said, "maybe they'd of picked me to do what you're doing now, Buel. But you must of been born lucky!"

"Is they anything you want to say, anything you want us to do?" asked Arthur Camp. "In case something goes wrong and you don't come back, is they any messages—"

They were standing in front of the house, Billy in the center of the circle, and now he bent his head in thought. Presently, he spoke, in soft tones:

"They's a girl over yonder in the mountains— But no, the best way is to send no news to her. She'll forget me pronto that way. The other way, maybe she'd have kind of a regret about it. No, best leave her out. About the other things—" he paused again and looked down. "Case you find me with my things on—well, these here spurs ain't so bad."

His eyes searched their faces.

"I'll leave 'em to you, Buck Martin. You look the lines of a man that could ride a hoss tolerable well and tolerable hard."

"I sure take it kind of you," said Buck Martin, "and if anything goes wrong, which I'm sure hoping it don't, I'll keep them spurs like they was part of my body."

"Thanks," and Billy smiled. "And this here sombrero is pretty well hefted down with gold lace and stuff. That and my gun is about all that's worth anything that I have in the world. My gun goes to you, Joe Walker." He nodded to the giant, who gulped in surprise. "Looks to me," went on Billy, smiling at the obvious astonishment of the big man, "like you and me might of had trouble if we'd hung around these parts together too long. That's because both of us is hogs, Walker, and want to grab all the glory, you know. But I see you got the hand and you got the eye—and I want to leave this old gat to a fighting man; so, if you find me lying on my face in the woods, my gat goes to you, Walker. And treat it kind. I've fought a hundred times with it, and it's never failed to shoot clean and straight. It's got a touch like the grip of a friend's hand, and it's got an action—well, you just make a wish, and the gun goes off—that's all! So the gun goes to you, old-timer!"

Joe Walker gasped. He could do no more.

"About this hat," said Billy in the same half firm and half careless manner, "I guess the hat ain't right for any of the gents. Besides, if I go down I'd like to have you nail it up again' the wall in the big room, and when you look at it you can say to yourself that it stands for a gent that didn't die with no regrets, because he liked fighting a pile more than he liked living. And so I guess the hat would go to you, Art Camp."

The head of the house nodded gravely.

"I'll sure set a pile by it," he said, "and if things go wrong with you I'll see that folks in these parts keep the memory of you green."

"They's one thing else," said Billy Buel. "I got a hoss. And you, Art Camp, have got a daughter. Will one of you fetch Sally and somebody else fetch my hoss Lou?"

It was done without comment. A man about to die, as all of them thought Billy probably would before the deadly guns of Ames Benchley, had a right to make singular requests. And the mare was led from the stable at the same time that pretty Sally Camp ran out from the house.

Billy took Lou by the mane and the girl by the hand and brought them face to face, two deliberately graceful creatures, bright of eye and gentle.

"Sally Camp," said Billy, "maybe it ain't

misknown to you that I might be about to take a long trip from which I won't come back, and if I don't they's only one thing on earth that my ghost'll worry a pile about, and that is my mare, Lou. Which she ain't no ways fitted for the common run of folks to ride. She follers your voice a heap more'n she ever wants to foller the rein. She got a mouth as tender as a lady's mouth, you see; and it don't need no wrenching and pulling at the reins to turn her or stop her."

The mare interrupted the words at this point by resting her chin on his shoulder and blowing her breath down his back. He pushed her nose away, laughing at her, and she stamped in mock anger. The eyes of Sally Camp, watching, filled with tears.

"You see," said Billy, "she's more of a pal to me than she is just a hoss, and when I got to thinking who I could leave her with I thought about pretty Sally Camp, because her eyes are kind of straight and gentle, like Lou's. So will you take her Sally, and keep her and ride her and learn how to talk to her?"

"I'll promise—with all my heart," said the girl, "if—if anything goes wrong. But nothing must go wrong, Billy Buel! You've got to come back to us! You've got to come back to us!"

"Sure," said Billy. "Sure I got to and I hope to. But I'm darned sight from certain. That's all. Well, folks, so long."

And flushing a little, as though he feared he had made too much of a scene out of his departure, he turned on his heel and made off through the woods with his gay whistle blowing behind him.

As for the others, Buck Martin stood trembling with eagerness like a horse about to dash off from the start. And Slow Joe Walker kept mumbling stupidly: "I dunno just how to make him out—his gun! To me!"

And the Camps stood solemn of face and gloomy of eye, for it did not forebode good fortune when a champion started his adventure with a mind as gloomy as Billy Buel's seemed to be on this day.

Only pretty Sally Camp threw her arms around the neck of the bay mare and wept, against the glistening silky mane; and Lou, who would have leaped away from a gesture half as violent in another person, merely turned her beautiful head and watched with bright eyes while the master disappeared among the first trees down the winding road.

That was the tableau which Billy Buel saw when he turned his head just as he went out of sight, and the picture which affected him the most was that of the bay mare and her lifted head.

But, now that he was quite alone, the gloom which had fallen upon him while he was making that singular "last will and testament of Billy Buel" was quickly dissipated. All about him the forest was growing a dark and a darker green in the deepening of the twilight. And, indeed, when he came into a thicket of the wood it seemed to him that sudden night had come. Only when he looked up did he see that the treetops were still a fresh green with the glow of the evening sky.

In the meantime, he was alone and bent on his greatest adventure. He was in health, his step was firm and light, his muscles played smoothly and easily, his eye was clear, his hand steady as rock when he willed it to be so. Why, then, should he not fight as he had never fought before? And surely he had never had so many incentives. The tired face of Margery Camp and the grim face of her husband rose before him in distinct pictures.

Suppose he should be the direct cause of restoring Nell to the arms of her true mother? That would be glory enough and achievement enough for one man, he felt.

The thought raised his spirits another notch. The whistle which he had forced at the beginning now flowed as freely as the song of a bird in the spring of the year, a bird happy it knows not why, and whistling foolishly one gay, glad phrase of music over and over, without meaning except pure happiness. And so it was with Billy Buel.

He could easily follow the way, for it had been pointed out to him that he had only to keep his eye on the tallest of the big Soutar Mountains, and then he would inevitably come to that big blade where the white birches stretched in a ghostly circle. There he would find Ames Benchley waiting for him.

The pleasant and tingling atmosphere of danger for which he had always lived his life was now the very air in his nostrils, and he loved it. Once or twice he took out his gun and weighed it, and each time the weight of the familiar weapon raised the confidence. He would have preferred to fight in the full blaze of daylight rather than in the shifting and uncertain shadows of the evening; but, let that be as it might, here he was suddenly in an open stretch, and round about him marched the ghostly ring of the birches just as he had been told.

Yet his whistling was not even now abated, and, sauntering to the center of the clearing, he looked calmly about him until he was aware of a motionless figure at the lower end, a figure more than half obscured by the thick and slanting shadow which fell across it.

Billy Buel stopped whistling.

"Hello!" he called. "Are you there, Ames Benchley?"

The figure moved out into the light.

There was no mistaking the lofty carriage of the head and the way it was placed on the wide shoulders.

"I'm here."

"Are you ready?"

"At this distance?"

"Any distance you say, pardner. My gun will shoot that far."

But Ames Benchley was still approaching, growing more and more distinct as he spoke.

"What's the signal for the draw?" he asked, halting in ample easy range.

"Any signal you pick out, Benchley."

"I've done all the picking and choosing. I've got you on my own ground and at my own time. Make one choice for yourself, Billy Buel, and Lord help your soul!"

"He'll give me all the help I need," said Billy somewhat blasphemously, "but if you want a signal, here's one. You heard the owl hoot a while back?"

"Yes."

"Then get ready. The next time he hoots we go for our guns. Does that suit you?"

"Nothing better."

· XXI ·
THE BETRAYAL

They remained watching each other in perfect calm, in silence. It was that time between twilight and dark when it is still possible to see things at a distance, but even things near at hand are by no means entirely distinct. And the white birches seemed to glimmer with a phosphorescent light, a thing contained in themselves and far brighter than any illumination they could have received from the thickening skies above. Very ghostly trees, indeed; very ghostly watchers.

But Billy Buel gave them little heed. To his mind the universe was included in the big and muscular figure of the man before him—close, now; very close. It was no question of good marksmanship. Billy would have preferred that infinitely, because in his skill he had the most perfect trust. But at this distance it was a mere matter of who should get his gun from the holster first.

And on that question he was more open for argument, since there was, in Ames Benchley, a suggestion of nervous energy pent and ready for the lightning movement as great as that in Billy himself. At a gun play Billy was an artist, and being an artist he could see and appreciate the artistic mastery of his rival's style. He admired the easy manner, also, in which Ames Benchley allowed his arms to swing freely at his sides; no tense fingers gripped the revolver butt, waiting for the instant of the signal and dulling the nerve precision with the force of the finger pressure. That was one attribute of the true fighter.

There were other things that appealed to the eye of critical Billy Buel. For instance, Ames Benchley was not painfully erect but stood very naturally, as though he had merely by chance paused for a moment of careless conversation. And he did not fix his stare with painful intentness upon the form of his antagonist, but allowed his glance a small compass through which they wandered about and above and past Billy and gave the impression of a man who was not only perfectly at ease but was even enjoying the beauties of Gloster Valley at this charming hour of the evening.

And the heart of Billy Buel swelled with a responsive admiration. He would have liked to step up to this man and wring his hand; he would have liked to go to him with a profession of undying friendship; he would have liked to choose him for a partner till they were separated by death.

In a moment the warm emotion passed. Whatever else he might be, above all Ames Benchley was a foeman worthy of Billy's steel. And by that token he should have measured heartily to the full limit of Billy's ability.

It was he who broke the silence first.

"Benchley," he said, "the owl don't seem in any hurry. Seem like she wants to give us a chance to chin a bit. For my part, I got this to say—if you're unlucky and drop, I'll give you with all honor right back to your folks. And if I drop I got to ask that you don't take anything from me by way of a souvenir, because I've promised away everything from my sombrero to my spurs."

And Ames Benchley answered: "I give you my word, Buel. The minute you've dropped, I'll treat you like a brother. They ain't any anger between us, Buel, nor any grudge."

"That's man-talk," said Billy.

And the silence fell again. But the scene was changing quite rapidly. The shadows were deepening. The birches were now faint pillars of marble with a black, nightlike canopy supported above them, a crushing burden. And in Ames Benchley there was a change, also, it seemed to Billy. The big man was growing more rigid. His right arm crooked a little, and the hand was raised close, close to the butt of his revolver. Once he raised his left hand and settled his sombrero with a furtive quickness. Again he raised his left hand and flicked it across his forehead.

And Billy, thrilling, knew what the gestures meant. The careless ease was passing from Benchley, and in its place was a desire to stare close and closer into the face of the foeman. And thoughts and imaginings were springing up in the mind of the big man. He was hearing, in anticipation, the hoot of the owl. He was seeing, a dozen times, the dull gleam of the guns as they were drawn. He was hearing the bark of the exploding cartridges. Even, perhaps, he was feeling the blow of the bullet and the hot stab of pain as the lead tore through the flesh.

Did not Billy know? Had he not, a dozen times in the beginning of his wild career, felt similar emotions in somewhat similar circumstances? But that was long ago, and the school of battle had steeled him and made him impregnable to such weaknesses. His nerve was iron, his eye was steady as a spirit level. And a fierce, hot exultation swept through him as he guessed the weakening of the man before him. The battle, he felt, was over—it was ended. Ames Benchley and all of his glory would fall, and all of the glory would descend on the shoulders of the victor! And the teeth of Buel flashed in a smile, a slow and cruel smile.

Then the signal came, sudden and harsh, it seemed, tearing the soft air of that quiet place. And he saw the convulsive movement of Benchley's arm. It was a swift draw, done in a flashed part of a second. But, no matter how fast, it seemed to Billy that the hand of his enemy was chained and weighted in its place compared with his own speed. It seemed to him that his revolver was clear of the leather, his finger curled on the trigger, before the muzzle of Benchley's weapon was out.

And then it happened—strangely, stupefyingly strange!

A blow struck him across the head, a stunning blow, and on its heels came the deep, roaring report of a gun, deeper and louder, and louder, it seemed to Billy as his senses went out, than any revolver he had ever heard in his life before. His finger pressed the trigger and sent the bullet away, but he was firing into a cloud of darkness. Then all things went out. The ground beneath him rose, bedded him gently—the rest was darkness.

As for big Ames Benchley, he stood in a daze with his undischarged revolver hanging a limp weight in his hands. It seemed that an instant before he was about to die, under the incomparable speed of Buel's draw; and now a bolt from heaven had struck the terrible young fighter down, and here was he, given a new lease on life.

Then a figure leaped from the covert at the side of the clearing and ran toward him, carrying his rifle swinging at his side. And he heard the familiar voice of Hal Moore saying: "You ain't hurt bad, Ames? I didn't hold that shot too long? I seen your hat jump off. Did he nick your head?"

Ames Benchley looked stupidly behind him. There lay his sombrero on the ground, and he vaguely remembered the wrench with which it had been torn from his head. Hal Moore was picking it up.

"A hole right through the top!" he said. "Ever see anything like it, Ames? And he fired while he was falling! It sure would of been a bull's-eye and the end of you, Ames, if he'd had all his senses with him when he shot!"

Ames Benchley took the hat and replaced it on his head. Gradually his mind was clearing, and the truth was coming to him. Hal Moore had slipped away on his heels when he left the house and had hidden quietly here to end this decisive battle by a stroke of stealth.

"He's dead?" he asked hoarsely.

"He sure ought to be," said Moore complacently. "I had a dead center on his head. But I dunno. Seeing him stand there so quiet and easy, it got my nerves, and my hand began to shake like I had buck fever for the first time. He sure was some fighting man."

"I know, I know!" said Ames Benchley with a shudder. And he wiped his forehead; it was still wet with the perspiration of that long and terrible wait.

"And if he's dead," he said calmly, "you die with him, Moore. As sure as they's night and day, you'll die too, if I'm able to drill you."

"Ames," gasped the younger man, recoiling, but never thinking of a self-defense against terrible Ames Benchley, "didn't I plumb save your life? Wouldn't he of drilled you clean if I hadn't dropped him first?"

"He sure would," said Ames Benchley, "and don't you think that I'd rather be dead than to have him shot down by a trick? Didn't he meet me fair and square, and wasn't all the Camps square behind him? Couldn't they of done what you've done? Go to him, Hal, and if he's sure dead, start praying!"

Hal Moore dropped his rifle and scurried to the fallen body where it lay on its face. He turned it over, fumbled at the heart, leaned his ear close to the lips of Billy Buel. And in a moment he rose on his knees and shouted: "He ain't dead, Ames! He ain't dead! He's sure got a hard skull. The bullet just glanced off the top of his head, that's all!"

Ames Benchley groaned aloud with his relief and hurried to the place. It was indeed true. Billy Buel was senseless from the impact of the bullet rather than from any death-bringing wound. The scalp wound bled freely, and the bullet had bitten deep in the bone, so that there was no telling how really serious the result of the wound might finally prove to be.

Between them, they made a bandage and stopped the flow of the blood, but still Billy showed no inclination to open his eyes. His breath was irregular; his heartbeat was alternately a death-beat and then a hurried flutter.

"We got to get him where he'll have care—and we got to get him quick! Run back to the house. We're closer to our place by a mile than we are to the Camps. Run back as fast as you can and tell 'em to bring a wagon and help!"

"Run back nothing. Wouldn't that show that I been here—and what I've done here? I ain't supposed to have been anywhere near. It's you that dropped Billy Buel, Ames!"

Ames Benchley started.

"D'you think I'm going to take any credit for this? No, sir, I'm going to the Camps and tell 'em man to man that they been tricked, and that the fight don't count, and that everything is back where it was before."

Hal Moore groaned. He saw all his good work undone at a stroke.

"Listen to me while I talk a bit of reason," he pleaded. "D'you want that Nell should stay with us or go to the Camps?"

Ames Benchley sighed. And he thought of how Nell had run through the bars of sunlight down the hall and come to him and to fierce old Jacob Benchley, his father. To take her from the Benchley house would be like removing a continual and pleasant music. Even if justice should be done to Lew and Margery Camp, her rightful parents, they had done without her all these years, and they might do without her for a longer time.

"It don't mean that I'm giving her up," he said gloomily. "We can go right on fighting for her and keeping her the way we've done up to now. But I ain't going to take no credit where no credit is coming to me. I'll never let a men in the world believe that I shot down Billy Buel in a square fight."

"But where's the harm? Between you and me, they ain't any man alive that could drop him in a fair fight. D'you think it's going to ruin him to be dropped by you?"

He pointed to the bared chest of Billy Buel where they had exposed it to give him air.

"Look at them scars—bullets, Ames. And look

at that white streak across his forehead—bullets, Ames. I tell you here and there he's been dropped many a time. Maybe that was when he was just a kid and wasn't anywheres near so handy with his gat. But the fact is that he knows all about what it is to be beaten. It won't break his heart. But he'll start right in and try to get another whack at you!"

Ames Benchley caught his breath with something like a groan.

"And if you want to do the square thing," said Moore, "you're doing it plenty by leaving him alive, because he'll never leave your trail, partner, till you or him is under the dirt!"

There was a spirit of prophecy about the speech, and it chimed in with all the thoughts that were passing through the mind of Ames Benchley.

"Besides," went on the tempter hastily, "what harm does it do? We take him home. We nurse him till he's well. And maybe that way we teach him that all the Benchleys ain't skunks. And maybe that way we get him over his grudge against you for shooting him down. And at the same time, the Camps have sure got to admit that their man is down and beaten, and they got to give up the war. And they got to give up Nell. And we keep her. And listen, Ames!"

He came close to Ames Benchley. He was pleading for his own chance of success with Nell Benchley, and therefore he was pleading with all his heart and soul.

"Listen! Who'll get the glory? Who is it that gave Nell to the Benchleys? Who is it that gave peace to Gloster Valley? Who'll everybody praise and talk about? You, Ames!"

"And every word'll be a lie." Ames Benchley groaned.

"No, because you deserve to have them things said about you. Who else has kept the Benchleys together and give us a fighting chance against them man-eating Camps? You, Ames. It's all been your work. Start back for the house! I'll stay here and see that nothing goes wrong with Buel. When I hear you coming back with the wagon, I'll sneak off into the woods, and nobody'll ever know that I ever been near the place."

"I can't do it!" said Ames Benchley.

"You got to," declared Hal Moore.

· XXII ·
AMES' HOMECOMING

The forest had been cleared away from before the big Benchley house. It was a work of military precaution to keep an enemy from sneaking up too close for a surprise rush. And that, indeed, was the ghost which never ceased haunting the Benchleys. Outnumbered in the open, beaten everywhere except when they fought single duels here and there through the forest of Gloster Valley, they were continually anxious lest the enemy by some cunningly concerted plan should eventually break open the gates and get at the interior of the house itself. Then would be that last terrible battle in which no quarter would be given, and in which the house would run red; but in the end, numbers prevailing as they surely must, then Benchleys would die, and the Camps would conquer.

For that reason the forest had been cleared away to a considerable distance before the building, and on the rooftop, in strongly walled little bullet-proof towers of logs, there was always at least one watcher; and on dark and stormy nights fitted for surprise attacks, there were generally two. There were two now, but they were both straining their eyes in one direction—eastward down Gloster Valley.

On the ground below the rest of the clan were gathered, man, woman, and child, all who had answered the ringing of the bell which might mean good news or bad, but at any rate meant an instant gathering of all who prided the Benchley name and fame. And all of these, too, stared steadfastly eastward toward the trees. Martha Benchley, with her little boy in her arms, stood strongly, with a grave, imperturbable face, though here must have been the greatest agony of all. And there beside her was Alice, trembling in every limb and holding Nell close to her. And old Jake Benchley sat in his wheelchair close by, patting one of Nell's hands from time to time, while his aged wife, Katherine, mother of all his long line of children, leaned on her cane on the other side of the chair.

And the common concern was—who will appear from the skirting of trees? Will it be Ames Benchley, returning, and therefore victorious, to announce the end of the war and the permanent settling of the question of Nell's parentage, or the claim to own her? Or will it be that other, that stranger, Billy Buel, come to claim Nell as his right and lead her to the waiting hands of the hated Camps?

The dusk had grown; the house was growing black even to the windows behind them when at last the long and shrill wail of a lookout above came thrilling down to them: "They's a man coming!"

Not a breath of answer was heard for a long moment. Then, from Oliver Lord, he, next to Ames Benchley, being the staff which supported the Benchley fortunes: "What's he look like?"

"Can't make out nothing much but just a man."

"Is he tall or short, big or skinny? This Billy Buel, young Runyon says, ain't more'n ordinary size and sort of skinny. And the Lord knows everybody up here in the Benchley house ought to know what Ames looks like—you ought to be able to sort of sense him down the wind! Can't you make out?"

"He's getting clearer—nothing sure yet!"

"Try to guess, for Heaven's sake, lad!"

And still the pause, until now everyone could see the approaching figure as it climbed above the hilltop. And still another heart-breaking pause, then a semi-shriek from Martha Benchley: "Heaven be praised! It's Ames! It's Ames!"

She would have run forward to meet him, but in the general groan of relief and joy Oliver Lord held her back.

"Are you sure, Martha? Because it'll bust your heart if you run out there and find that you're wrong!"

"I'm sure, Oliver. Oh, I'm sure by the walk of him. They was never another man that walked the way Ames walks—my Ames!"

And, breaking away from the restraining hands, she raced forward across the clearing.

But she was not alone. Every soul there swept forward, with old Katherine Benchley hobbling in the rear, last but not least to take her boy and her hero in her arms. Only old Jacob Benchley remained moveless in his wheelchair and stroked his fleshless chin to cover a grin.

It was, indeed, Ames Benchley. They broke around him like waves around a rock. They danced and shouted; they clung to him. And poor Alice, out of a heart full of gratitude and relief, was kissing his big, strong hands and stammering vague words. For now, at the last, Nell was hers, all hers, and forever.

So the crowd gathered around two main points of interest—Ames Benchley and Nell, for if Ames had won the great battle for them, Nell was the great prize. And there were men and women there who had lost their nearest and dearest in the long nine years of combat, but none of them grudged their sacrifices when, through the gloom of the day, they saw the face of Nell, radiant with a sort of inward light—and laughing and weeping at once—and holding out her hands to them—and thanking them one by one for all they had done to keep her for the mother she loved. There is about great beauty an element of the holy; and the bright face of Nell sanctified the war and the end of it.

But, strange to say, there was no joy in the face of Ames Benchley. He had never seemed taller, he had never seemed stronger. But, striding through the midst of them, tears and shouts and laughter and clapping on the back were no more to him, literally, than dashings of spray against the mightiest and most deep-rooted of rocks. He had no raised hand and answering bellow, such as they all had heard full often when Ames Benchley came back safe and victorious from a skirmish against great odds. Instead, his large and solemn voice went booming across their startled heads and by the first surmise took half the joy out of them.

"They's a man down in the hollow yonder where we met—yes, it's Billy Buel. And he may be dying for all I know. You, Oliver, if you was ever my friend, get your fastest pair hitched to a buck-board and go down the valley at the gallop. If we lost that man's life, I'll never smile again. Quick, boys, help us!"

Several thronged with him. The rest swirled here and there in a dance of triumph. It was true. Ames Benchley had met the enemy, and, as always, Ames Benchley was returning safe and sound, and his enemy lay bleeding, dying on the ground behind him!

What had it cost? They were soon to know.

Ames Benchley leaned over the chair of his old father.

"Did you have a hand in it?"

"A hand in what, lad?" asked the ancient.

The hat of Ames Benchley was caught by a gust, loosened on his head and blown away. Someone was bringing lanterns from the house, and the breeze tossed the flames in the chimney-throats and filled the hillside with wild flickerings. And with the dancing crowd it was a gay crew of madmen, or the bewitched.

"A hand in what I think you know about," said Ames Benchley, unheeding the riot, "because if I ever find out that you did, I'll forswear my name and get another and leave you forever!"

And, so saying, he turned and strode away, heedless of the wind which was rising now, blowing his hair up on end.

Someone had picked up his hat, but, before they

followed, their eyes caught on something that checked them; there gathered an instant circle.

"Here's what you nearly cost, girl!" shrilled an old woman. "Come here, Nell!"

She came, and old Mrs. Runyon dragged her to the center of the circle and held up the sombrero. The lantern light streamed straight through it, from side to side, showing a neatly clipped hole.

"Just half an inch too high," they were saying, "or maybe it clipped his hair. Who knows?"

"I know," breathed Nell. "And I only thank Heaven that no other man will ever be in danger for my sake again!"

The roar of the wagon disappearing through the gate of the corral drowned any further opportunity of speech. It was a big buckboard holding four men, and it was drawn by two horses galloping as fast as the whip could drive them. And when the rattle of the wagon died away down the hill, old Jacob called: "Hey, Moore! Henry Moore! Will you take a hoss and ride for the Camps and tell 'em soft and low that Billy Buel is down—and that he's been took to our house. And that if they want to come and fetch him they can whenever they want. And tell 'em that the war's over— damn 'em! And tell 'em that we're as glad as they'll be, and it was never worth fighting from the first!"

But while he spoke this last his arm was around the waist of Nell, and he was chuckling up at her.

He went on with his orders as Henry Moore ran toward the corral, glad of the distinction which had fallen upon him. Oh, to bear that message among the haughty Camps and to see them grind their teeth and wince under the relentless whip of words!

And now Jacob Benchley was issuing new orders.

"Get the big south room ready. Hey, Nell, you look to that, will you? And get it fixed up pretty, because if this Billy Buel was good enough to fight for all the Camps, why, now, when the fight's over, he's good enough to get the best we can give him. Hurry it up, and then come down here and wait beside me till we hear the wagon bringing him up. Oh, this is a day, this is a day, Nell!"

She scurried away with half a dozen of the women after her.

And Jake Benchley fell back into a soft monody: "The fences'll start marching down the valley now. Gloster Valley is my valley, Heaven spare me five years more. It ain't much to ask—the Lord knows it ain't much to ask!"

The strange old man raised his face to the stars which were beginning to burn more clearly in the sky of the young night.

Someone touched his shoulder.

And a whispering voice said: "Here's Miriam, come looking for you, Mr. Benchley!"

He quaked at the words, a sudden terror seeming to take possession of him at once.

"Miriam?" he echoed. "Miriam? What's she come for? What's she want?"

"I dunno. She just says that she wants you."

"It ain't luck," said the old man, shrugging his shoulders as though to rid himself of a bitter chill. "They ain't no luck when Miriam's about. And her to come on the happiest evening of my life! Take her away!"

The answer was instant: "It ain't no good trying to handle her, not when she's made up her mind. You know how she is!"

"Is she that way tonight?" whispered the old man with a childish awe in voice and in face.

"She's tolerable set on seeing you," was the response.

"Lord in heaven!" breathed old Jake, pressing a lean hand against a still leaner chest. "What's she want? What does she know? What has she said?"

"Nothing. Nothing, but that she wants to see you!"

"And croak at me some of her black news!" groaned the old man in a fury. "But I won't see her. I don't want to have her turn my blood cold this night of all nights!"

"Then I don't want the job of telling it to her. And you better change your mind. You know how she is when she's crossed!"

"I know!" echoed the old fellow again and drew his coat more closely around him.

"All right!" he exclaimed suddenly. "Go and call her, but first tell 'em to take that lantern away. Do they think I want to see her face?"

The strange order was obeyed, and as the lantern was carried off it passed by Miriam. She was being led forward, a mere slip of a girl of nineteen and the youngest of the children of Jake Benchley. She was very pale indeed, and she walked with a faltering step as though she were weak. Yet she was pretty enough—far more than ordinarily pretty, indeed. What could explain the horror which the old man felt for her? Perhaps it was her eyes, for as the lantern passed by a high light was struck into the great, blank, dark, wistful eyes; but in spite of that flash of the lantern-light she did not blink, did not turn her head.

That, and in addition to it the straightforwardness of her glance, were enough to explain that Miriam was quite blind.

· XXIII ·
ART CAMP INVESTIGATES

She had been born blind, and from the first time he looked into her face she had affected her father with the same peculiar mixture of horror and aversion. All the blind, indeed, troubled him in much the same way. It was as though the old man to whom faces were an open book in all of their varied meanings was baffled and thrown back by eyes which could not meet his.

And, when, in the midst of talk, a blind man paused, old Jake Benchley was full of trouble, feeling that what he had last said was being taken into consideration and treated with acid tests in the inward laboratory of the other's mind—but what the result was, who could read in blind eyes? It was not only that she was unapproachable that made him dread Miriam more and more as she grew toward womanhood, but also other qualities which baffled and perplexed him and baffled and perplexed all the rest of Gloster Valley as well.

At any rate, as she was led toward her father the old man shrank away in his chair as far as the side of it permitted, and then, with head lowered and face working, he watched her coming as though she were a mortal poison being carried for his drinking.

But none of his disgust and fear was reflected in the girl. When she came to a little distance from him she stretched forth her pale hands—those indescribably affecting hands of the blind!—and, leaving the woman who guided her, said softly: "I can find him now!"

How could she find him now? thought Jake Benchley. Many a time he had seen her brought close to an object, and suddenly a light would pass over her face as though nearness to a thing were to her the power of sight. Indeed, all through the house of the Benchleys she was never at fault but could walk where she would with no fear unless a chair or other article of furniture were put out of its accustomed place. But, if that were not done, there was no need to pay attention to Miriam. She walked and even ran about in the assured places, and there were even regions about the house where she passed by herself; and it was one of the familiar sights of the evenings to see her seated on the hillside with her hands clasped about her blind face raised to the setting of the sun.

And she came straight and sure to her father now, in the dimness of the late twilight. Truly, the very greatness of the hard old man's detestation of her merely seemed to make her love for him greater and greater. And when she found him with a few deft touches of her finger tips—so swift and light that they did not seem to be made at all—which enabled her to locate him exactly, she knelt beside him on the turf and held his chilly hand.

The others flew back in a wide and wider circle from about the two. They knew the feeling of the old man for the girl; and they also knew that he hated to have anyone near who might spy out the expression on his face when she was about him.

Besides, they wished to take their mirth where there would be no damper. So, about the old man and his daughter there fell a gradually widening silence. And finally in the quiet he asked her gently: "What's wrong, Miriam?"

"I dunno," said the girl in her usual soft, rather mechanical voice. "I just sort of wanted to be with you. Is it all right?"

"I guess so."

"You ain't got anything to do right now?"

"I guess not."

"Then I'll sort of sit about near you for a while, and that'll make me happier."

She always sought him when she was in the least trouble. That was the peculiar horror, the peculiar irony in their relationship, that in her the appeal from blood to blood was almost incredibly strong, and in him there was no response at all.

"But ain't you happy?" he asked. "Ain't you heard the news?"

"I heard the news," said the girl, "but I ain't happy. Matter of fact, I think it was the news that started giving me this chilly feeling."

"How come?" asked old Jake, and then, striving to drive away the morbid curiosity which swept over him, he added with a feeble attempt at laughter: "Never mind trying to explain. It ain't nothing. Just one of a girl's fancies. Which you have uncommon piles of 'em, Miriam."

She did not reply to the last part of his speech, but to the first she answered slowly and gravely: "I'm kind of glad that you don't want me to explain, because explaining would be terrible hard about this, I guess!"

The curiosity which he had successfully fought back for a time now overcame him in a wave.

"Tell me," he said. "Tell me all about it if you can. Right from the first when you began to get what you call that chilly feeling."

The girl sighed and lowered her head against the arm of his chair. It was all he could do to keep from shuddering at the nearness of her as he looked down to her hair, softly glimmering black in the late twilight. At least there was one advantage in her position: He did not have to look into the blind face or even through the darkness catch the sense of those wide, dull eyes and the pallid skin and the lips, tense and parted for speech even when no words came.

And as long as this was spared him, he could endure much. It was chiefly when he became acutely and visibly aware of the struggle of the spirit that went on inside her that he was perturbed. Others in Gloster Valley thought Miriam insane in a harmless fashion, and still more considered her simple minded; but to her father she was neither, but simply a strong brain turned back upon itself.

"I'd a pile rather not talk about it," said the girl. "But if you want, I'll try to tell you. You see, when they brought up the good word that Ames had won, I jumped up to my feet all ready to shout out and sing. But no singing came, father, no singing came up to my throat."

She stopped with a sigh, and the old man rubbed a furtive hand across his forehead.

"Instead, they was a sort of a cold hand closed up my throat. Do you see? And inside of me something black came up big, and out of the blackness they was a sureness that Ames hadn't won!"

"That's talking fool talk!" exclaimed the patriarch. "Don't you hark to 'em singing over yonder—as far away as they can get because you put a cloud over 'em? But still they're singing because Ames's won. Didn't he get out and fight? Didn't he come back safe except for the bullet hole in his hat—which it was a narrow miss enough? And ain't they gone down now to get Buel and bring him up and take care of him?"

He laughed aloud, rubbing his cold hands together.

"Ah, that's what pleased me the most; more, almost, than the ending of the war—it's that I beat the champion of the Camps, and after I beat him I took him in and nursed him and got him all well and sound. Showing that I can beat the Camps and despise 'em while I beat 'em! Ah, they'll never get over that!"

"They'll come no good out of that fight," said the girl. "They's no good come out of it now."

"Miriam, are you plumb out of your head? Don't it mean the end of the war? Listen to 'em now—there's the creaking of the buckboard down the hill, and they're bringing up the champion of the Camps to be took care of. Can't you hear the wagon wheels, girl?"

"I hear 'em," said the girl. "And I hear a lot of other things inside of me like voices talking."

She rose slowly to her feet. And in the chair beside her the old man literally cowered.

"You ain't going to have a spell, Miriam?" he pleaded, touching her arm as a child might touch the arm of an angry parent.

"I can hear a lot of things!" she was saying to herself over and over again, paying no heed to him.

The wagon was approaching the front of the house, and the crowd was gathering in an expectant silence to receive the wounded man whose fall, as they believed, at the hand of Ames Benchley, had ended the war. A joyous and grateful silence, in fact for it seemed that Billy Buel had actually brought them a great gift.

Suddenly, Miriam started forward. Two men had lifted a limp form from the bed of the wagon, a form around whose head the white bandage glimmered faintly, and the body had been given into the strong arms of Ames Benchley standing beside the vehicle. It was at that moment that Miriam started forward, and Jacob called: "Kate! Kate! It's Miriam gone wild again. Watch her. Have 'em take her away. She's bad!"

The shrill cry of the old man suddenly divided the interest of the waiting group. Half of them flocked around Ames Benchley as he carried the wounded man toward the door of the house. And when they flashed a lantern in the face of his burden they saw a pale face with the eyes closed, a young and handsome face.

"Why," they exclaimed, "he ain't no more'n a kid. And for him to stand up to Ames Benchley!"

"Ay, and near bring him down, as his hat speaks for itself. But how come the Camps trust to him?"

"And look how light Ames carries him, like he weren't no more of a weight than a sack of crushed barley!"

But the other section of the crowd split away and met the coming of Miriam. Her hands were extended before her, and by the vague lantern light there was seen something in her face that made the others recoil. Many a hand was stretched toward her, but not a finger's weight was laid on her to stop her forward progress.

So she fumbled her blind way to the door and turned there, leaning against the boards.

"Brother Ames!" she called.

Dead silence fell over the Benchleys and their men.

Then came the voice of Ames Benchley as he bore his helpless victim toward the door: "I'm here, Miriam. What's wanting with you, girl?"

"Are they bringing him in the house?"

"Bringing who?"

"Him you fought with?"

"Billy Buel? Yes. He's here. I got him here close before you."

The girl cast her hands before her face as though sight had been suddenly given her and blinded her with what she saw in the first glimpse.

"Ah, ah," she moaned, "I can tell it. They's a smell of blood about him, Ames. It's on him, and it's on you, and it's on all the Benchleys. They's a smell of fire and of smoke, and the house is burning. Ames, the house is burning, and the men inside of it!"

She no longer cowered before the horror of her vision but stood straight with her arms cast above her head, and the silent, terrified crowd raised lanterns so that the white, working features of her face were visible. And she seemed to tower above them, larger and stronger than Ames Benchley himself.

"Take him away, Ames. Leave him out yonder in the forest. What care is it of a Benchley when a Camp dies? Leave 'em to find him dead and bury their dead. But if he enters your house they'll be no good come of it, but all the war'll start again, and worse'n ever before. They'll be burnings and shootings and slaughters by night, because this Buel ain't no common man. Take him inside, and he'll live—they ain't no doubt. And he'll be like the snake that you brung in out of the night and warmed, and it bit your heel. He'll be like that.

"Oh, I can see a thousand things, all shadows inside of shadows, and every one of 'em worse'n the other. I can see 'em all, Ames. And worst is that I can see you and this Billy Buel standing up to face each other some day. And I can see the guns drawed. And I can see the flash of the sun on 'em, and I can hear the shots, and I can see you fall, Ames. And I can see Billy Buel run and lean over you and laugh like the devil he is. Oh, Ames Benchley, bring him inside this house and you kill yourself and you send Nell to the Camps and you burn the house of my father!"

The strength went out of her. She dropped to her knees, cowering against the pillar in the doorway, and Ames Benchley, shifting the burden in his arms a little, leaned over her.

"Poor Miriam," he said, though his wife was white. "She's sure been took bad. Take her away, some of you womenfolks, and let me get by!"

But Katherine Benchley had come hobbling between them.

"And who knows if they ain't some truth in what Miriam says?" she asked. "I felt my blood stop running while she talked. And it seemed like every pain I had at the birth of all my boys come back to me; and it seemed to me like I seen 'em drop, one by one, and always this Billy Buel standing over 'em as they fell, and laughing!

Ames, ain't they some other place you can take him and get him healed up?"

"This is all a pile of nonsense," said Ames angrily. "I can't stand here all night holding him. Open the door, mother, and get Miriam taken care of. But it's right in this house and no other place that Billy Buel is going to get taken to bed and kept till he's well!"

They were too accustomed to obeying the dictates of Ames Benchley to dream of disobeying him now. Even his mother, shaking her head, moved silently to one side, and with the aid of two other women carried the helpless form of Miriam away into the house, and after them went Ames Benchley, carrying Billy Buel.

"Who takes charge of him?" asked Oliver Lord, pausing on the threshold before going inside.

"I've made the arrangements, and I've give the order," said the old man. "But who's them that's coming yonder?"

Out of the night two horsemen approached at a rapid gallop up the hillside. They swung into the range of the lanterns—Henry Moore, and beside him no less a person than the head of all the Camps—Arthur, the chief of the house.

A hush greeted him. Instinctively, the women drew tensely back, the men laid hands on their weapons. But Arthur Camp dismounted and advanced with one hand extended in sign of peace, that age-old token of surrender and amity.

"Gents," he says, "I've heard what Henry, here, has got to say, and I've come under a truce to see for myself. Where's Jake Benchley?"

"Over here!"

Arthur Camp approached. For the first time in nine years the leaders of the rival houses were face to face, the one withered in the extremity of age and wise old experience; the other in the full flush of the solid strength of middle age. The one peered down with a frown; the other peered up with a smile.

"Jake," said the younger man, "I got to ask you to show me the body of Billy Buel, living or dead! Will you do that?"

"Otherwise, they ain't much chance of the peace going through, I figure?" suggested the patriarch.

"None in the world."

"I'll go up with you," said Jake Benchley. "Billy Buel's just been took inside."

They wheeled him, accordingly, into the big hall of the house and to the south end.

There, as they were about to lift the chair from either side and carry him up the stairs in it, as usual, he made a sign that they desist.

"Art," he said to his guest, "it's a sight of time since I walked up them stairs. But with you to help me, maybe I could manage it. You see I'm a tolerable old man, Art."

Art Camp nodded with a grunt of half pity, half suspicion, while Jake Benchley turned back the rug which protected his legs and leaned forward to rise.

And he could have risen easily enough, for in those withered muscles of his there was a reserve of power which would have astonished any in the hall had he cared to call upon it. But now he did not care to do so. And he allowed his arms to shake and tremble as the weight of his body came upon them—until Art Camp, with an exclamation, caught him under the armpits and lifted him carefully to his feet.

"You better not try them stairs."

"With you to help, Art, I think I can manage—with you to sort of lean on."

Art Camp nodded, and passing one arm around the frail body of the seer, he began to help Jake strongly up the stairs.

It was a well-laid plot on the part of the ancient. It was one thing to have a nominal peace with the Camps, a peace which could be broken at some pretext and the war continued for another reason than the possession of Nell, and hotter than ever before. It would be quite another thing to conciliate this proud chief of the Camps and make him feel that there was no insolent triumph in the Benchleys because of their victory.

"You see how I am, Art," breathed Jake as he labored up the stairs with a difficulty threefold what it might have cost him. "I ain't long for this world. No, sir, I ain't long for it."

"The devil you ain't," said Art kindly. "You're a tough piece, Jake. You'll outlive all of us."

"What? Me?" exclaimed Jake. "No, son, the only thing that's kept the breath of life in my body has been the hope that I could see peace once more in Gloster Valley. That's all! That's all, Art."

"They's always been ways of coming at peace, Jake," said the other a little sternly. "And some of the things you've done—"

"Ay, I've done terrible things—right terrible things," agreed Jake, sighing and shaking his head.

It was an amazing confession. Art Camp glanced sharply down at the white head near his shoulder and wondered.

"You see, Art, you have the strength of numbers over me. And I had only tricks to keep up my end. So I used the tricks. Ay, Art, I'll have a long account to answer for when I get to the other world!"

An admission so great could not fail to bring a response from a man so much younger, so much stronger.

"They's been faults on both sides. We ain't none of us tried to fight too fair and square till this young Billy Buel come into the valley and shamed us."

"And I'm thinking," said the old man, "that we both owe a tolerable pile to Billy Buel for bringing us peace."

"And to Ames Benchley for suggesting the

fight," replied Art gravely. "No, Jake, it ain't easy for me, being a tolerable proud man, to see the Camps lose, and lose Nell as well. But peace means a pile to me and to Gloster Valley. And I thank Heaven that the time is coming for it."

It was progress toward good will so great that the heart of old Jake leaped in him.

"You see how it is, Art," he said, "I'm weak, and you're strong. But, if you and me was to put our heads together, my having the knowledge of a long life, we could do a tolerable pile in Gloster Valley—ah, a tolerable pile, Art! And it looks to me like they's a sort of meaning in the way you help me up these stairs. It shows how the Benchleys and the Camps is going to work side by side after this."

And in his heart he added softly: "Till I've got my strength and money back—and then one push, and out the Camps go!"

But they had come to the big south room where he had ordered Billy Buel to be placed and now they stepped into it. Billy Buel's wound had already been freshly bandaged. He lay straight in the bed, with his hands folded on his chest, his eyes closed, his handsome face pale from loss of blood.

Arthur Camp went to the bedside.

"I see with my own eyes," he said. "This is Ames' work. He won fair and square. Well, Jake, I dunno what the Benchleys figure, but I'll answer for the Camps. We'll keep this truce—this peace, better call it. When Buel's able we'll take him back down the valley till he's well. And—I guess that's all. I just had to see for myself."

He stepped back from the bed, and so doing, his eyes fell on Nell Benchley, half in shadow, half in lamplight that chiseled her profile with a golden warmth. Long and steadily Arthur Camp stared at her, and then, without a word, he turned on his heel.

But at the door he laid his large hand on the skinny shoulder of Jake.

"Keep her close, Jake," he said. "And for Heaven's sake, don't let any of the young Camps see her for a while, or the war'll break out all over again. Me myself—well, Jake, I can see why we been cutting throats for nine years. They was a reason, and a strong one!"

· XXIV ·
IN THE SICK ROOM

They passed down into the long hall below where the servants were lighting lamps to illumine it, and, reaching the great and stretching level of the floor, they heard, through the open window, the singing—for man and woman, mother and maid and child were singing for a victory of Ames Benchley and the end of the feud—singing out of the fullness of their hearts.

But as they stepped into the hall a big man walking hurriedly and with head down almost ran into them. He stepped back with an exclamation of surprise. It was Ames Benchley himself, but there was no exultation on his face. It was gathered in a frown of impenetrable gloom. The radiance which should have been his after the great victory was not there, and in its place the shadow of something akin to guilt was over him. He stared upon his father and the head of the clan of Camp with unseeing eyes as he sprang back. It was Arthur Camp himself who spoke first, though that duty belonged rather to the archenemy and son of his host.

He advanced with his hand outstretched.

"Ames Benchley," he said solemnly, "it sure appeared like the day would never come when I'd offer to take your hand in peace. But I got to do it. You beat Billy Buel fair and square, and the war's ended. You beat him with equal chances and—"

There was a sort of groan from Benchley, which interrupted him, and the champion exclaimed: "How's Buel coming?"

"Still out of his head, but a good, steady pulse!"

"Thank Heaven for that! I'll go up to see him."

He was about to brush by them but recollected himself at the last moment and turned hastily to Art Camp.

"I'm glad to see you under my father's roof," he

said in a constrained manner. "I'm glad I've shaken hands with you."

"And me, Ames," said the other eying closely that face which had always been the dread of the Camps. "But of all the Benchleys you've always been the one that we feared the most. I ain't ashamed to tell you that—and that we've put the most trust in you."

There was a muttered word of thanks from Benchley, and then he pushed past and hurried up the stairs.

Old Jake and Arthur Camp stared at each other in amazement. Ames Benchley had always been considered the very essence of courtesy in the whole range of Gloster Valley. What had happened to him to-night?

"Don't take his acting-up to heart none, Art," said Jake eagerly. "He don't mean no harm to you, nor no insult. But he's had a lot on his hands today, you see. I'll tell you the straight of it: The only man he ever feared to meet was this same Billy Buel, and I guess the relief of getting it over with is too much for him."

"Maybe," said Arthur dubiously, "but he sure did look like a gent that was none too happy. I got to go back now, Jake. Back home they's one broken-hearted woman, and they's a brother of mine that'll never really learn to lift his head again since he's lost all hope of having the girl."

In the meantime, Ames Benchley had mounted

the stairs swiftly and come again to the big south room where Billy Buel lay.

Nell alone tended him, since for the sake of a greater quiet she had banished all others from the room; and her dark head was bent above the recumbent figure now. She looked up slowly as the shadow of big Benchley fell across the bed, and then she smiled into the face of her uncle. For the very reason perhaps, that he had always been gruffer with her than any other in Gloster Valley— and also for his inherent manliness—he was her favorite in all the household. And there was a little touch of awe in her eyes, also looking on the fighter, and then down to his reputed victim and the crimson-stained bandage around the latter's head. How close the death had come, sped from the hand of Ames Benchley! How near the shadowy wings had brushed across that face which was still immobile from their close passing!

But Ames Benchley had no eye for her. He leaned over the slender figure of the sleeper. In his anxiety, it seemed to Nell, he actually dropped upon his knees and placed his ear to the breast of Buel. Then he raised a face contorted with a sudden agony.

"I don't hear the heartbeat, Nell!" he whispered.

A flash of concern crossed her face, and she touched the wrist of Buel with the tips of her fingers. Then she nodded and smiled.

"That must be because your own heart is beating

so hard and fast, Uncle Ames. There's a very firm, steady pulse. He'll be waking up in a minute or so more!"

There was a positive gasp of relief from the big man as he staggered back to his knees. And yet, as though to make sure, never moving his eyes from the face of Buel, he circled around the bed and came to the side of Nell.

"You ain't making any mistake, Nell?"

"None, Uncle Ames."

She wondered with all her heart at his concern, and yet it warmed her to the soul. Certainly it proved that Ames Benchley was capable of fighting without malice and blood-lust. And in his concern he seemed to her more leonine than ever, a noble head, a noble man in every respect. She would have poured out a flood of questions to another; but Ames Benchley, as always, touched her with that chilly finger of awe which restrains the speech—just as Miriam affected her, without the real terror which Miriam inspired.

"Thank Heaven," said Ames again, "thank Heaven for that. If he gets well, I'll make you remember it. That gray two-year-old hoss you liked in the corral the other day—you remember?"

"That dark gray? That lovely thing? Yes, yes!"

"The minute Billy Buel gets up out of bed and puts on his boots, that hoss is yours."

"But I can't take him. He's the last of the strain,

242

Uncle Ames, and I know you were training him up to be your own horse."

"Never mind that. But if you let Buel die—and they's nobody in the valley that knows nursing and the care of wounds the way you do—if you let him die, Nell, I'll make it a dark day in your life, and never forget it!"

She lowered her eyes gravely under the threat, not as defying him, but certainly not shrinking from the danger.

"I'll not forget," she said simply.

The big shadow of Benchley moved across the bed as he started for the door, but he turned abruptly, and, yielding to an uncontrollable impulse, of which he was apparently ashamed in a measure, he came back and sank into a chair beside the sleeper. There, one elbow supported upon his knee, he stared into the face of Billy Buel very much as some great painter might study the work of a great rival, wondering at the secrets which he saw half revealed, half guessing at their nature, half feeling that they are beyond his scope. There was all of this in the intent stare of Ames Benchley.

At length he shook his head and spoke without looking up.

"Nell!"

"Yes?"

"Come around here."

She obeyed, and as she approached he reached

out blindly for her and drew her close to him, his arm passing about her waist, and his big right hand catching her own right hand. So he held her quite close. And she looked down to him in amazement. There was no caress in the gesture, she knew. There was no tenderness in it. But rather it was the act of a man bewildered and seeking an explanation and striving so intently for a solution to a mystery that he felt that even physical nearness might be an aid.

And the girl, studying with her wise young eyes the intent, downward bend of that great head beneath her shoulder raised her left hand and gently stroked the tangle of rough curls away from the forehead. And she was dreaming as she did so, how, during those long nine years, this man had been the great power which had preserved for her the place she loved and kept her among the people she loved. What power was in that large neck, and how the huge muscles sloped and swelled and made play along his broad back and shoulders! Ay, he was a man among men! But what was wrong with him now? And why did his hand, holding hers, increase and decrease its pressure as though a pulse of nervous fear were in him?

"Nell!" he said, speaking always in the same husky, subdued voice.

"Yes?"

"You got an eye for men."

"Thank you, Uncle Ames."

"Oh, yes, and for women, too. You ain't one of these thin-brained young fools with a pretty face and no brains inside of 'em. No, you're furnished out tolerable well with a mind, Nell. They's more man in you than they is in nine-tenths of these young fools that think they want to marry you. Well, girl, I've seen you read men at a glance. I've seen you weigh 'em and judge 'em. Now look down at this gent on the bed. Look down at this Billy Buel and tell me what you think!"

She obeyed; and, to enable her to examine him more freely and closely, Ames Benchley released her. She stepped closer to the bed.

"I've been looking at him," she said gravely, "ever since they put him to bed and called me in to dress the wound. You know, they've always called me to take care of the boys when they're hurt, so that I have quite a little experience."

"Ay, girl. You have the touch. I remember when that big hound of a Joe Walker put the bullet through my forearm—they's a score I hate to see go unsettled—and you fixed me up. They was feathers in your fingers, they was that soft. Well, go on."

"It was a painful wound to dress," she said. "It must have hurt him a great deal when I was cleaning it. You see, the bullet drilled out a deep gash, and I had to work thoroughly and carefully for a long time. Well, even brave men, Uncle Ames, will groan when they are unconscious and they feel a great pain, if they are conscious enough to feel it at all. Now Billy Buel felt all of the pain. I saw his face grow pale. But instead of groaning he set his teeth—and then smiled!"

"I believe it," said the big man heavily. "I believe every word of it!"

"He's the strangest man I've ever seen, Uncle Ames. I thought at first that he was hardly more than a child. But then I looked closer, and, you see, in spite of all the softness of his face and in spite of being so handsome, he's much older than he looks, and there's a little touch of sternness in him."

"Girl, he's all man," said Benchley. "All man, and never you forget it!"

"Also," said the girl, "I saw this."

The sheet was turned back low on the chest of Billy Buel, since the night was warm, and the throat of his nightshirt was open. On it glinted the white of a long scar, and the girl, gently widening the gap, revealed to the curious glance of Ames Benchley a chest literally covered with scars.

"It looks as though he'd done nothing but fight for his life since he was a child," said the girl.

But Benchley, awe-stricken, was analyzing the wounds.

"That was a knife. Not half so ugly as it looks, but tolerable nasty at first flash. And they's where a bullet glanced across his ribs. That's big, but not so much. But here—look here, Nell—there's where a slug come close to the heart of him. You see that big silver spot, big as a nickel, almost?"

"I don't want to look, Uncle Ames. It makes me a little ill."

He closed the shirt across the body of Billy.

"Ay, he's fought a hundred fights, I guess, or pretty near that."

"But most of all," said the girl, turning hastily to a more agreeable subject, "I've wondered at his hands. Did you ever see such hands?"

She took up one in both of hers as she spoke and turned it gently to and fro.

"He's never done hard work with those hands. He's never worked much even with a rope, because that raises callouses, and his palms and his finger tips are as soft as the hands of a baby, Uncle Ames. Just feel!"

He did, with a broad finger tip, and shook his head with a soft oath of wonder.

"And see," she went on, "there doesn't seem to be very much bone or muscle in those hands. They're just a mass of nerves in the shape of hands!"

"Ay, just twin pieces of lightning, them hands."

"And—and—forgive me, Uncle Ames!"

"Well, what is it? Out with it, girl!"

"You see, I've been studying him here so long that even as he lies asleep he seems so terribly proud and fearless that—that I can hardly imagine even you, Uncle Ames, shooting him down."

And to her astonishment Ames Benchley turned

pale. He even shook his head and dragged down a great breath.

"You'd wonder still more if you seen him as I've seen him, Nell, standing in front of a gun smiling and happy and like a youngster about to have a dance with the girl he loves, and the band playing his favorite tune for the dance. That's the way he stood up to my gun, Nell, and never another man in Gloster Valley has ever done it."

He looked down at the bed, and she could have sworn that a shudder passed through his body.

"Who is he?" asked the girl.

"A hired gun fighter—that's all I know."

"A hired gun fighter?" exclaimed the girl, her lips curling with scorn at the thought of the mercenary entering Gloster Valley and the feud.

"Ay, that's him." And Ames Benchley went on, to himself more than to the girl: "But it was never the money that hired him. Never the money. It's the love of fighting that hired him At the house of the Camps he sat and stared at me like a hungry wolf, and he kept running his eyes up and down me with a funny sort of little smile. D'you know what he was doing? He was picking the places where his bullets would land. He was killing me a dozen times as we stood up, man to man. Nell, he fights the way another man would dance. And here's one more secret to lock inside that trusty little brain of yours, Nell—he's the only man I've ever feared before I fought him!"

"I don't believe it," declared the girl loyally.

"And did you hear what Miriam said?" asked Ames Benchley.

"No. But after all what—Miriam—"

"I know. We never believe her, but ain't she turned out right nine times out of ten?"

"I know. It's strange, Uncle Ames. And what did she say?"

"That because we've taken in Billy Buel he'll be the cause of the house burning and half the men in it—and he'll first kill the best of us in open fight—and she named me, particular, dropping with Buel's bullets plunging into the flesh!"

The girl gasped.

"Ay, not pretty, Nell. But maybe true? I dunno! I dunno! The Lord knows to-morrow, and we don't more'n half guess. But do your best for Billy Buel, girl, though I'm half thinking that him you nurse and care for will be him that tears you away from the Benchleys and gives you to the Camps whether you will or not!"

▪ XXV ▪
SOWING SEEDS OF DOUBT

He left abruptly after this. The girl made a step after him as though to call him back for an explanation of all his warnings, but she changed her mind and came slowly back to the bed. She herself had more respect for the strange prophecies of Miriam than other persons showed for the blind girl in her moment of frenzy. But was it possible that this slender fellow lying so helpless before her could work all the great things that were declared? The scarred breast and the long-fingered, nervous hands were witness that he could be terrible indeed. And more than all that, Ames Benchley himself had declared that when he faced the youth he felt the first fear he had ever known in battle.

In the meantime, it was her duty to nurse him back to life. It would not be difficult. Plainly, there was nothing the matter with Billy Buel save that insignificant cut across the head, and, if he recovered from the unconscious state and showed no effects of shock, he might be about on his feet and as active as ever in a day or so.

She moved back the lamp on the table so that the light cut less directly across the sleeper's face. And as she did so he moved, yawned, and sat bolt upright in the bed!

In spite of the fact that she had just assured herself that he was not so seriously hurt, it was a grisly effect—almost like the dead arising—and Nell stared aghast into his face. It was wild of eye and stern of lip, and there was a peculiar and hungry joy about him.

"Now, Benchley, it's my turn!"

As he spoke his hand made a convulsive movement which was arrested at once, while Buel glanced down, bewildered at his empty fingers. Plainly, he had thought that the battle was still in progress, he had just struck the ground under the impact of the bullet, and now, awakening, he was ready to drive his own shot at the foe.

When he raised his head again, slowly, it was to stare with horror at the girl. And while he stared, understanding, miserable understanding, flooded his face.

"He beat me," said Billy Buel, his lips barely parting for the words. "He beat me?"

She could not answer. Fear and dismay and a peculiar pity which was surprising her, stopped up all the speech in the hollow of her throat. And while she paused, a lightning arm darted out, and strong, slender fingers fastened about her wrist. She was drawn close to the bed, and there were the dark eyes burning into her.

"Tell me the truth! He beat me? Benchley?"

Still she could not speak, but she managed to nod, and the effect was as though she had caught up a club and beat it into his upturned face. Billy Buel dropped back into the bed, turned, caught his face in the hollow of his arm, and lay in a quivering agony.

It was more than any long speech. It gave her an insight into the very soul of the man and all his mortal pride. She understood, then, how it is that some men will die a thousand times rather than be shamed once. But what shame was it to be beaten in open fight? What shame, above all, to be beaten by such a man as Ames Benchley? And should not this fellow be rather thanking Heaven that his life had been spared?

There was obviously no thankfulness in Billy Buel. When at length he turned and allowed her to see his face, the agony was still in it, controlled, but impressive for that very reason.

"I'm sure considerable of a man," he said, and the ghost of a smile came about the corners of his lips. "I get beat up, and then the gent that beats me up pities me."

He paused with his teeth set and his eyes half closed while the misery of the thought ebbed away in him.

"He takes me home and he sets his womenfolk to taking care of me—and when I find out what's happened I just lie down and quit like a dog under a whip!"

And into his eyes came a positive hatred that she should have seen him in his moment of abasement.

Her first tremor was passing. She came to him firmly now.

"You'll have to lie quietly," she said. "You mustn't move about, you mustn't talk of these things, or you'll have yourself in a fever very quickly."

"I'm in no fever," he answered. "I could sit the saddle for twenty miles right now. Feel my pulse.

It's steady as a clock. And look at my hand—they's no shake to it!"

He extended that long, fragile hand as he spoke, and what he said was true. It was firm as though carved from stone. And she wondered at him, seeing, vaguely and by glimpses, the working to the iron will in the man.

"Besides," he added sharply enough, "what d'you know about bullet wounds?"

She had never, really, been talked to in this fashion, so directly and coldly, as though she were a man speaking to a man. In a way it angered her, in a deeper way it pleased her.

"I've had a good deal of experience," she said quietly, "but I'm afraid that you've had even more."

He touched the scars on his face.

"Practiced on myself," and he chuckled. "Yep, I've had experience enough. But who are you? And where am I? And—you don't talk the regular lingo of these parts, lady?"

Before she could answer, he replied to his own question and raised his hand to check her response. Then, sitting up in bed again, he peered closely and more closely at her. One would have said that he was peering through a fog and making out, more and more distinctly, the landmarks of a strange and wonderful country.

"I see," he said slowly. "When I first come in and heard all the talk, I didn't believe it. I thought

253

all the gents in Gloster Valley was plumb loco. But now I savvy the way of it. You're Nell, I figure?"

"Yes."

A smile came across his face, a smile so gentle and so bright that it astonished her. And then he held out his hand.

"I'm the Camps' hired man," he said cheerily. "And my name's Billy Buel. I'm sure glad to meet you, Miss Camp."

She stared at the name and at the inference.

"But you know—my name is Benchley."

He shook his head, unconvinced.

"D'you ever see your father and your mother?"

"Of course!"

"I mean Lew and Margery Camp."

"But they're not—"

He raised his hand.

"When you see 'em you'll understand that they're right that Lew is your father and Margery is your mother. I take it it's nigh onto nine years since you've laid eyes on 'em?"

"Yes, all of that time, but—"

He went on smoothly, resistlessly:

"When you see 'em, you'll understand. I can see it the minute I look at you. Why, they stick out all over you. Your father has the same way of holding his head, straight and high; he has the same way of turning it quick from one side to the other. Not the same sort of bird-motions that you got, lady, but the real type of 'em. And your mother is printed in you deep and strong."

She had attempted to listen without hearing, at first; but now she was listening with all of her heart and soul. There was a calm conviction about this man that went to the root of her being and called up deep instincts and made her pulses tremble. After all, the rest were heated arguers, but here was a man from the outside world who could look on and judge from a distance, so to speak.

"Take the sadness out of her face," said Billy Buel. "You got to do that, to begin with. Take all the years out of her face—you got to do that, too. But you can lay to this, lady, that a woman that's once been beautiful is beautiful all the rest of her days. Beauty ain't just the way flesh and bone is put together. Not by a long shot. It comes from the inside, I tell you. Sure as shooting it does. Like a light shining through the chimney, and even when the lamp chimney gets all smoked up, you can't have any doubt about the flame inside!"

He paused, nodding in utter conviction, and the girl listened, wholly fascinated. Other men did not talk in this manner, or, when they talked of beauty, they flushed and were embarrassed, for they were speaking directly to her. But there was an element of the impersonal about Billy Buel which made all he said gospel truth, so it seemed.

"And Margery Camp is still beautiful," he went on. "And take away the years and the sorrow, I tell you, and you get down to a girl that would of made the hearts of men jump, lady. Matter of fact, wasn't she the prettiest girl in Gloster Valley in her day? You come from her, they ain't any doubt. Even your voice has a sort of ghost of her voice in it. And, except that her lids are all wrinkled and her eyes are dull, your eyes are her eyes. And her chin has the cleft in it that your chin has."

Her thoughts whirled wildly. All he had said about Margery might be mere guesswork—and indeed everything he said about her was true, Alice Benchley—the same complexion and all—but not that faint cleft in the chin. And for the first time a real doubt entered her soul, to remain there forever!

He was still talking, all the time peering at her and seeming to become more sure every moment of his talk.

"And the same forehead and—Lord bless me!—the same hands, pretty near!"

It was another shock to the girl, for she had often wondered at the hands of Alice Benchley—formed well enough, but heavy and strong and rather made for work than to be looked at.

"Take one or two things, and it makes the case out tolerable clear," went on the relentless persuader. "But take it all together, and they ain't a single doubt. If they was only the hands and the eyes, it'd be pretty good cause for thinking that she was your mother, lady. But take all the things together—hands, eyes, brow, voice, and the cleft chin—and more than all of these put together, sort of the same feeling about the two of you—why, when you see her your heart'll jump in your throat, and you'll want to have her arms around you, because every drop of blood in you'll be saying: 'Here's my true mother—Lord bless her—found at last!'"

The girl cried with a sob in her voice: "Stop! Stop! I can't hear you any longer. I mustn't hear you. I'll leave you and—"

"Are you afraid of finding out the truth?" he asked with a sudden sternness. "No, you're just scared because you see that it maybe is the truth!"

"But it mustn't be! These people have fought for me all these years!"

"And haven't the Camps fought to get you?"

"But my mother—she loves me—and I love her—and all—"

"And think of them other two, your real mother, lady, and your real father! Ain't they been in hell waiting for you and hoping for you?"

"Don't!" pleaded Nell.

"And right now, because they think that they've lost you for good, me having been beat. I tell you what—Margery Camp is lying at the door of death, lady, and it's you that's brought her there." A sudden and grim inspiration came to him. "This woman of the Benchleys that you call mother, if she was to lose you do you think she'd die? No, she'd cry a pile and she'd be plumb wild for a time, but she'd get over it. It's only when they's blood mourning for blood that folks die, lady. You can sure lay to that!"

"But you don't know that Margery Camp is dying?"

"Don't I? And didn't I see her face when I started out to fight Ames Benchley? If ever they was a woman praying, it was Margery Camp. And I tell you, lady, if you was to go to her now you could lift her right out of her sick bed, and with one touch of your hand you could keep her living and hoping. Will you do it? Will you go with me to the Camps just for one visit and see for yourself?"

She was shaking her head, but still he could see that she wavered. Her face was raised so that light cut strongly across her profile, and his eyes roved swiftly down the lovely lines of that face, over brow and nose and lips and chin, to the throat that disappeared softly in a cloud of yellow muslin, thin as silk.

"I mustn't go. They—they wouldn't let me come back!"

"I'd be your warrant for that!"

"No, no!"

"But I say, 'Yes, yes!' It's working on you, lady. And you'll do the right thing, because they ain't nothing wrong in your make-up. You're thinking of your mother lying near dead and grieving. And you know you could make her well. And then you can come back here. You got to come back here because—because the Benchleys have won. But, once seeing her, you'll know the truth. And can you ever rest easy till you've known the truth?"

Instead of replying directly to that fiery pleader, that insinuating and swift voice, she murmured: "Was Miriam right? Was she right? She said that if you came inside the house you'd undo again all that had been done—you'd start the war again— and you'd ruin the Benchleys. And is this the way you're going to do it—through me?"

"They's times," said Billy Buel, "when words can do a pile more'n bullets. And maybe this is one of the times. I dunno, but I begin to pretty near forgive Ames Benchley for shooting me down. That brought me here and give me a chance to put the seed in your mind."

"I'll never let it grow. I dare not let it grow, Billy Buel."

"You're too brave to put a good honest doubt out of your head," he replied. "No, you'll keep thinking. About the other thing—well, I'll beat Benchley next time we meet, and that'll wipe out the disgrace of this!"

"You'll meet him again?" breathed the girl, "after he's brought you so near death once?"

"Meet him again? I'll never breathe free till I've met him again with guns! He beat me this time. I dunno how. I could of swore when we stood up there that I had him. I seen him begin to weaken."

He was leaning forward, speaking softly and passionately.

"And when I made the draw I was plumb sure that I had him. The fight was as good as over. I had my gun clear before his draw was half made, it seemed to me. But—somehow—some queer thing happened. Anyway, I felt the bullet strike, and that's the end."

He added: "But the next time they ain't going to be any miracles. I'll win!"

And the girl remembered the gloomy face of Ames Benchley as he had repeated the prophecy of Miriam concerning his death.

"Hush," said Billy suddenly. "They's someone coming to the door, and I don't want to talk to anybody but you for a minute or so. I ain't waked up yet, you see?"

He sank back on the pillows and instantly composed his face so perfectly that Nell herself was half deceived.

· XXVI ·
ALICE BENCHLEY CONFESSES

The door opened the next minute on Alice Benchley, and Nell looked at her with an emotion more curious than any she had ever felt before in her life. Instinctively her glances went to the places which Billy Buel had pointed out for her.

260

She looked at the forehead, broad, indeed, but far lower than Nell's. And she looked next at the chin, strong and well made, but without that telltale cleft. How much indeed did it tell? And she saw the hands, as always a puzzle in their size and their lack of delicate finish. But last of all she looked for that thing which Billy Buel had laid the greater stress upon—that note of personality as distinct as the note of music—that inner light—that peculiar and intangible thing for which no words availed—the thing which would assure her that this was indeed her mother.

And for some reason the familiar face which had been for years so dear to her was now lacking in the main essential. And she wondered how great a part habit played in her affection for Alice Benchley. Without the name of "mother," how would she feel toward this woman?

In spite of herself she pushed Alice away to a distance and looked at her with dispassionate, cold eyes. A lifetime of custom had made her feel that she revolved around the will of her reputed mother. Remove the certainty of that relationship and what remained? Certainly there was something lacking, and the usual overflow of affection which she felt when she saw Alice Benchley was now quite lacking.

Naturally she felt no gratitude to Billy Buel for having opened her eyes, if indeed there were a single iota of truth in what the "hired man" had said. But she looked at the man on the bed so perfectly feigning sleep, and wished to Heaven that she had never laid eyes on him, for had she not been happy before in the people around her? Had she not accepted Alice Benchley as her unquestionable mother? And was not Jacob Benchley her grandfather, and was not Miriam her aunt, and was not Ames Benchley, the strong, her uncle?

In a dizzy swirl of doubt and hesitation she smiled vaguely at Alice Benchley. The latter had come in nodding, happy, and looked at once to the wounded man. Then she smiled to Nell.

"He's sleeping?" she whispered.

"He—yes," said Nell.

"Still stunned?" asked Alice Benchley, and without waiting for a direct answer, but raising her voice carelessly, and secure from being overheard, she went on: "I'm kind of curious to see him close, Nell, this man who decided things for the Camps. D'you think I could come up close and look at him without waking him up?"

"I—" began Nell, but before she could complete her answer the other rattled on:

"I guess they's no danger of waking him. He's dead to the world right enough."

And she approached the bed, while Nell shrank back a little and looked, so to speak, from a mental distance. There was a contrast greater than words could express between her mother and the limp, slender figure on the bed. Truly a devil had told Billy Buel how to teach her to look for the faults in a woman she had always considered as mother. And truly the same demoniac power made Alice Benchley, at this time of all times, come so close to the bed of the injured man. For in Billy Buel, Nell had felt all the fineness of the thoroughbred. She saw it now and more strongly than ever in the clean chiseling of his features—in the thin, straight nose, in the fine making of the mouth and the lean chin, in the depth of brow above the eyes, in the height of the forehead, in the long and meager hands. And in contrast the woman who leaned above him seemed commoner than the common. Her very curiosity had in it something that was painfully vulgar to the girl.

"And him the best the Camps could put out!" scoffed Alice Benchley. "Well, he ain't much to my way of thinking, daughter, and anybody with half an eye would say the same. I'd like to see them hands and them arms"—and here she picked up one of the limp hands of Billy Buel and let it fall carelessly back—"I'd like to see him handle wheat sacks all day—five hundred wheat sacks the way I've seen my Joe, your father, do, Nell. Yep, I'd just like to see him! Well, the Camps used to turn out real men in the old days, but they've gone downhill, gone a long ways down, when they got to go outside of the valley and hire men to fight their fights. The whole matter of it is that they was plumb scared of Ames. That's all. They was plumb scared of Ames. And so he's given me my girl to have forever, without nobody questioning it!"

And going quickly to Nell, she caught the slim body of the girl in her arms and kissed her again and again. And the irony of it was—as it came to Nell—that at the very moment when the rest of the world was willing to submit and to accept her as the undoubted mother of Nell, the girl herself had begun to question.

"Now, Nell," said the other after a moment, "they ain't any sense in you staying up here and wearing yourself away on a man what you don't care a snap of your fingers about. You run off and play. And I'll tell you something. Hal Moore has asked if you can go out for a ride with him, this being the first time that a Benchley could ride the valley free of fear of bullets.

"They's a fine clear moon up over the trees, and Hal is sure set on going with you. Which he's a fine upstanding boy as any that ever walked in Gloster Valley, Nell, ain't he?"

The girl bowed her head. Too much had been poured into her brain this evening, and she wanted time to be alone—to think. She hated to hear Billy Buel pursue the arguments which her mother's entrance had interrupted, and yet with all her soul she yearned to hear them. It seemed as if this stranger had possessed himself of the truth, and, having seen beneath the surface, he was able to speak with full surety.

"I'm a little tired, mother," she said.

How that last word hung on her lips!

"Tired? Tired nothing! When I was your age, honey, and a youngster like Hal come along to take me out, I'd of gone with him if my bones had been falling apart with tiredness. Of course you'll go with Hal, and I'll stay here and look after this Billy Buel. I can do that as well as you can, but I can't please Hal as much by riding with him!"

It offended the girl again, this brusque cheeriness.

"Besides," she said, "grandfather Jake told me to stay with Billy Buel and look after him, and you know how grandfather is when he's crossed. I wouldn't dare to go till he gives me the permission to leave."

"Permission to leave! Silly thing, you know as well as I know that they's only one thing in the world that Jacob Benchley can't do, and that's hurt your feelings. You do what you want, and you know that Jake Benchley will never say boo."

It was an unanswerable argument. All the valley knew that Jake was wax in the hands of Nell. And the girl bowed her head a moment in thought.

"But why should I be going with Hal Moore?" she asked. "I've never been so much interested in him."

"Ah, is there somebody else?"

"Perhaps," said the girl, stung to anger and obstinacy.

"It's that Oliver Lord," said the older woman with heat. "Him with his lordly way and his high hand. When I was a girl I wouldn't have looked at the conceited fool twice! That's my word for it. And it's my word to you, Nell, that you pass him by! Oliver Lord—bah!"

"He's good enough, and a better man than Hal Moore ever dreamed of being," said the girl, driven back on this last line of defense, albeit unwillingly.

"Better at fighting, because he's bigger and older. They's other things than fighting in this world, lass; and, besides, when Hal is the years of Oliver he'll be a bigger and a better man. That's what he will! Ain't I a judge of men, I ask you?"

Every syllable she spoke jarred on the ear of the girl.

"Perhaps you are," she said slowly, "but I don't think I care to go riding with Hal Moore. Not to-night. Perhaps to-morrow."

Little did she know of the talk between Hal and Alice that evening, and how Alice had promised Hal a quick reward for his service in shooting down the champion of the Camps.

"Nell," said her reputed mother, "you're acting plain foolish. Is they a better catch for you in the valley than Hal Moore?"

"A catch!" the girl shuddered. "Do I have to think about being married so soon?"

"And why not? I was thinking of it when I was your age."

"Perhaps—we're different."

There was a meaning in that sentence which quite escaped the attention of Alice Benchley.

"Different? Not much! I know girls. They're all alike. Some a bit more fuss and feathers, but under the surface all looking for a husband, the best they can get. Tush, Nell, be getting over your foolishness and open your eyes and look about you. Are you waiting for a prince or some such matter?"

"I'll tell you flat, mother," said the girl with heat. "I don't care enough for Hal Moore to go riding alone with him in the moonlight, and I don't think I shall ever care enough for him to do it!"

She was surprised to see that Alice Benchley was by no means ready to give way. Usually the pronounced will of Nell was law in the household; man, woman, and child gave way before her. But it seemed that there was a strong basis for the obstinacy of Alice Benchley. Now she regarded Nell from beneath lowered brows.

"You're young, and you're foolish," she said, "and I see that I have to give you better reasons."

"Better reasons?"

"Stronger reasons, Nell! Are you glad to be with us still? Are you glad that you're still a Benchley?"

"Mother!"

"Or would you rather that Ames Benchley—your Uncle Ames—had been shot down?"

There was a gasp from Nell.

"Shot down and you taken to the Camps to be cared for by a strange man and a strange woman that would call you daughter?" And she added hastily: "And perhaps they'd come to tuck you in at night, same's I've done all these years, and tell you they loved you, but never with the same words I've used, and never pouring their love over you as I've poured mine, sweet Nellie!"

It was an irresistible appeal, of course, and the girl melted to tears before it. She took Alice Benchley in her arms.

"Are you asking me if I love you, dear?" she said. "Oh, you don't have to be told. But why are you talking in this way about Hal Moore? What's he to me? What's he to you? Hal Moore —why, he's a boy!"

"A boy?" exclaimed her mother. "He's six years older'n you, my dear. He's as old as this fellow here that the Camps thought old enough to be their champion and carry all the weight of their cause on his shoulders. Come, come, get up and into your things and get down to Hal. He's got two hosses tied up under the big spruce south of the house, and he's just waiting till you come down into the hall before he starts out."

"I'm not going," said the girl suddenly. "There's

268

no use arguing. I simply don't want to go with him."

Her mother eyed her gloomily.

"Suppose," she said at length, "that there was a good reason for you to go?"

"A good reason?"

"That's what I said."

"How on earth could there be a reason?"

"Do you owe something to the man who kept you with the Benchleys?"

"I owe it to Uncle Ames, bless his great heart!"

But she found that the other was nodding coldly and wisely as though she could tell much if she chose.

"You owe it all to Ames Benchley, do you?"

"And to who else? Certainly not to Hal Moore!"

The girl made an imperious gesture to the inert figure on the bed. In her great excitement she had long since forgotten that Billy Buel was not truly asleep, that his unconsciousness was purely feigned.

"Do you think for a moment," she exclaimed, "that Hal Moore would dare for an instant to stand up before this man here, this man with the scars covering his chest, this born fighter, this Billy Buel?"

The challenge stung Alice Benchley out of caution.

"Do I think so? Ay, I know so! You think that Uncle Ames Benchley went out and faced this hired murderer and shot him down? You think he did it single-handed? I tell you he didn't. He had help!"

It came stunningly home to the girl. What was the cause of the profound gloom of Uncle Ames? And what, on the other hand, had been the explanation of the surety of Billy Buel in describing the battle, his absolute surety that he had Ames Benchley beaten and ready to kill? What was it that he had ascribed to miracle? The sudden blow on the head?

"He had help!" Alice Benchley was repeating in a sharp whisper. "And that help came from Hal Moore! It's Hal that's kept you here for me—for all of us! It's Hal Moore that's ended the war. And, oh, lass, this is gospel secret. For Heaven's sake never breathe a word of it or Ames Benchley would die for shame. And him on the bed—I thought he moved!"

She ran to the bed as she spoke, and as she leaned over the sleeping figure Nell could see her face. And it was convulsed with strong passions. Providence indeed must have helped Billy Buel had it been discovered that he was awake, for there was murder itself in the face of the woman who bent over him. And the sight of it curdled the veins of Nell.

Close bent Alice Benchley, and when her ear had remained for a breathless minute above the parted lips of Buel she straightened again and came slowly toward the girl.

"You mean," interpreted Nell slowly, "that Billy Buel wasn't beaten in fair fight?"

"Would we take the chance, little fool?" asked Alice sharply. "Did we want to lose you and all the nine years of fighting? No, it was me that thought of it. It was me that sent Hal to do the work unbeknownst to Ames, poor honest idiot that he is! I sent Hal, and Hal fired the shot that brought him down. And Hal says that Ames' gun wasn't yet clear of the holster when Buel was ready to fire. Lucky Hal was there or we'd have had a dead Ames Benchley, and we'd have lost you, and you'd have lost us! Even when he was stunned and falling, Buel shot offn' his hat! So up, Nell, and go downstairs and see Hal, and don't breathe a word of what I've said to you!"

"Mother," said the girl faintly, "I'm—stunned, and I feel odd inside. It's such a lot to know all in a moment. Will you tell Hal that I'll gladly ride with him to-morrow morning?"

"I'll tell him to wait twenty minutes, and then you'll be down," said Alice Benchley firmly. "And mind you're ready when I come up again. Get over this lightheadedness. It ain't like you, and it ain't worthy of you!"

"I—I'll try," whispered Nell.

And with that Alice Benchley left the room.

But the moment the door had slammed behind her Nell whirled toward the bed. She saw Billy Buel sitting erect in it, his eyes ablaze.

· XXVII ·
A COMPACT

Her first emotion was anger that he should have overheard so much by means of his simulation of sleep. Her second emotion was overmastering fear, and she ran to him.

"Billy Buel," she breathed, "you've heard nothing. You'll forget what you've heard?"

"Forget what I've heard?" And Billy smiled. He threw a tensed right hand above his head, and his lips framed a silent shout. "Forget it, when it shows that I was right, and that I wasn't beat in a square fight? When it shows that Ames Benchley ain't proved himself my master? Forget it? Never in a million years, lady!"

"But if you tell," said the girl sorrowfully, "don't you see that it means the war starts again? You've given the valley peace. Are you going to throw it into a murdering war for the sake of your own pride? And I tell you no one in Gloster Valley thinks it a shame to have been beaten by Ames Benchley!"

"But I'm not from Gloster Valley," said Buel coldly. "And I think it a shame! What's Gloster Valley? How big is it on the map? Why, it can't be found! It ain't the world—it ain't more'n a pin-head on the face of the world." His voice rose and carried a ring through the room: "Go out over the mountains and ask 'em about Billy Buel and how many times he's been beat in a square and fair fight—that is, since he growed up. It ain't been done, lady, and it ain't going to be done till more'n one man tackles me or till I grow old. I've seen 'em come a long ways to get me, but them that come riding with all their reputation around 'em—they stayed where we met, and it was me that rode off alone! I'm talking true, and they'll tell you over the mountains that I don't lie!"

She looked at him in amazement. She had not dreamed, before, how much true barbarism lay beneath the gentle voice and the young, handsome face. What had they said? That this man fought for the sheer love of fighting? She believed it! He made her think of some Indian brave of the old days chanting his deeds before he took the warpath.

"What have I lived for, and what have I fought all the fights for, lady? To be downed here in Gloster Valley and have Ames Benchley talk big about what he done to me—curse him!—when the thing that beat me was a skunk shooting from the side?"

She had drawn back little by little during this tirade until now a considerable distance separated her from the bed and the speaker. And he, seeing her wide, frightened eyes, changed suddenly.

"I'm sure talking brave," he said with a chuckle, "boasting to a girl like you. Do me a big favor and forget what I've said—only, it sort of riles me to think of that Benchley. It sure does, him and all his oily gang! They'll pay for what they've done. Oh, they'll pay rich for it, and you can lay to that!"

And again the prophecy of blind Miriam darted into the head of the girl. The burnings of the house with half the men in it—the death of the best of the Benchleys—and the death of Uncle Ames first of all. Yet for all her sick fear of him a peculiar admiration was warm in her blood. Here he was in the house of his enemies defying them and breathing threats of vengeance! How many other men would have done so much? She could see that he was a creature all of tinder and fire, ready to flame up and burn himself away in perilous experiments.

"Will you listen to me for one minute?" she said quietly.

He threw himself back on the pillows and stared at her.

"You're a cool one," he said admiringly. "You've a tolerable level head, I'll say. Are you going to try to persuade me in spite of what I've said?"

"I have to try."

"Then take this chair close to the bed and talk as much as you want. I'll listen. If I was made of wood and stone I'd sure listen to you, lady."

She obeyed, flushing a little, and sat there with

her hands folded in her lap, looking him gravely in the face.

"Do you know that this war has lasted for nine years?" she said first.

"I've heard tell about it."

"And do you know how many lives it has cost?"

"Ain't heard that."

"Over a hundred, Billy Buel. Not bad men, you see, but the people on each side were sure they were right. And the best of the Benchleys have killed the best of the Camps and then been shot down in turn. Boys that I've played with, men that have held me on their knee when I was little, I've seen them go out in the morning, and they've never come back at night. Do you understand what it means? And every mother who loses a son and every sister who loses a brother and every child who loses a father—they all turn to me, and even when they say nothing they blame me in their hearts, and they blame me with their eyes! Oh, if I had a thousand lives to give the world I could never pay back what I've cost! And—and I wish I were dead, Billy Buel. I've tried to kill myself, but—but I haven't the courage. I'm afraid I'm only a coward. But if I could, all the trouble would end.

"And now, don't you see? It's in your power to end the war by simply pretending that you didn't hear what was said in this room. I know it's asking a great deal, a very great deal. I know your honor is more than your life to you. And I know that you feel your defeat has shamed you. But no one in Gloster Valley feels that you are shamed. They are talking downstairs now about your courage, and how your bullet which you fired when you were falling drove the hat from Ames Benchley's head. No, no, they'll never accuse you of failing in that fight—not even the Camps will! They're glad of peace, and so are the Benchleys; and if you let the war start again it will be the death of me, I swear. For my own selfish sake, Billy Buel, swallow the shame, bear up under it, let the war stand ended as it stands now, and I'll pray for you, I'll bless you!"

He saw her gestures too late to avoid it. Before he could withdraw his hand it was captured in both of hers, and here she was leaning close to him with the tears rolling down her face one by one.

The heart of Billy Buel stood up in his throat.

"If you'll—you'll stop the crying," he stammered.

It only brought a greater flood of tears.

"If you'll stop, I'll promise anything. But stop in the name of Heaven!"

Just as a stern gust of wind scatters the clouds and lets the bright blue sky shine through, so in an instant the tears had ended, and she was very rosy with happiness and smiling at him.

"Heaven reward you!" she said. "You are the most generous man in the world!"

He lay there, stunned, realizing that his word

had been pledged, and sick with the knowledge of it. Here was the end, then, of the invincibility of Billy Buel. Here was the period put to the long career of the wild fighting. Many a year had passed since he had been overcome; and the belief in him had passed, in certain quarters, into something akin to a superstition. Now the tale would go out on wings, as ill tidings always travel. Billy Buel had been beaten in a fair fight. And he must go out of Gloster Valley and battle to regain the old height. No wonder that he sighed as he stared at Nell.

"And there is nothing that you can ask of me—" she began.

"There's nothing?" he broke in sharply. "D'you mean that? Nothing you won't do?"

She reconsidered, summed up eventualities. "Nothing," she reasserted.

He sat up again in his sudden way, all fire once more with a new purpose.

"Then get into riding clothes while I dress. We can slip out a side door and get to those two horses that Hal Moore has saddled and ready for you and him. To-night you're going to ride to the house of the Camps and give Margery and Lew their first and maybe their last sight of you. Will you do it?"

"Ride with you all the way down Gloster Valley? And you with this wound? Do you want to commit suicide, Billy Buel?"

"This scratch kill me?" He chuckled, alive with

excitement and his plan, now. "No, I'll tell you what would kill me, and that's to lie here in bed and think of Margery and Lew Camp near dead with grief and blaming me for it."

"But if I were to go," she breathed, "all of the Benchleys would follow at once and—"

"Not a bit," insisted Billy. "Moore probably left the hosses with just their reins throwed over their heads to keep 'em standing. We'll ride away soft and easy, and when Moore finds the broncs gone he'll just figure that they've strayed."

"But they'll find the room empty."

"First when you're about ready to start, send for Moore and tell him that you ain't riding to-night, and that nobody's to disturb this room because I'm getting along pretty good, but that I mustn't be waked up for fear of starting a fever or a relapse or something!"

He was like a child, rolling from side to side and laughing silently for pure joy in his invention. She watched him, somewhere between mirth and fear and admiration.

"I—Billy Buel, if something goes wrong—if I can't come back—"

"If you want to come back, I'll be your surety. Will I do?"

She nodded, trembling with excitement.

"And I'll never have to go again? And you think we could get back before morning without being discovered?"

"I know it. Give you my word!"

"Then I'm ready now."

"Good! Just turn your back, Nell, while I hop out of bed and dive into my clothes."

She went obediently to the window and stared into the jet-black surface of the night until she could make out the forest and then the rolling of the hills and finally, very dim through the glass, the stippling of stars across the sky.

Then all this was blotted out. She found herself listening to the swift motions of this wild adventurer. And finally—wonder of wonders!—she heard him humming softly and gayly.

At last: "I'm ready!"

She turned to see a brilliant figure, from the gold-braided sombrero which sat light above the bandaged head to the splendid belt, and down to shop-made boots and golden spurs. It was a flashing form that half dazzled her—until, a moment later, the childishness of his love of finery, the barbarity of it, set her smiling.

After all, it was in tune with the reckless pride of the man, this vanity in his dress. In a city he would dress the part of a dandy with exquisite manners and contemptuous air. But in the mountains his face was brown, his eye wild. But what she saw before her with her overwise lovely eyes was the type of gentleman adventurer who has gone down the history of the ages supplying brawn and brains to all wild chances and forlorn hopes and lost causes. The men who followed Hannibal from Spain were such fellows, no doubt; and such men rose for the king in Scotland; and such men spurred in the train of Cortez and conquered an empire and gambled it away. Not that all these exact images swarmed up into her brain, but the emotion was the same; and it seemed to her suddenly that she had known the brilliant youth all of her life—that she had read of him in a hundred books.

"Now for Moore!" he urged, and he was flushing and smiling like a flattered girl at the admiration he found in her eyes, or thought he found there.

· XXVIII ·
FLIGHT

Nell's own color was rising at the thought of the ride which lay before her, and her spirits rose likewise. Here, in the midst of the brawls which stormed through Gloster Valley, had been a life of singular inaction, for all that battling had been to provide her with a sheltered quiet. Time would come, perhaps, when wilder work than this would be nothing to her, but now it was much indeed; and there was something in her that responded as the harp-strings responded a murmur to a sudden chord.

"Into bed with you, then," she urged, "in case Hal should look in!"

"I'm sure a blockhead for not thinking of that!" exclaimed Billy Buel.

And flinging his hat into the corner of the room he dived beneath the covers of the bed and was instantly swathed to the chin. A second later, while the girl stood waiting at the door, she saw his face composed to its former pale and rigid calm of senselessness, save that one eye opened and winked with a sort of funereal solemnity at her.

She was choking with laughter when she opened the door and sent a long hallo down the hall.

It brought Hal Moore to her at once, very excited, his eyes dancing, and: "You're coming, Nell? Just for a canter?"

She tempted Providence by opening the door.

"Look, Hal. It might be the death of him if I leave!"

"But—"

"Hush. Whisper!"

"Is he still out of his head?"

"I don't know. That or a very deep sleep."

"Somebody else—"

"I can't trust to anybody else."

"Nell, the moon's a beauty. If you once put your head out the window and got the scent of the trees you'll—"

"Another time. Say to-morrow morning. And then I'll make it a long ride if you will, Hal."

She allowed herself to smile on him as she had

never before smiled on any human being, and then caught herself up with a start. But though she banished the tenderness from her eyes at once it was too late. Hal Moore was staring, breathless, and she saw one nervous hand clenched and unclenched.

"To-morrow, then," he whispered. "To-morrow sure. Will you shake on it, Nell?"

"Yes, yes!"

He held her hand for a long moment, swaying slowly, slowly, toward her, then caught himself up with a great effort and turned away.

Nell closed the door and turned thoughtfully to Billy Buel. He was already grinning with an impish broadness.

"Did you hear?" she asked, flushing hotly.

"Every syllable," said this irrepressible maker of trouble.

"You wouldn't," said Nell, stamping her foot and growing hotter than ever in the face. "It was all in a whisper."

"I heard," insisted Billy, still grinning as he rose from the bed and resumed his hat. "And, what's more, I saw!"

And all at once she found herself laughing. There was really no harm in his hearing and seeing, and he took such a childish enjoyment in it that it made her wish to laugh aloud.

"Now," he went on, "I think you knew what was coming tonight. That's the way with you women.

You read our minds. And here you are all dressed for the trip."

Earlier in the evening, in fact, she had changed from the yellow dress into a riding skirt and a rose-colored blouse as warm as a touch of sunset color. And now she found him surveying her critically as she put the broad-brimmed hat on her head.

"You see them yaller flowers yonder?" asked Billy, pointing to a small glass vase beside the window, overflowing with wild flowers.

"Yes?"

"Suppose you was to pin a few of 'em at the V of that blouse. D'you think they'd keep fresh till we got to the Camps' place?"

"Perhaps. But why—"

"I'll show you."

And he suppressed all protest by taking a few from the vase, and after directing her attention toward a mirror he held the spray before her. Yellow against rose—golden-yellow against rose—it made a charming combination. And in spite of herself she could not help turning and smiling up to him, for this was something worth knowing, and doubly worth while because he thought of it. She knew, a moment later, that she could hardly have trusted what Hal Moore might have done had she smiled at him in exactly that manner, but Billy Buel remained as finely impersonal as ever.

"Which way?" he was asking as she pinned the flowers to her dress.

And then, turning again, she saw him covertly draw the revolver which had been left in his holster and weigh it with the touch of one who feels the grip of an old, old friend. She caught all the connotations of that gesture, and it sent a chill through her blood.

"You'll make no trouble, Billy?" she said earnestly.

"Me?" murmured the gun fighter. "I'm as tame as a lamb, lady, and they ain't any use worrying about me."

"You promise?"

"Yes."

"This way, then. But, oh, what a wild, wild thing I've done in case they come up here and find that I've gone!"

"I'll show you how foolish that is as we ride. Quick! We ain't got any too much time if we want to get to them hosses before Hal Moore does!"

She hurried at the words, beset with fears. Through the door which opened to the right she led the way, and swiftly they went down the flight of steps which showed there until they stood, in a stride past the door, in the full silver of a new-risen moon. The house behind them became at once something hostile, black, huge, and strange, and compared with it the forest below was a friendly place of shades to hide them. To the left they could hear choruses of cheery voices, for this great Benchley day was not to end with the setting of the sun. It would last, far, far into the night to celebrate the ending of the feud.

Had they known that the two figures to the right of them, barely seen by those with narrowed eyes, were about to light the torches again, how quickly that mirth would have hushed! And something of this premonition came to the girl as she listened. Would the result of this journey mean the undoing of that day's work? But in spite of herself she was drawn on by a curiosity which she could not conquer, a curiosity which had in it something like the power of fate. The picture which Billy Buel had painted of Margery Camp had been strong enough. But for that matter she had a mother, so-called, among the Benchleys. But what would it be to have a father? And what was the face of Lew Camp? Out of her childhood she remembered dimly a rather short, very broad man with a kindly face and a great voice. That was Lew Camp, and, considering him as the years and as grief might have changed him, she could not remain away.

"Look yonder," Billy Buel was saying. "There are two hosses standing in the shadow of that spruce. Might them be Hal Moore's hosses?"

She followed the direction of his pointing hand. The moonshine glimmered faintly on the color of a red-bay; and it was ghostly bright on a gray horse.

"Yes, that gray must be Hal's horse."

"It's my hoss tonight, then. Now come. Not too fast, because they can see us from down yonder where the lanterns are. We got to seem like we belong here. We got to walk slow across this open stretch. That's so's we won't be noticed. Things that move quick always seem sort of guilty, I've noticed. Take in a free-for-all, the way to get a bullet inside of you is to jump for the door; the way to get clear with no harm done particular is to just stay where you are and sort of flatten against the wall. Understand? So take it easy. Here, hang on to my arm. That's the way. That's to steady you, not to help you walk. They ain't nothing to fear. They ain't no danger at all! But not down there straight toward the hosses. No, we'll head right on into the trees so's if they should notice us they'll never think we're heading for a ride. That's the way. Brave girl! I tell you what, Nell, you sure have got a steady nerve. You got the making of a man inside of you."

It thrilled her strangely to hear such praise. It thrilled her, also, to hear her name on his lips, though for that matter she remembered that she had been the first to use a first name, and a nick-name at that.

A moment later they stepped through the outer wall of shadow and were under the trees.

The moment they reached the new strategic situation Billy Buel changed.

"Now, quick," he urged her. "Seconds are what count. Moore must be on his way, curse him. Better for us that he don't find us. And better for him, too!"

There was a soft grimness about the last of this that shocked her into a new awe of the situation. And she stopped short after beginning to run.

"What do you mean by that? If we're followed—if we're followed by Hal Moore, would you shoot?"

"Did he follow any rules of fair play?" asked Billy Buel hotly. "Nope, he shot from out of cover against a gent that didn't dream he was anywhere near. Why should I act fair with him? No, curse him, if he follers too close he takes his chance. I ain't the kind that takes to follering as easy as all that."

"You'd shoot?" breathed the girl. "You'd shoot? Then I don't follow a step, for there comes Hal Moore!"

She pointed behind her. A figure had left the swirl of dancers, the swirl of lantern light, and was sauntering slowly toward the trees. She was recalled from her glance in that direction by a strong, biting grip laid on her arm, and she twisted about and looking up, found the face of Billy set like iron. None of that softness of eye and mouth that had attracted before and baffled her, was there now. Looking at him she was aware for the first time of the full quality of the fighter.

"Listen to me!" he said fiercely. "You come, and you come quick, otherwise I pick you up and carry you and put you on the hoss."

She flinched away. His grip held her like a vise, the fingers cutting through soft flesh to the bone.

"I'll call!" she breathed.

"That'll bring plenty of 'em," he said unmoved, "and it'll bring plenty of fighting. I almost wish that you would, because it won't mean I'll be caught, but it'll mean that a pile of Benchleys will have cause to know that Billy Buel is in Gloster Valley!" He added as softly and coldly as before: "Will you come by yourself?"

And, since there was no alternative, driven forward by her own first steps in the foolish flight, she was obliged to race ahead of him toward the horses.

He followed half a pace behind. They came to the bay. His hand was under the arch of her foot, and she was floated up into the saddle. Before she was more than half settled in it she saw Billy Buel reining Hal's gray beside her.

"Now take it slow—no using of the spurs!" he was cautioning her. "But just drift like a fog into them trees, and I'll be right behind you, watching for accidents!"

· XXIX ·
NELL YIELDS TO TEMPTATION

She cast one glance behind her past the stern face of Billy Buel, through the thin wall of tree shadow, and beyond at the approaching form of Hal Moore. He was still at an appreciable distance, and considering the fact that he was newly come from the flashing region of the lantern light, it might well be that his eyes could not pierce to the exact position of the horses. But if they did, and if he saw them start away, would he raise a shout?

She loosened the reins. The bay started slowly forward. There was no outcry behind them. In a moment an impenetrable wall of shade had formed, and to the left, glimmering like stars, she could make out only the lanterns with the black tree trunks drifting thickly across them.

Not a word behind her. Once she turned, and vaguely she made out the line of glimmering white under the brim of Buel's sombrero—that line of the bandage which she had put on with her own hands.

She turned again to face the front and weave the bay through the thicket of trees, her eyes blinded with sudden tears of self-sympathy. This was her reward, then?

A voice from behind: "Now tickle the bay with the spurs! Ride, Nell!"

They had come through the denser hedge of the trees, and now a region of comparative clear lay before them; and a wild thought came to Nell. In the upper rim of hills about Gloster Valley, the only district where the Benchleys could ride safe from surprise at the hands of the Camps, many a time she had ridden and matched the speed of her nimble-footed bay against the best of which Hal Moore's gray was capable of putting forth. Why not try them again now? Why not touch her sensitive baby's flanks a little too deeply and let him bolt? It would be dangerous work, with the trees flashing past on either hand and the treacherous footing of the forest mold beneath them, but after a time, when he had distanced the gray and Billy Buel, could not she circle and come back toward the house of the Benchleys? That surely would be far preferable to venturing on in company with this wild man whose thirst to kill had been so recently revealed to her. Easier by far to return and make full confession into the forgiving ear of Grandfather Jacob Benchley than to continue on to the dwellings of the terrible Camps and be held there, like as not, with or without her will!

No sooner had the impulse come to her than she obeyed it. At the first keen prick of the steel the bay threw up its head with a snort, flirted its heels high, and then bolted with the speed of the wind. The sharp start flung her sheer back against the cantle of the saddle, and by the time she had steadied herself in the saddle the trees were in a mad whirl on either side of her from the velocity of the bay, and when she pulled on the reins to establish her control of the animal she found that the horse had taken the bit in his teeth.

It gave her one thrill of terror. Then, looking behind, she made out that the gray was being distanced, and her heart leaped. A few more minutes of this, and she could detour to the left, when the terror of the bay had abated and the beast was under control again. Certainly the gray could never maintain this whirlwind pace for the distance of half a mile. So she threw herself as far forward in the saddle as possible in order to lighten her weight, and did the best she could to sway back and forth and so influence her mount into what seemed to her the best courses.

She kept straight on resolutely and forbade herself the luxury of a single glance behind for a full five minutes of such wild riding. Then, when she turned, it was not to discover if Billy Buel were still in sight, but because from the distance behind her she made out a crackling of dead twigs under foot, as though someone were approaching. Had Hal Moore so quickly sensed her flight, and had he flung himself on the back of one of the finest of the Benchleys' horses and come so suddenly in pursuit?

She turned in the saddle. Not far behind a gray

horse shot across a clearing, bright with moon-light—Billy Buel!

Her head was whirling when she swung about to urge on her mount. What had happened to the gray?

Vague stories came into her mind from the past about master horsemen who could lift their mounts to super-deeds. Was Billy Buel one of these? Had those long and nervous fingers meant some uncanny skill with the reins, some myste-rious manner of telegraphing strength and wisdom to the brute brain of the creature he rode?

In a frenzy of panic she put the spurs again and again to the bay. She gained, indeed, but when she looked back even in the forest shadow the gray was still in sight, drifting ghost-like among the trunks of the trees.

What, indeed, had happened to the gray? In the old days many a time she had flung away from him in the first mile of running. Now the bay was stretched to the full and, having his fill of running, was rapidly coming to the point when she could have stopped the runaway with the first strong pull on the reins.

There was one good explanation. Hal Moore was thick of chest and solid of body, the sort of man who weighs around fifteen or twenty pounds more than he seems to weigh, and every ounce of him muscle; so much so that among the Benchleys it was said that, next to the terrible Ames himself and Oliver Lord, Hal Moore stood third among their champions both for strength of body and expertness of hand and quickness of eye. But compared to the solidity of Hal, Billy Buel was a very wraith. He was a creature of nerve rather than either muscle or bone; and doubtless his weight was a slight thing in the saddle. More explanation than that was needed. She looked back at the next broad clearing and found it.

Billy Buel rode inclined recklessly forward, like a jockey, well nigh. His left hand gathered the reins high along the neck of the horse, and his right hand was stretched forward along the side of the neck. It was as though one hand guided, and from the finger tips of the other hand five streams of electric energy were pushing into the body of the gray and spurring it on.

He was holding his own. He was doing more than that. With a despairing heart she saw the head of the bay come up, sure sign that he had passed the full of his strength. And the gray gained steadily from behind, maintaining that whirlwind pace.

It was marvelous riding plus the lighter weight of Buel that made the difference, she knew now, and, good horsewoman though she was, she recognized defeat and pulled the bay back to a canter. The poor horse was so thoroughly spent by that heart-breaking gallop that he came to hand readily enough, letting the bit come up from his teeth, and in a moment the gray was beside her.

They swung through a shaft of moonlight, and it flashed on the face of Billy Buel, deadly pale, deadly set and determined. Only then she remembered his wound. He had seemed so unconscious of it, so gay at the beginning and so savage when Moore had appeared, that she had entirely forgotten that he was badly hurt. She could tell by his pallor, however, that he had been suffering torments; and her heart went out to him with a sudden pity that overcame her fear. He was smiling steadily, mirthlessly.

"Once you make up your mind," he said, "you sure make it up strong. I wouldn't of thought that you was in such a hurry to reach the Camps."

She tried to read his expression, but they had swept on into a region of steep-falling shadows, and she could make nothing of him. So she changed the subject, rather clumsily, she felt.

"I forgot about your wound. This wild riding. Billy—has it opened the wound again?"

"Nothing—hardly a trickle."

"Hardly a trickle! Oh, I'll never forgive myself if—"

"Listen," he broke in gruffly. "It don't amount to nothing. Forget about me. I'm going to last fine to the Camps' house. Just keep cutting ahead."

"But suppose Hal Moore follows and actually comes to the house while I'm there?"

"Do you think he'd dare to come inside?"

"Of course. There's a truce now. Better than that, the war's ended."

There was a little pause, and then came the voice of Billy Buel so muffled and hard that she knew he was speaking through set teeth.

"I don't figure that he'll come inside the house, unless he's a better man than I make him out."

He added a moment later: "What sort of gent is this Hal Moore?"

"You hate him and despise him," said the girl thoughtfully, "and of course you have reason for it. Neither can I respect him. But I've always found Hal Moore honorable. You see, it's the effect of this feud. It has poisoned the minds of the men. They no longer really understand fair play. And that's why Hal Moore did that—"

"Never mind," broke in Billy. "Just tell me some more about him. Maybe he's pretty much of a fighting man?"

"Next to Ames Benchley and Oliver Lord, I think he's more respected as a fighter than any other man among the Benchleys. And since he's so young—he's hardly older than you are, Billy— who knows what he may become when he gets older?"

"Who knows how he may turn out?" echoed Billy. "It'd sure be a shame to put a frost on a promising young gent like that so early in the game!"

She caught the ring of rage and hatred in the words, but he covered it deftly by continuing: "Now in a couple of minutes you're going to be at the house of the Camps. You'll find 'em tolerable downcast, likely. Like as not they'll have some black looks for me. And I got to bear 'em. I got to bear 'em like I had really lost a fair fight to a better man."

He paused, and she saw that he was writhing with mental anguish in the saddle.

"But you go in," he went on, "and give 'em a talk right from the shoulder and tell 'em that you're sorry for all that's had to be done about you, and that you hope that good times is coming, and—but you'll find the right words when the right time comes. I'll trust to you. Only tell me how you feel. Steady!"

"My throat is choking a little," she answered. "And—and—"

"And you're a little cold in the pit of the stomach?"

"Y-yes!"

"I know. That's the way it always is with any of us when we're up against something hard. But when you see Margery Camp d'you think you can manage to smile at her?"

"Ah, yes! Surely I can do that without trying, and I half love her for all the useless love she has given me, Billy."

"I'm glad of that, I'll tell a man! But don't let

your nerve go for a minute, you understand? Keep your chin up. And mind you this, that they're a wild-headed bunch, these Camps. They're more used to fighting than to talking, and before you've been there more'n a minute, like as not somebody'll up and suggest that they don't let you go back now that they got you."

The girl cried out in terror.

"And then what can I do?"

"Then you trust to me—and keep behind me. If it comes to the pinch, you'll find that they won't try to ride over me."

"One man against so many, Billy? And you wounded?"

"I ain't wounded so bad I can't handle a gun. And even if I been beat by Ames Benchley"— there was another pause of agony while he fought away the desire to curse—"even if I been beat by Ames Benchley they know that I ain't no man's easy meat. They ain't going to pay for you all that they'd have to pay to take you away from me. And you can lay to that!"

· XXX ·
NELL MEETS THE CAMPS

She nodded, and on the heels of his last words they swung out onto a moon-whitened road, at the end of which sprawled the ungainly and large outlines of the Camp house. The girl cried out beneath her breath, and Billy Buel brought his horse to a walk. At that pace they proceeded.

"We'd better go back," pleaded the girl softly. "They—they've all gone to bed, Billy—and—"

"They're not all in bed. But they've got no cause to light up the house and holler the way the Benchleys are doing tonight. All asleep? You'll be seeing a pile of Camps that ain't asleep in about five minutes, lady!"

As he spoke, he dismounted, and the girl followed his example. She stood looking up at the ungainly outline of the building.

"It's all so changed, so much smaller," she whispered at last. "As I remembered it, it was as large as some old castle."

"Nine years since you've seen it?"

"Yes."

"It's you that's changed, then. Now come with me."

"Will you give me one minute—only half of a minute, Billy, till my heart stops beating so fast?"

"Half an hour if you like. But we'd better get this through with and start back as soon as we can."

"I know. I'll try to pull myself together. But the thought of seeing those terrible Camps, who've murdered so many of my playmates and so many grown men I've known—and being under their roof and in their power—"

Suddenly she was clinging to him and whispering

swiftly: "You won't let them take me, Billy?"

He slipped his arm around her. It was a purely brotherly caress, and the smile with which he looked down to her was amazingly gentle. Where was the tigerish face which she had seen at the beginning of the ride?

"I won't let 'em. Trust me."

"I do implicitly."

"I don't quite foller that last word. But I sure got the drift of your smile, Nell. You lay to it that you'll be all right. Are you better?"

"Yes, as long as I can keep my hand on your arm."

"Then I'll knock?"

"Y-yes!"

He raised the big iron knocker and smote with it against the door once, twice, and again, and in the pause that followed they heard the dull echo strike faintly through the quiet of the house.

There followed a pause.

"I told you," murmured the girl. "They're all asleep."

But as she spoke their ears caught the sound of a heavy footfall slumping down the hall and toward them. There was a sound of iron grating on iron as the door was unbolted—for in Gloster Valley the strength of a simple lock had not been trusted for these nine years back—and then the great door, ponderously thick and iron lined so that a rifle fired at short range could not pierce it, swung back with a groaning of hinges for a short distance. They saw no face, they saw no form against the jet blackness of the hall within, but they caught the glinting of a feeble moon ray on a barrel of a gun, and it was like an evil eye watching them, a snake eye in the gloom.

Billy felt the girl's hand tighten on his arm.

"Open up!" he called cheerily. "I ain't a burglar, and I ain't come to jimmy the safe. Open up. I'm Billy Buel come back!"

The door was jerked suddenly wide.

"Billy Buel," boomed a tremendous voice which literally thundered out of the air above them.

And looking up, Billy Buel made out the lines of a gigantic body which could not be other than that of Slow Joe Walker. The girl, at the sight of that huge apparition, so faintly and terribly guessed at among the shadows, shrank closer to the side of her protector. Her blood had turned suddenly to water.

"Billy Buel!" continued the giant, swaying toward them and coming into the white flash of moonlight. "And who's with you?"

The last words came out with a gasp of breath. And then a roar filled the ears of Billy and the girl like the crashing of storm waves in a cave, and the huge voice of Walker boomed back through the house.

"Art, Buck, Bill Camp! Buel's come, and Nell's with him! Nell's with him!"

"Billy!" pleaded the girl, "I'm dying with fright. What shall I do?"

"Keep your head up, girl. Just that and no more is what you need. Now, step inside!"

She obeyed, but they had taken hardly half a step when the arm of the monster keeper of the door swung about them and literally lifted them in the hall as a wave picks up a dangling bit of wreckage and flings it with one great and impatient lunge upon the beach. The door was sent smashing to behind them, and as the bolts fell clanging back into their places there was a clatter of steps, a booming of voices along halls, murmuring in distant rooms, and breaking out suddenly with the opening of doors.

Lights appeared—at the head of the spacious and winding stairs—and at a doorway on the right—and at another door toward the end of the entrance hall—lights that glimmered about them uncertainly and splashed the hall mirrors with yellow streaks and showed to the oncoming crowd the figure of Billy Buel with the white bandage about his head, and at his side the form of a girl in a rosy blouse with a cluster of yellow flowers.

And this was Nell Benchley—Nell Benchley! This was the cause of the war which had so lately ended?

After that first pause of staring they crowded about her from all directions. Men and women, and the lesser followers, the hired men, the servants of the house, formed the background and choked the doorways. And still others were coming. Great, cheery voices shouting far away. It seemed to Nell that a whole host was gathering and focusing upon her, and all she could do was cling to the arm of her protector with a beating heart and wish heartily that she had never left the security of the Benchley house. There, if men had dared to gape upon her in this fashion, old Grandfather Jake would have banished them forever from Gloster Valley.

She was ranging her frightened eyes across stern, bearded faces and stern, young faces of men, and the murmur of Billy Buel named them. That was Buck Martin, he with the flame of hair and the intolerably bright blue eyes. Many and many a wail had risen in the ranks of the Benchleys because of the deeds of Buck Martin. And the giant himself was no other than that almost fabulous hero, Slow Joe Walker. Ah, what tales she had heard of him—how he had been cornered once on a hillside, and how he had worked loose two enormous stones and sent them rolling—yes, and the tale should be believed, looking upon those shoulders and upon those incredible hands! And yonder was a wise face—it was he to whom the Benchleys attributed all the great successes of the Camps—that serpent tongue of persuasion, that inexhaustible fertility of invention, that man of the many devices, William Camp.

He came swiftly toward them. And yet, when he came closer, it was a kindly face, and the smile was everything that was gentleness. Were all the devilish tales that were told of him true? She began to suspect it the moment he spoke. It was like the flow of water through a quiet forest glade, so smooth was that voice of William Camp.

"I've seen brave days in Gloster Valley, Nell," said he, "but never a day as fine as this one that ends the feud and gives us a sight of you all at once! Do you know me? I'm William Camp. Tush, my dear, don't shrink from me. I know that the Benchleys have given me a coat of black. I admit I've done hard things during hard days. Now it's over. Don't fear me, Nell. Look here, I've considered myself your uncle so long, these nine years or more, that I can't get over it all in an hour, no matter how the fight come out that gives you to the Benchleys."

There was something infinitely reassuring about such a speech. At the very beginning he was recognizing the battle between Ames and Billy as the true decisive judgment from which there was no appeal—the period to war.

He took her by the hand.

"Here's Art coming. He's another that's been used to looking on you as kith and kin, Nell, and he'll make you welcome for the sake of that, and as much more for your pretty face, my dear. Art, here she is, and if they's a man in the room that grudges the nine years we fought to have her for our own, I say he ain't a man, he's a snake!"

And what a deep, hushed murmur there was in response to that speech!

As she advanced to meet Art Camp she saw the gathering of men and women fall back before her. She searched their faces eagerly, with a timid smile that offered kindliness and hoped for a return; but there was no answering smile.

The wind had blown the brim of her sombrero well back, and the light from the lamps and the gathering lanterns shone full in her face and tangled in her hair and glistened when she turned her eyes. Nell found herself passing women whose expression was simply an incredulous surprise that made them gape foolishly, and men who stood as though struck and stunned and awakening to a hunger of eagerness.

And so she came to Arthur Camp. He was, she saw, a big man, a manly man, with a short and thick brown beard in which the fingers of his right hand were tangled while he studied the girl who came toward him. He had the air, it seemed to the girl, of one who was very tired, tired to death of what he had met and seen, and some of that weariness lasted over to confront even Nell herself.

He took both of her hands and held them well apart in his own.

"So you're Nell?" he asked. "So you're Margery's girl?" and he added swiftly, while she colored: "At least, you're what we thought was Margery's, but we've forgot all that. You're just the girl the war has been about, and the war has proved that you belong to the Benchleys. Well, we take the opinion of the war, and they won't be any more talk! This is my wife. Maybe you don't remember her, you being kind of a kid when she last seen you; but here she is, she that used to think you was her niece."

Nell found herself before a big and queenly woman with a set, handsome face and a peculiar steadiness of eye. She seemed to be thinking very much as a man thinks, with a sort of muscular force behind it, instead of that light and surface thinking of a woman. Nell found it difficult to shake hands with her and meet her eyes. There was too much reminiscence behind them.

"And here's my daughter, Sally, that used to think you was her cousin."

Nell found herself before a pretty, dark-eyed girl, very eager, with a smile playing fitfully around her lips. And she was charmed at once by the reception she met.

"And you're Nell? You're Nell?" the girl was saying. "If I'd only seen you as a stranger, I'd have known."

And how Sally Camp wrung her hands! Certainly this was not the cold eye which she expected to meet from the women of the other clan. And then she found herself to one side.

"And Billy," Sally was whispering. "What of him?"

"Haven't you seen him?"

"They say he brought you. I haven't dared to look."

"Why?"

"Because they say that he's been badly hurt."

"Not very badly. At least he won't admit that it's bad."

"Ah, but that's Billy. You know, he wouldn't admit."

"I thought Billy Buel was a newcomer. But you talk as though you'd known him for a long time."

"It doesn't take a long time, do you think, to know Billy? He's all right there to see on the surface!"

Nell drew a trifle back and looked at the girl and saw the glistening fire in her eyes. It was plain that Billy Buel was no stranger to her, and for some reason it contracted the heart of Nell to see.

"Perhaps he is. To me he seemed quite mysterious enough!"

Sally laughed in her excitement.

"But he's won, after all," she insisted, "just the way I knew he'd win. Didn't I tell them when they grinned about his going out to meet Ames Benchley? They said he'd go down. But I said he'd win. And even when they brought news that he'd lost, I knew that something was wrong. Why, it doesn't take two looks to see that Billy couldn't lose. Don't you think? And the proof is that he's brought you here to us! Isn't that proof enough?"

And in spite of herself it cost Nell a pang to say: "It isn't because Billy won that I'm here, but simply because I have something to say."

That word was caught up by Art Camp, who had remained close enough to hear all of the talk.

"You have something to say. Then we'll hear it."

He sent down the hall a long, wavering cry with a peculiar power of penetration to it. And in answer to the cry a wave of silence passed along the assemblage and left them with all faces turned toward Art Camp and Nell.

"Gents," said Art, "here we got Nell that all the fuss has been about, and she's come to say something to you. So let's keep quiet and hear her. Nell, it's your turn. Here, you go up on a chair so's they can see you. Asking your pardon for saying it, but seeing you is a pile more important than hearing you!"

And before she could resist he had taken her under the armpits and swung her easily onto a chair. She stood there, laughing with the sudden excitement and balancing herself uneasily and all unaware, poor girl, of the eyes of stern men gazing at her.

Neither did she see Art Camp draw apart and talk to his wise brother, William.

"This is what I've prayed wouldn't happen, William. I told you I seen her in the Benchley house. And I told you that if ever our young men laid eyes on her the war would start all over again. I told you what she looked like!"

"You tried to," said Bill, "but you made an all-fire poor job of the description. She's a queen, Art. Look at the boys. They're near crazy with watching her already."

"And here's the tail end of the works of your man Billy," said Art Camp gloomily. "First he goes out and loses the war for us with his first fight, pretty near. Then he comes back and brings with him enough trouble to start the war all over again. Mark you me, Bill, the war ain't ended. I seen Buck Martin draw in his breath; and I seen Slow Joe Walker's face light up like they was a fire in front of him. No, sir, the war ain't ended, and they'll be more dead men still before the story of Nell is ended. And there's Billy Buel standing over yonder looking proud of having been licked."

"Wait, easy," answered William Camp. "Don't read Billy too quick. All that's showing here to-night I dunno. But you can lay to it, Art, that Billy didn't get Nell to come with him for nothing. They's something behind it. Maybe the girl will say when she talks. Maybe she won't. Let's wait and see."

"Hush!" said Art Camp. "She's talking already!"

· XXXI ·
NELL SEES THE TRUTH

It was a slow and quiet voice that they heard, not shrill with excitement nor broken with nervous laughter. It was a steady and slow voice. Lanterns and lamps were raised through the spacious hall, and there was a steady light falling upon the face of Nell. And still, as she talked, from that small eminence of the chair, they saw her arms go out, and they saw the flicker and gleam of her hands as though inviting more light, more to show upon the inside of her mind. And it seemed that the same light played with continual variations upon her face as she spoke.

"I've come here like an enemy," said Nell, "into an enemy's house. But, oh, I take you to witness that there's no enmity in my heart. There's nothing but gladness, my friends, that the war is over, and nothing but sorrow that it has lasted so long. Who was right in the beginning, and who was wrong, I cannot even guess. All I know is that many people have been unhappy for my sake, and many people have fought, and many, alas, have lost their lives. I am sorry for it. I wish that there was in me enough riches and strength to repay all those who have lost. But I have no such riches, and I have not such strength. All I can do is to come to you and tell you how I grieve for you and with you,

309

and to ask you humbly to forgive for the griefs which I have brought on you.

"Oh, I know that there are those among you who will sneer and be hard with me, and to those I can only say, over and over that I have never willed it, that I have never wished it. I know that it has never been truly for me that the war had been fought, but for something beyond me. It was something far more important, of course, and to that thing of pride or sternness or whatever it may be, my name has been attached.

"Do not hold me too close to it. And believe me when I say that for every tear the Camps have dropped, I too have wept. And every brave man who has fallen in this long and costly war I have mourned for, knowing that I am the small cause of it all.

"Perhaps you will wonder why I have come to-night. It is not to gloat over those who are defeated. It is rather to see you face to face and tell you the truth as I know it, to hope that this day will see the end of the cruelty. And, above all, I have hoped that to-night I may see face to face those who have stood for my parents among the Camps. Do not think that I have foolishly mis-judged them, but believe that I have always known that they are too kind and generous of heart, having adopted me. And I wish to go to them now, not proudly, but on my knees, and beg them to forgive the sorrow which I have caused them, and, if I cannot be their daughter, at least I wish them to know that I am open to them.

"All of this is because the man you sent to us was Billy Buel, and if ever there was a fine and upstanding man it is he. He has brought me close to you, although he is not one of you. And he has filled me with the desire to make you understand me and so to force this to be a lasting peace in more than name. Oh, my good friends—and I know that I have friends among you—help me to make this truce a lasting peace, and help me to make you all understand without malice."

She ended in the complete silence which comes after many have listened. And though every face was lifted, there was no response. It was Arthur Camp who spoke at last for the crowd.

"Nell," he said, "what you've said stands well enough, but the main thing is for you to see Margery and Lew. You may wonder why they ain't down here with the rest of us. I'll tell you. It's because Margery is pretty nigh onto death, and Lew is watching over her. It may be they ain't your father and mother. It may be that they are. But either way it may mean the turning point for Margery to see you close. Will you go up and see her?"

While he spoke Nell had gotten down from the chair, and now she looked around her. She saw many a keen-eyed man, she saw many a curious woman, but there was only one face which spoke

311

to her in the crowd, and that was the face of Billy Buel. She sought him at once.

"Shall I go?" she whispered to the man with the hired guns.

"Go and go quick," said Billy Buel, "because Hal Moore might come on your traces almost any time."

And he led her through the crowd to the side of Arthur Camp.

"Mr. Camp," she said faintly, "will you take me to Margery Camp and her husband?"

The leader of the Camps looked down to her with a smile.

"They was a time," he said, "when I expected to see you here and saying that same thing not as a Benchley but as a Camp, and, though you ain't here now in that way, I think I understand. Come with me, Nell, and we'll find 'em, and Heaven teach you to think as kindly of them as they think of you!"

"I'll go," said Nell. And she added softly: "Don't leave me, Billy!"

"Not a second," he assured her instantly.

Under the guidance of Arthur Camp they gave way before her, the rest of the crowd. There was a species of awe which attended this quiet-voiced girl. And as the women turned back to the right and to the left, so did the men also. And out of this soft-footed turmoil she found what she was approaching, having mounted a stairway and turned down a long hall, a new part of the house. They ended before a door where Arthur Camp himself paused, stroking his curly beard.

"Nell," he said, "inside of this door the two of 'em are. Here's my brother that's been figuring all these nine years that he's your father. And here's my sister that's been thinking all this time that she's your mother. Maybe me and some of the rest, like William and the judge, could convince Lew that he's had the wrong idea, and that because Billy has lost in the fight it must be that Joe Benchley and Alice was mother and father to you instead of Lew and Margery. But no matter how much we could talk to Lew, which he's a reasonable gent, no matter of talking could ever make us sound with Margery. Keep that in mind when you come to her. Be soft with her—be terrible soft with her, Nell!"

And, as he spoke, he thrust the door softly ajar.

What Nell saw was not the dull-tinted room and the low-rafted ceiling; neither did she look to the squat and ponderous furniture; but she saw, first of all, a grim-faced man of middle age with broad shoulders that were obviously meant for the lifting of burdens, and she knew, without asking questions, that this was her pseudo father, Lew Camp. Pseudo father? Indeed, he was more than that! Sincerity looked at her from under his deep-shadowed brows, and sincerity spoke from the low voice which said:

"Whatever foolishness you gents may be up to, and whatever rejoicing you may have because the war's over, for Heaven's sake take the noise of it some other place in the house, because Margery ain't up to it. She sure ain't up to it, being dead closer than she is to alive! Go where you want and do what you want, but don't bring your noise close to Margery!"

The last words came as he saw the face of Nell in the crowd. And suddenly he had come to her, brushing aside those who intervened, and stood holding her by the shoulders with his two big, brown hands.

She heard a voice with a fiber in it such as she had never heard before: "Nell! And have you come to us now, girl, in this time of all times? Have you come to us now, Nell?"

There was a sob in her voice as she answered: "What shall I do, and what shall I do that's the right thing to do?"

The slender form of Billy Buel made his way to her out of the crowd, and he stood beside her, pointing with an outstretched arm.

Ordinarily it might have been hard enough for her to understand what he meant by the gesture, but now it was not hard, and if there had been any doubt it would have been dismissed by the steady voice which was saying to her: "Look yonder to the wall, Nell. Before you do anything and before you so much as say a word, look yonder to the wall!"

She obeyed his pointing arm and his steady eyes, and the others in the room obeyed the same direction. They heard the voice of Billy saying: "Keep the rest of 'em out of the room, Camp. Keep the rest of 'em clear so's the girl can do some thinking on her own account!"

Art Camp, without a word, turned on the herd behind him and began, not too gently, to urge them toward the door, and for those who resisted there were softly voiced curses so pitched as not to reach the ears of the woman who lay on the bed with her arms helplessly outstretched and her eyes fixed on some indeterminable point in the ceiling, with its myriad cracks which ran this way and that.

But finally the crowd was pushed and hurried out of the room, and the door closed with a jar as Arthur Camp turned back upon the little assemblage.

"Now, Billy Buel," he said gravely, "suppose you make it clear why you've brought her here, which I sure want to state that I don't see any reason why she should be here. Speak up, Billy, and let's have a look inside of that mind of yours, if you don't mind."

And Billy Buel answered simply enough: "If I could answer you with words, I'd sure be a happy gent to do it, but sometimes words fall down a pile, and, we got to look to something else. That's what I look to now, and that's what I ask the rest of you to look to, and then turn around and look at the girl that a pile of fools has called Nell Benchley, which she ain't any more of a Benchley than I am."

He paused and lowered his voice, for Nell was going steadily, slowly, as though impelled by a volition other than her own, straight toward the bed where Margery Camp lay.

"It's an instinct working in her and showing her the truth even more'n I can show it to the rest of you. But there's what I mean. There is the shadow on the wall!"

As he spoke he caught a lamp from a stand beside him, and, raising it well above his shoulder level, he advanced a pace or two toward the center of the room. The illumination fell at once in the bed corner of the room and showed more distinctly than ever the worn, weary face of Margery. It showed, also, the thing to which Billy Buel was pointing.

It was a picture of Margery taken some twenty or more years before, and enlarged. She was wearing the stiff bodice and the quaintly high-shouldered sleeves of that period of fashion, so that the whole picture had an indescribable air of primness. But the face and the throat, with the edging of soft ruffles about its base—nothing could change their beauty. And many an older man, looking to the worn woman on the bed and then up to the picture of her beautiful girlhood, felt his heart leap with pity. It seemed only yesterday that Margery had been the cynosure of all eyes, the observed of all observers. It seemed only yesterday that they had wooed her so hard and long and had envied Lew Camp so bitterly. And now what a change! It seemed pointlessly cruel of Billy Buel to call attention to that poignant contrast.

But he was saying: "And now look at Nell and you'll see what I see, or else I'm half-blind!"

For Nell, beside the bed, had turned and was looking down into the face of the prostrated woman with an expression of the most perfect sympathy; and so doing, her face was turned to the crowd, now edging into the room again, in exactly the same profile that the photograph on the wall above them showed. And then the full meaning of Billy Buel rushed over every man and woman there.

It was the same profile. Seeing them in full face, there were vital differences apparent between Margery's youth and that of Nell; but the profile struck out the difference and left from brow to chin and throat the identical pure and steady line. And, unconscious of the rest of the room in her rapt attention to the sick woman, Nell seemed to be instructed by a spirit at this moment to take the broad hat from her head. And the result was a gasp that ran around the circle in the chamber. Now that the hat was gone, there remained no chance for doubt, it seemed. It was not only the same face, it was the modeling of the head and the posture of it that were the same, and by a freak of chance each of them wore the same type of hairdress. It was drawn low across the forehead, and the shiny masses were coiled at the base of the neck.

There was a moan from Lew Camp. The next moment he had sprung to the side of Nell, and, taking her by the shoulders, he turned her toward the wall, pointing with a trembling arm.

"Look, Nell," he whispered, "and Heaven give you the power to see what all the rest of us see! There's Margery when she was a girl just after she was married—there's Margery, and that's your mother, girl!"

It seemed to Billy, and it seemed to the rest, that the recognition must be instant, but Nell remained for a long time staring and staring and staring. The only way in which they could tell that she was more and more deeply moved was the manner in which her hands closed tighter and tighter over the big, brown hands of Lew Camp, until at length she slipped to her knees and they saw her hand glide under the head of the woman on the bed.

Then: "She's going to wake up? Tell me that she's going to wake up!"

There was a stir and a movement from the older woman, while every man and woman in that room leaned forward, breathlessly intent.

"Who?" she whispered faintly. "Who's calling? Lew?"

"It's Nell," answered the girl. "And my eyes have seen the truth at last. Oh, my dear, my dear!"

Billy Buel whirled on the crowd, and his voice was a snarling threat.

"Get out!" he commanded harshly. "Get out! We ain't needed!"

And they turned without a word, each with a shining face, and sifted through the doorway with careful and noiseless steps, leaving the three huddling close together in the far corner of the room.

· XXXII ·
HAL MOORE COMES

"Look to Buel!" said William sharply as they stood, wondering, bewildered, bright of eye, in the hall beyond.

For Billy Buel, his work ended, was leaning against the wall with a face deadly white. The pain of his wound, the weakness, the effort of the ride, had drained almost the last remnant of his strength; and one thin mark of red passed down the side of his face where the bandage had slipped a little and a corner of the wound had opened.

"Look to Billy Buel!"

There were others nearer to him, but Slow Joe Walker came to life and cuffed his way to the place, sending men reeling right and left. So he split a way to the side of Billy and scooped up the latter as though he were a child.

"And now what?" he rumbled to Will.

"Take him downstairs and put him on a couch. He ain't in a bad way. But he's near fainting from being so tired. Nobody but a crazy man like him would be riding so quick after being near shot to death!"

With Walker leading the procession and the others trailing behind, William pressed to the side of his brother Arthur.

"And now," he said, "have you changed your mind? Is Buel worth his salt? Was I a fool to pick him for a champion? Has he done so bad? Here we've been fighting for nine years. Have we done as much in the nine years as he's done inside of a day?"

"The day ain't ended, and neither is this visit of Nell's," said Arthur Camp gravely. "You was always an optimist, Will. But here Buel's stepped out and taken Nell away from her home after the peace come on the valley. Who knows what trouble'll come out of this? What if the Benchleys have found out already that she's gone? What if they've started out, every man of 'em, to take her back from us?"

"Started out to take her back?" and Will grinned. "Not unless they've changed their color, and the leopard'll change his spots quicker! No, Art, the Benchleys won't never see the day when they'll come out to tackle us! Sneaking behind trees like Indians—that's more their style!"

"But by the peace, Will, we've guaranteed to give up all claim on Nell."

"Give up all claim? Sure we do! What do claims amount to so long as Nell's found out the truth about her parentage?"

"The Benchleys'll never let her come near Margery again."

"Won't they? They won't be able to help themselves, Art. She's found her mother, Art, and you can lay to it that they don't build stone walls thick enough to keep 'em apart. No, sir, kin calls to kin tolerable strong! And they can't keep them two women apart!"

"But how long will it be before the fighting starts again?"

"What fighting?" queried Will. "Ain't the fighting over, Art? Ain't that what to-night has brought us? They'll be no more fighting, Art."

But Art Camp shook his head.

"I seen Buck Martin when he looked at Nell; and I seen Joe Walker when he looked at Nell. It's been a long time since they laid eyes on her, and she's a-blossomed like a flower, Will."

"She sure has," agreed the craftiest of the Camp clan.

"And Martin and Slow Joe had fire in their eyes. Don't ever think that they'll let her stay peaceable with the Benchleys. No, sir, they'll be up and after her, and that'll mean fighting, and fighting'll mean that we've got to back up friends like Martin and Walker, and backing them up'll bring on the whole feud again."

He sighed and went on:

"I don't see no way out. Maybe it's a good thing to have Nell here. The Lord knows it sure pleases me to know that she's my niece, and to have her know it. But when I seen her to-day in her own house by the bed of Billy, where he was sleeping, I sure said to myself that if our young men ever seen her as close as that they'd be trouble popping till one of 'em had her for his own wife! And even then maybe the killings would keep right on! I tell you what, Will, a pretty woman is bad enough to make trouble, but a beautiful woman like Nell is worse'n the lower regions turned loose in the world! You can lay to that. It's gospel."

"Maybe," said the practical William, "but I ain't looking that far ahead. All I see is that Gloster Valley is at peace to-night and that in spite of the fact that we've lost Nell in name we've really won her in spirit. And that's what counts, particular with women. What the law says to 'em don't count, but what their hearts say to 'em means everything!"

He had hardly finished when the knocker on the big front door set up a lively clangoring that sounded and resounded through the lower rooms of the house. Some of the crowd which had followed big Walker and his burden into the lower hall turned aside, and the door was opened to an impetuous figure who pushed straight through to the foot of the stairs and then cast a wild glance around him.

Dust of hard riding was on his face and his clothes, and the fire of his haste shone in his eyes.

"Look," said Art Camp gloomily to his cunning brother, "after all you've said, there stands a Benchley. And he's come here all alone on the trail of Nell, it looks like!"

In fact, at that moment Hal Moore caught sight of Art Camp coming down the stairs, and he raised toward him a hand which was half a threat and half an appeal.

"Camp!" he shouted. "I've come here on a trail all by myself. I went for two hosses that I'd tied in the woods near our place, and I found the hosses had gone—strayed off, I thought. So I took another hoss and followed as fast as I could, ranging around through the woods, till finally I got an idea that maybe they hadn't strayed at all—they'd been ridden! And they was only one place they could of been ridden to. So I headed straight here, went outside, and there I found the two hosses standing, and on the ground I found a handkerchief that every Benchley knows belongs to Nell."

His voice rose and became shrill with rage.

"You've planted your hired man, your Billy

Buel, to steal her, but, Camp, you've got to give her up! You've had a pretty fair name for an honest man, Camp, and now I say you got to give her up, or you'll be thought no more of in Gloster Valley than a skunk!"

"He's right," said Art sadly. "Send for Nell, one of you. I didn't do no planning; it all come out of Buel's head, Moore. And what he does is enough to save the life of Lew's wife. Do you grudge her that much—just one chance to see her daughter?"

"Her daughter nothing!" exclaimed the fiery youth. "The fight to-day proved whose daughter she was!"

"It proved nothing," said a fierce, low voice.

Buck Martin was coming swiftly toward Hal Moore.

"It proved nothing!" said a vastly larger voice, whose great volume, indeed, filled the entire hall to quivering; and Slow Joe Walker was seen striding in the same direction.

Hal Moore had his share of courage. The one cowardly act of his life, perhaps, had been that of the day; but he lost color when he saw these two formidable fighting men approach. Not that he exactly feared them, but there was something in the combination of two such mighty men, famous for their skill with all weapons, that made them seem invincible. Even Ames Benchley might well take thought before he faced either of these.

"It proved nothing!" said Walker again, arriving first by virtue of his superior length of leg and steam-roller straightness of direction. And folding his arms lightly, he glowered down from his immense height upon Hal Moore.

"And I say it proved everything and finished everything!" insisted Moore.

"Go upstairs, son, and take a look at her in the arms of her mother. Nope, you can't turn a man into a snake, and you can't turn a Camp into a Benchley without being found out pretty soon. Nell has found out, and the whole world'll find out pronto!"

Hal Moore had paled at this news.

"Some more of the Camp tricks!" he cried fiercely, and with an oath on his lips he glowered angrily back on the darkening faces of the men about him.

Ordinarily it would have been far above the reach of his courage to dare such a thing, but now he was fighting desperately for something which he had felt to be almost in his grip—a priceless treasure—now swept away.

"Them words are big words to come out of a small man's head," said the giant, sneering, "but words that ain't backed up don't mean a pile."

Battle madness swept over Hal Moore. He was swaying and trembling.

"I'll back 'em," he said, "against you or against any two like you. And I mean it, Walker."

"Step outside with me," said the giant with evil meaning. "They're a tolerable bright moon out there waiting for us. And—"

"I have the first call," said Buck Martin fiercely, breaking in upon them. "I called him first. And he's mine, Walker."

"You be hanged, you and your first calls," said the giant hotly. "He's all mapped out for me, and I'm going to have the job!"

"I'll take you both, one after another," said the Benchley adherent dauntlessly. "I'll take you, both of you, and you can throw a coin to see who's first."

"Wait!" said a feeble voice far down the hall. "I guess they won't be any need to throw coins!"

All heads turned, and they beheld Billy Buel rising from the couch where he had been placed, saw him brush aside the hands which attempted to restrain him, and now he was staggering straight down the hall and toward them.

"He's gone crazy," said William. "He can't hardly hold up his head, but he wants to fight."

"They's all gone crazy," said Art sadly. "It's the girl, Will, just as I said. Look at young Moore. Think he'd ordinarily have the heart to stand up for one second to gents like Martin and Walker? Why, Ames Benchley himself would have to think twice before he took on Walker. And there's that little game-chick trying to get himself killed because he thinks that fighting is the way to get on in the eyes of Nell. But they mustn't be any fighting. Break 'em up, will you?"

Broad-shouldered William sped instantly to the heart of the scene and pushed between Walker and Moore.

"Walker," he said, "you sure are big enough to have more sense. The war's ended. No more shooting scrapes. You'd ought to know that, Moore, if you got a grain of brains. Hold up your hosses right where you are before you get hurt and get hurt bad. You ain't made for gun fighting in the same class with Walker. I know you, Hal. I know you're a fine hand with a knife, but this ain't Mexico, and this ain't a knife-work crowd. Guns are the things, and if you stand up to Walker with guns you know you're no better'n dead. It ain't a question of backing down, it's a question of common sense. I say they's going to be no fighting to-night, and I mean it."

"What you mean," said the feeble voice of Billy Buel, "is interesting, all right, but it ain't a bit important. I got something to say about whether or not they's to be a fight to-night, and I'm right here to talk out loud. Stand aside, gents, because I sure mean business."

And business, unquestionably, he did mean. He was quite white with exhaustion. Always slender, he seemed positively fragile now from his pain and exertion. But determination stamped in the set of his mouth and the frown which shadowed his eyes. He came slowly, with a fumbling and uncertain step, and his actual physical strength was plainly at low ebb. Yet men gave way before him. The glamour of achievement was about him. He had done what no other of the Camp adherents had dared—he had met Ames Benchley alone and face to face, and, though he had lost, yet rumor was already telling how he had blown the hat of Benchley from the latter's head. Chance, it seemed, had beaten him rather than lack of skill, as even in his weakness he seemed fully as formidable as any man in the big hall.

Straight to Hal Moore he made hesitant and lurching way and paused close to the champion of the Benchleys.

The latter gave back a pace, his face working. The first of his fighting fury had passed, and, looking in Buel's face, what he saw was not the wounded man before him, but the man seen in the twilight glade when Billy's gun had come into his hand like a sudden magic, and when only the superior speed of powder and lead had saved the life of Ames Benchley. Now Billy Buel was weak, but it required no great strength to draw a gun and fire it.

"If they's to be trouble," said Hal Moore, "can't the Camps find a sound gent to put up against me? I don't want to do a murder on a gent that's been beat once already to-day and sure needs a bed and a long sleep!"

"They'll be no fighting at all," insisted the large voice of Art Camp. "Buel, go back where you were. Moore, you came here for a thing that's due you and the rest of the Benchleys. Nell don't belong to us by right of the fight to-day. I'll send for her and let her go along with you. Hey, up there, call Nell!"

There was a dull growl from the young men among the Camps, and then the sharp, light voice of Billy Buel cut in above the murmur.

"Hey, you up there, stay where you are!"

"What right have you to give orders in this house, young man?" asked Camp.

"By the right of the strength that I've paid down," said Billy grimly. "But they's more reasons. Nell goes back to the Benchleys, but she don't go with this skunk. I wouldn't trust him around the corner with her. She goes back with him that brought her—meaning me!"

"He won't fight a cripple," said Art Camp. "And even if he would I wouldn't let you fight. You're about played out, Buel!"

There was a sort of moan of rage from Billy, and his face flushed dully with his anger.

"Don't talk about what you'll let me do, Camp, and what you won't let me do. Hear me talk—gents—I'll do what I please. That's my style, and I ain't yet found gents big enough in Gloster Valley to keep me from it!"

It was a braggart speech, but plainly Billy Buel

was not in his sound senses. There was fever in his cheek; there was fever in his eyes; and the voice in which he spoke shook and trembled up the scale with his excitement.

"And as for Moore, I'll give him cause to fight me!"

"He ain't coward enough to do that, Billy!"

"Wait," said Billy Buel, and he drew a long step nearer Hal Moore.

"Moore," he said, "are you ready?"

"This is a good bluff that you're putting up," said Hal Moore with simulated scorn, "but you know well enough that I can't fight with a gent that's been already knocked out. That's why you talk so big."

Billy Buel showed his teeth as he smiled.

"Moore," he said, "I know everything!"

Those who were watching attentively declared afterward that Hal Moore shook under the impact of the word as though he had been struck in the face with a heavy fist.

"You know what?" he whispered.

"Everything," said Billy, "and the mark of the bullet is across the head, and not from front to back!"

What that meant was a mystery to those who stood about, but the effect upon Hal Moore was even more marked than that of Billy's preceding speech.

"Curse you," he said at length. "I'd like to have one minute with you!"

"You can have ten times that long, but for our sort of work it won't need more'n a split part of a second to tell the tale. But have as long as you want, pardner!"

"Are you going to let a cripple take this fight with him that's insulted us all?" asked Buck Martin of Art Camp.

But the older man was studying the two enemies from under dark brows.

"Shut up," he said. "Leave Billy Buel alone. He's strong enough to pull a gun, and as long as he's strong enough to do that I figure that he ain't going to shame us none!"

Hal Moore was reasoning in the same manner. And, against such magic speed in gun play as he had seen Billy Buel show in the twilight of that same day, he knew perfectly well that his own skill was thrown away. And he fenced eagerly for a loophole of escape and finally found one. There was one sphere in which he was unequaled, and that was in knife-work, and he knew that the ordinary cow-puncher knew nothing at all about that vicious science.

"If you're dead set on a fight, Buel," he said at length, "I'm sure you're a man. I see you wear a knife. Pull it out, and we'll see who's the best man!"

It brought a dead hush over the crowd and then a cry of "Shame!" The wizardry of Hal Moore with cold steel was well known. He could throw a heavy hunting knife with near as much accuracy as a good shot showed with a revolver; and the effects were terrible. He had been seen to sink the blade half-way to the hilt in strong wood. What would the result be if the edge struck flesh of man?

Billy Buel studied his adversary. He knew well enough that the latter had chosen a sure means of victory. He knew, even if he were an expert with a knife, that in his weakened condition he could not move about with sufficient agility to match his adversary. And yet, the longer he stared at Hal Moore, the more passionately he became determined that he must fight the man. There was a veritable ache in his bones that led him on.

"Moore," he said suddenly, "maybe you guess that I ain't any expert with a knife, and maybe you can see that I ain't quite the man I ordinarily am, but I'll tell you how I'll fight you with knives.

"Let 'em put out every light and close every shutter. Let 'em get up on the stairs and lock the doors and windows of this room where you and I will stay. Then we'll walk out into the darkness till we find each other, and we'll fight till one of us dies. That makes it pretty much chance, and the lucky man wins, if you want to put it that way! Are you game, Moore?"

The horror of the thing made Hal Moore blink, and then, remembering that he was sound and strong and the other was injured, he nodded.

"I'll take that fight that way," he said, "and Heaven help you, Buel."

"Amen," said Billy Buel. "Did you hear, Camp?"

· XXXIII ·
THE FIGHT IN THE DARK

There had been rough fights in Gloster Valley, and there had been horrible frays hand-to-hand, with knife and club and even hands and teeth, but those had been the results of long battles. This was to be a cold-headed horror, which made all the difference in the world. Art Camp gaped and then shook his head. But William came to him and took him to one side.

"Let the fight go on," he said. "I've just had a new idea, Art. This great Billy himself is kind of interested in Nell. And if I'm right, that means he'll stay on in the valley of his own accord. And so long as he's here we'll have trouble. Maybe it means the end of Billy here to-night. Better have it that way. And they's another thing. He talks as though he had something he knew private about Hal Moore—something important. I seen Moore's face all wrinkle up when Buel spoke to him. Well, maybe this fight'll bring it out. I say let 'em go at each other!"

"And Buel near dead already? You're sure a cold fish, Will!"

"Sure I am. But, whether you want to or not, d'you think you can keep Billy Buel from doing what he wants to do?"

The chief of the clan looked down to his hired man, and one glance convinced him.

"If Buel dies," he said with a gathering excitement, "I'll sure have the dream of it to my deathday. But he's asked for it, and I'll let him have it!"

In fact, the fighting lust had seized the whole assemblage. They were fighting men of the most brutal description. They had been reared for nine years so as to be hardened to the thought of killing in every form, and here was a new method to try on their professional palates. By mutual assent the few women withdrew hastily. The men began to take the places which Billy had suggested for them on the staircase.

"Gents," said Art Camp, swept away with the excitement, "I'm going to give Buel his way. Stay up here, all of you, and don't set foot in the hall except me and Will. We'll put out the lights and close the shutters, and then we're coming back here with the last lamp. The minute that's put out, it's the signal to begin. Heaven help him that loses."

The instructions were obeyed at once. He and his brother went the rounds of the shutters and closed them securely to keep out the moonshine. The lamps and lanterns were put out, and then they returned, carrying only the one last lamp, and climbed to their places on the stairs.

Looking down the staircase and up it, there was a glimpse of dark, savage faces of the onlookers, and Slow Joe Walker murmurerd: "He has all the luck! He has all the luck! Why ain't I down there?"

And in the center of the room, each man with the sleeve of his right arm rolled up, stood Buel and Hal Moore facing each other, but at a significant distance. And in the right hand of each man the light gathered and dripped along the blades of heavy hunting knives, razor-edged and needle-pointed. A thrust would drive that blade home to the hilt; a slash might sever a throat clear across.

In the postures of the two their minds could be read. In the face of Hal Moore there was savage and hungry eagerness as of one perfectly confident in success; and in the face of Billy Buel was a sort of disdainful calm, as though he despised the brutal type of battle which he had himself suggested.

"Ready!" boomed the voice of Art Camp, and his breath the next instant extinguished the light.

Blinding and utter darkness rolled across the eyes of the watchers at first. Then, straining their ears through the silence, and straining their eyes through the dimness, they made out vague noises and vaguer lights.

The wind had risen somewhat, and from the

shutters along the walls it raised a continual, soft jargon of stirring hinges, very rusty. The breeze in the forest beyond made a sound like the rushing of water, infinitely soft, infinitely distant, but a cool sound of peace. And for light there was the haze of moonshine which filtered through the shutters and made about each window square a dull ghost of an illumination extending not more than a few inches into the pitchy blackness of the central room. Indeed, there was just enough light to make that blackness horrible and thick; and there was just enough of whispering sound to make the silence deadly.

But from the men who must be somewhere on the floor of the room, stalking and listening and stalking again, and striving to look through the blackness with the power of listening, there was no faintest sound.

And up and down the stairway rose a sound of heavy breathing where the watchers leaned against the balustrade, and now and again there was the mutter of a curse as the strain of waiting grew too intense for human nerves to endure.

But what of the two who stood in the black room?

To Billy Buel, as the battle fever ebbed in him with the extinguishing of the lights, it seemed that his last fight had come. His strength of body was not a third of what it normally was. And in his hand, even had the light of day been there, was a weapon with which he was distinctly unfamiliar. Like all frontiersmen, he had played with a hunting knife now and again, but he had never made the close study which the art required. Hal Moore, if he became tolerable sure of the location of his foe, could let drive with the heavy knife from a distance, and, having buried it in the body of the foe, he could keep away and wait for Buel to die. But Billy Buel could do nothing but come to close quarters—and coming to close quarters meant the almost certainty of both giving and receiving stabs.

Thinking it over quietly, he regretted with all his heart the wild challenge which he had given, but, now that the challenge had been issued, there was nothing for it but to stay with the game.

In the meantime the darkness was stifling thick. If he extended his own knife a short distance before him, he lost all sight of it. His hand, held an inch or so from his face, was an indistinguishable and ghostly blur. How, then, could the best of hunters hunt? And Billy was far from a great hunter.

One thing at least was certain. While he was standing in the open floor, danger threatened him from all sides. By the wall there would be danger only from the front.

With that in mind, he dropped lightly to his toes and one hand, feeling his way with the hand on the floor, and keeping his weight well back on his toes, so as to be able to spring up or to the side as need arose. And in this fashion he crept softly, softly, toward the wall, with the hunting knife poised in his right hand and ready for instant use.

One thought came to him during that progress: He had been carrying the weapon in the time-honored fashion in which painters have shown dagger-wielders. But with the blade projecting down and the top of the hilt caught at the root of thumb and forefinger, it would require two motions to deliver a blow, an upward lift to acquire a sufficient distance and then the down stroke. Moreover, the range of the blow would be strictly limited to the length of his arm. But if he carried the knife with his thumb pointing down the hilt—in other words, if he carried it as though it were a small sword—he could thrust out with the smallest loss of time. Also, he would have the blade in position for slashing in any direction.

In that fashion, then, he immediately gripped the knife and continued on his journey.

At first he had striven to an aching weariness to pierce the darkness with his eyes, but the result of all his straining had simply been that a red blur grew up across his field of vision, with illusory points of light glancing in it. The eye, apparently, was helpless. He must depend upon the ears unaided.

For that purpose he fixed his glance downward toward the floor, and abandoning all effort to penetrate the gloom with his sight he felt his way along through the power of touch and the energy of sharply attuned ears. Even should a contact be made with the enemy, it would be better to fight blindly.

And still there was no noise except that maddening and soft chuckling sound as the wind worked the shutters back and forth ever so gently.

Then suddenly there was a sound of feet landing with a jar on the floor, and the light swish of an arm driven with all the speed of which a man was capable through the air.

Billy Buel gathered himself, tense. It was very plain. Hal Moore had been roaming the room ceaselessly, straining his eyes, hungry to get at his foe, and confident in his ability with a knife, until at length that constant straining of the vision through the darkness had made phantoms rise before him. And at length he had leaped foolishly at what seemed to him a shadow among shadows.

So much was certain, and Billy made up his mind on the instant. Gathering himself on his crouched legs, with part of his weight supported by the finger tips of his left hand, he leaped toward that place near by where he had heard the sound. His body drove forward as close to the floor as possible—the knife in a space as high as possible trusting that when Moore found his own weapon cleaving nothing but thin air he would remain an instant numb with the surprise and the shock of disappointment.

At any rate Billy leaped low and struck high and in a circle. And in the very center of his swing the knife drove through something soft, and the hilt jarred heavily home. He had indeed found his target.

And as the sharp, short yell of Hal Moore sounded, Billy shrank back tugging at the handle of the knife. He could not move it. His ebbing strength, sufficient for the blow, was quite too small to enable him to withdraw the blade. His fingers slipped from the handle, and Billy, disarmed and helpless, cast himself face down, hoping to avoid the return blow.

His plan worked even better than he could have hoped. The answer of the pain-maddened Moore was a rush. A foot struck Billy heavily in the side, and Hal Moore crashed over him and against the wall.

Billy started to his feet and fled to a far corner of the room. He was quite helpless now. He could have found a chair and used it as an effective club, but the rule of the fighting was with knives, and, having been disarmed of the chosen weapon, he could not in honor take up a substitute.

Crouched against the wall, he heard the deep-throated murmur of horror from those who waited on the stairs the outcome of this grisly battle. And then came the cursing of Hal Moore. He was stumbling here and there across the floor of the room, begging Billy to stand out and fight. Pain and the danger of the wound no doubt were maddening him. And from the sound of his coming Billy drifted here and there—cautiously.

What had happened? Had he wounded Moore dangerously, or had it been only a glancing thrust and a surface scratch? He had not the slightest idea where his knife had found lodgment. It might well be that it had been the veriest scratch, and now Moore, a weapon in each hand, was roving like a wolf through the darkness, sure to find his foe before long and end the battle at his own cruel leisure.

He had hardly reached the thought when a long and shrill-drawn cry sounded from the far side of the room. "Help! I'm done. For Heaven's sake bring a light! I'm dying! Bring a light! I'm through!"

It seemed that half a dozen hands were ready with lamps and matches, and Billy, drawing himself up stiff beside the wall, saw a sudden flare of light.

What it showed was Hal Moore in the very center of the room. There was a knife in each hand, and across his chest and body was a big and growing spot of crimson. He took a step—there was a trace of moisture where his foot left the floor. Plainly, he had been badly hurt high on the chest.

He cast out his armed hands toward the lights and began to run to them as though the darkness had been a horror and a trap to him. But his wavering course led him close and closer to Billy Buel, standing motionless in the growing lamplight—and in the very act of passing the wounded man swerved and leaped with a curse at Buel.

There was no escape then for Billy Buel. His own wound, his own weakness, the fatigue of the ride, the terrible nervous strain of the fight, had depleted the last of his strength. He was numbed with weariness, and all he could do was see the blow coming and wait for the end. But as Hal Moore loomed large before him, with uplifted knife, there was an explosion of a revolver from the staircase, and Hal Moore slumped heavily forward upon his face at the very feet of Billy.

And Billy Buel, turning to the right, saw William Camp quietly putting up his revolver.

After that there was a moment when his mind was almost overwhelmed in a maze of shadows; and when the shadows broke up and the light entered his eyes again he found that he was still standing in the same spot, but many stern-faced men had gathered about him. They had turned Hal Moore upon his back, and they were staring down into the ashen, tense face of the dying man.

"You got about three minutes to live," William was saying. "Which is a long time for a skunk like you to stay in the world. But before you kick out, if they's anything you want we ain't going to have it said that the Camps let even a dog die without doing what they could for it, so speak up!"

Hal Moore closed his eyes.

As for Billy, he felt beneath his arms the hands of Slow Joe Walker and Buck Martin, and he heard their voices, made gentle, at his ears: "You better come along, partner. You're about played out. And you've sure done enough since you hit Gloster Valley to-day to tire out ten men. Thank Heaven, you've come through this O.K.!"

"I'll stay here—a minute longer," insisted Billy. "He may say something that I want to hear!"

· XXXIV ·
THE PASSING OF HAL MOORE

In fact, at that moment the eyes of Moore opened again, and he murmured: "They's one thing you can do for me, boys. Send for Nell—pronto!"

"Bring her down here to this shambles?" said Arthur Camp. "Never!"

"Send for her," said Billy suddenly. "After all, he's dying for her, in a way!"

"And you talk up for him?" asked Art Camp, raising his head in wonder. "Well, Buel, what you say to-night is law. You've earned the right to it. William, will you bring down Nell?"

He went at once, running, and the dying man

turned his eyes with a great effort to the face of Billy Buel.

"Thanks," he said and closed his eyes again.

There was something terrible about that expression of gratification from the slain to the slayer.

After that there was not a sound. The wounded man did not speak; old Judge Camp was busily working to stanch the wounds—an impossible task. And so there sounded the heavy pounding of William's returning feet, and the light tapping of Nell's heels as she ran down the stairs.

Straight through the group she went, the men giving way in awed silence at her coming. And then they thrilled to her little choked cry of horror and pain.

"Hal, Hal! They've trapped you and murdered you!"

And there she was on her knees beside him, and gathering his head in her arms. "Hark to me," said the dying man very slowly and yet very distinctly. He looked up to her face with a peculiarly happy smile, and yet there was something sadder than sorrow in it. "I've got what was coming to me. I've earned it twice over, and all on this day. But it was for your sake, Nell, that I went bad, and for my sake listen to what I say!"

"As if it were Bible talk, Hal," said the girl earnestly.

"Devil talk is what it'll sound like, I'm afraid. But here's the truth: Ames didn't drop Billy. I went out. Alice got me to go and promised me to get me in strong with you if I dropped Billy. And I waited there by the side of the hollow. When it come to the gun play Billy had Ames beat a mile. His play was like lightning. I got in my shot just in time—and I wish to Heaven that I'd killed him. That would've ended everything at once. But it was only a grazing wound—"

His voice was drowned in a deep murmur of rage and satisfaction mingled; and every head turned for one glance at Billy Buel. Then they looked back to the white, lovely face of the girl, and the white, dying face of the man whose head she was supporting.

"If they'll look under the bandages they'll see the mark of the bullet is across his head. Ames couldn't've fired it from in front the way they was standing. But here's what I got to say most of all, Nell—and will you promise me something?"

"Say what you want, Hal, and Heaven forgive you for what you've done!"

"If you forgive me, I'll take my chances with Heaven. But here's what I mean to say: Nell, Billy Buel won you for the Camps to-day. Stay with 'em. A lie don't do no good to him that tells it. The lie of that fight ain't done any good for the Benchleys to-day. It has near ruined Ames. He ain't crooked. He didn't want to take the credit of dropping Buel, but it was a pretty big temptation, the idea of ending the war and keeping you for the

Benchleys all in one act. So that's why he didn't confess.

"But as long as you stay with the Benchleys the Camps will keep on murdering. And as long as you stay with the Camps the Benchleys can do nothing. They ain't strong enough in numbers to come out and attack. They got to stay at home and wait. Nell, keep quiet here. They've won you—let 'em keep you. Otherwise the war'll go on. My brother'll go down. Oliver Lord will go down. Nell, this has been the only day in my life that I've done sneaking things. Let me wind it up by one good thing and know that I've kept my brother and my friends safe from out of this war. Will you promise?"

"I give you my hand," said Nell faintly. "And it isn't the matter of the fighting that makes up my mind, Hal. It's because I've seen the truth!"

The dying man closed his eyes, but he opened them almost at once.

"Nell!" he whispered.

She leaned forward suddenly and kissed his lips; and when she raised her head a smile appeared on his face, wavered, and went out. Hal Moore was dead.

· XXXV ·
"LIKE A KING"

It was a bright twilight on a day not many weeks after this. Billy Buel sat the saddle on his bay mare, Lou, in front of the house of the Camps, and Arthur Camp and his two brothers stood beside the horse.

There were no other farewells to make, for the remainder of the Camps were at the dinner table within the house. Only these three had been whispered out by Billy Buel.

"You having come here to get Nell for us," said William Camp, "you've sure wound up your work in good style, Billy, and here's the money we agreed on, and a bit more beside. But it ain't with money that we're paying you. It's with a heap of thanks, too. And in the days ahead if you ever find that you need a place to lay up and rest and do nothing but eat and sleep and ride where you please and be king of the land, come to Gloster Valley. I think the Benchleys won't raise their heads after this. You've brought me peace, and some day I hope you'll come back and enjoy it with us."

But Billy Buel, opening the heavy little canvas bag, took forth only a small handful of the golden coins.

"I come for money," he said, "but I've got more

than money can give me out of Gloster Valley. I'll take this for traveling on. But I don't want the rest. I'll tell you why—it's too much like blood money."

There was an exclamation from Arthur Camp, but William raised his hand for silence.

"Let him have his way," he said. "They's one man in the world we can afford to owe something to, and that's Billy Buel. But why are you clearing away so quick, lad? Are you tired of Gloster Valley now that peace is here?"

"I dunno," said Billy, pushing back his sombrero with its flashing load of gold braid. "I dunno. But it seems like they's a road off yonder in the mountains somewhere that I'd like to ride along."

"And that girl you spoke of, most like, at the end of your trail, Billy?"

"Ah, maybe that, maybe that," said Billy joylessly. "Good luck to Gloster Valley."

"And good luck to you, Billy! And come again!"

He waved his hand, spoke softly to the mare, and was gone, a flash of light among the trees and out of sight around the curve of the road.

But he had scarcely made that curve when he was stopped by a figure which ran out from among the trees with raised hand. With an exclamation Billy drew up his horse before Nell Camp.

She was dressed as he had first seen her and as he would ever remember her—in a blouse, a touch of yellow flowers at her waist, and her hair coiled low at the base of her neck. For a moment he sat in the saddle staring down at her.

"So you knew?" said Billy Buel.

"I knew," said the girl sadly. "I knew days and days ago, and I've been waiting for it to happen. But why, Billy?"

"Because," he said, smiling in his quiet way, which was more with the eyes than the lips, "I'm pretty much afraid to stay, Nell."

She considered that statement for a long and thoughtful moment, and then raising her eyes again, she flushed deeply.

"But why?" she murmured again very softly.

"Because," explained Billy, "I'm a wandering man, Nell. I got to follow the road. And if I stay here long in Gloster Valley I'd be apt to get anchored."

"Anchored."

He leaned a little from the saddle.

"They's a tolerable bad fever in Gloster Valley," he said slowly. "Most gents catch it after a time. I've been exposed to it for quite a spell, and I'd better go on before I come down bad with it—which I'm not far away from it now, Nell!"

"And—and you're coming back, Billy?"

"I don't know."

"Billy!"

Instead of answering, he brought Lou deftly a step forward by the sway of his body, and leaning from the saddle he swung Nell lightly from the ground. She felt his lips pressed to hers, found herself swung back to the ground again, and then she was staring after the figure of a wild-riding horseman growing dim and dimmer behind a cloud of dust. And so he wound into the trees and disappeared.

He toiled on until he had reached the summit of the tall range beyond. And there he halted for the night. He found a natural clearing. And through the sparse pines on the side he could still look down on the hollow of the valley he had just left—a hollow which was now rapidly pouring full of the dusk of the night.

He started a fire, but he had no heart either to cook or to eat. He watched the flame tossing, he listened to its fluttering. Then a wind began to rise and sing among the trees. It was a pleasant night enough, but Billy had never been so dolorous. He had left something behind him in the valley—part of his body—part of his soul.

His head had fallen wearily back on his shoulders, and he was looking straight up to the stars, when he heard a sharp snapping of a twig behind him. He looked around upon no other than Nell herself.

There was no escort with her. She was surrounded by the night alone, save that behind her the head of her horse was lifting with pricked ears. And Billy rose like a man in a dream and went haltingly toward her with his arms outstretched.

Center Point Publishing
600 Brooks Road • PO Box 1
Thorndike ME 04986-0001 USA

(207) 568-3717

US & Canada:
1 800 929-9108
www.centerpointlargeprint.com